Andrea Boeshaar has long been one of
of heartwarming romance is compell

—COLLEEN COBLE
AUTHOR OF THE HOPE BEACH SERIES

If you enjoyed the first book in Andrea Boeshaar's Fabric of Time
series, you'll love the second, *Threads of Faith*! As always, Andrea
offers her readers a cast of believable characters, a rich and inspiring
story that overflows with faith and hope, and a conclusion that will
leave them breathless...and looking forward to the next book in
the series. Dust off your "keepers shelf," folks, because this is a
novel you'll want to hold on to!

—LOREE LOUGH
BEST-SELLING AUTHOR OF NEARLY NINETY AWARD-WINNING NOVELS,
INCLUDING *FOR LOVE OF ELI*, PART OF ABINGDON'S
SOON-TO-BE-RELEASED QUILTS OF LOVE SERIES

Threads of Faith by Andrea Boeshaar is another fabulous, page
turning winner with its spunky heroine, hunky hero, and sweet
romance. A real keeper.

—DEBRA ULRICK
AUTHOR OF *NEW YORK TIMES* AND CBA BEST SELLER *A LOG CABIN
CHRISTMAS*

Sweet, heart-tugging, page-turner; these are words that Andrea
Boeshaar's books always bring to mind. *Threads of Faith* is no
exception. Boeshaar has given us a beautiful and complex heroine,
a compelling plot, and a heartfelt reminder that family ties are
strengthened through forgiveness and grace.

—SANDRA D. BRICKER
AWARD-WINNING AUTHOR OF LAUGH-OUT-LOUD FICTION FOR
THE CHRISTIAN MARKET, INCLUDING THE ANOTHER EMMA RAE
CREATION SERIES THAT BEGAN WITH *ALWAYS THE BAKER
NEVER THE BRIDE*

Ambition, family, and honor are at the heart of *Threads of Faith*—
the story of a man who has prospered at the cost of his family and
faith and comes to realize what matters most in life. Heartwarming
and touching, this is a book to "cozy down" with and enjoy.

—KATHRYN ALBRIGHT
AUTHOR OF *THE ANGEL AND THE OUTLAW* AND
THE REBEL AND THE LADY

Rich detail, lively dialogue, and downright smart storytelling make
this second book in the Fabric of Time series a marvelous read.
Andrea Boeshaar delivers another masterpiece!

—SHARLENE MACLAREN
AUTHOR OF FAITH-BASED CHRISTIAN FICTION
LITTLE HICKMAN CREEK, DAUGHTERS OF JACOB KANE,
RIVER OF HOPE

THREADS
of FAITH

BOOK TWO

FABRIC of TIME

SERIES

ANDREA BOESHAAR

REALMS

Most CHARISMA HOUSE BOOK GROUP products are available at special quantity discounts for bulk purchase for sales promotions, premiums, fund-raising, and educational needs. For details, write Charisma House Book Group, 600 Rinehart Road, Lake Mary, Florida 32746, or telephone (407) 333-0600.

THREADS OF FAITH by Andrea Kuhn Boeshaar
Published by Realms
Charisma Media/Charisma House Book Group
600 Rinehart Road
Lake Mary, Florida 32746
www.charismahouse.com

All Scripture quotations are from the King James Version of the Bible.

The characters in this book are fictitious unless they are historical figures explicitly named. Otherwise, any resemblance to actual people, whether living or dead, is coincidental.

Cover design by Bill Johnson

Visit the author's website at www.andreaboeshaar.com.

Library of Congress Cataloging-in-Publication Data:
Boeshaar, Andrea.
 Threads of faith / Andrea Boeshaar.
  p. cm. -- (Fabric of time ; bk. two)
 Summary: Julianna is running for her life, and she hides in a crate on London's dock, only to be loaded onto a ship bound for America. During the voyage she falls in love with Capt. Daniel Sundberg when he treats her as a person and protects her from his crew, but his plans for the future do not include marrying a stowaway on his ship -- Provided by the publisher.
 ISBN 978-1-61638-841-6 (trade paper) -- ISBN 978-1-61638-842-3 (e-book)
 1. Stowaways--Fiction. 2. Ship captains--Fiction. 3. Self-realization--Fiction. 4. New York (N.Y.)--Fiction. 5. Wisconsin--Fiction. I. Title.
 PS3552.O4257T477 2012
 813'.54--dc22
                2012025903

First edition
12 13 14 15 16 — 9 8 7 6 5 4 3 2 1
Printed in the United States of America

Much research goes into my novels, so I'd like to thank the volunteers at the Wisconsin Maritime Museum who discussed clipper ships with me, as well as everyone over at the West Bend Public Library. I appreciate your time and support. Another thanks goes to Anne M. for keeping me on track with her candid critiques.

Most of all, I'm grateful to my husband, Daniel, for driving me all over creation so I can get my facts in order. And a shout-out to the fiction team at Charisma Media.

Now faith is the substance of things hoped for,
the evidence of things not seen.

—HEBREWS 11:1

CHAPTER 1

June 1877

*T*HE YOUNG MASTER's come home, dearie, and he's asking for you. Run, if ye know what's good for ye. Run far and run fast!"

Eyes wide with fear, Julianna Wayland needed no further warning from the plump cook waving her floured rolling pin. She had taken quite a risk in warning her. But Cook had kept an eye on her ever since Flora was turned out of the master's home.

Bolting from the tiled kitchen, Julianna made her way through the servants' doorway at the side of the brick mansion. Her heels clicked against the cobbled pavement as she ran down the bustling, cart-lined lane in which hawkers sold their wares. But where could she go? Certainly not to Flora's home.

As she thought of her sister's cramped room with its single cot above the Mariner's Pub, dread sank like a stone inside of her. Was her fate to match her older sister's? Flora always said it was just a matter of time.

"You, up there, stop!"

Julianna glanced over her shoulder and saw the young master's manservant. No doubt he'd been sent to fetch her. Well, she wasn't about to let what happened to Flora happen to *her*!

She hastened past shoppers until she turned onto another street. Perspiration trickled down the side of her face, and the jiggling threatened every pin in her thick hair tucked beneath the white, floppy cap. With one hand holding it in place, she managed to look behind her again, only to see that Horace still trailed her. If he caught her, punishment would be severe—and that's before the young master got ahold of her.

Julianna zigzagged her way down one street and up another until she reached London's wharf, where a row of warehouses lined the Thames. Thankfully the wind had shifted, so the stench of dead fish and human waste wasn't as sickening as in days past.

Rounding the corner of a warehouse, she paused and leaned against the wall, fighting to catch her breath. Had she outsmarted Horace at last? She thought of the prayers she heard every Sunday when the crusty old master of the house, Mr. Olson Tolbert, insisted all his household staff attend Holy Eucharist. It was much to do about nothing, since she couldn't understand what the ritual had to do with her. But she believed there was a God in heaven, and if He could hear her now, she prayed that He would keep her safe from the clutches of the young master, Olson Junior.

Memories of his dark, soulless eyes, watching her every move as she served dinner last night, and then his icy touch upon her hand and forearm when she'd set down his plate of food, were all enough to propel her onward. The man was old enough to be her father—even though Julianna hadn't ever known hers. Perhaps her real father was twice Olson Junior's age. Flora couldn't recall. She'd just said he'd been a seafaring man—just like the young master.

Oh, why had he come home now?

The rapid approach of footfalls brought Julianna from her musing. Had Horace found her? Her gaze darted around. What should she do? She eyed the various-sized crates stacked against the brick wall of the warehouse. Hiding was her only hope.

She moved toward the stockpile, when all at once she spied a box in which she'd likely fit. Hurrying, she scrambled onto a nearby apple crate and peered inside the tall-standing container.

Empty.

Julianna vaulted over the side. Once within its narrow-slatted confines, she gathered her skirts and tucked her black dress around her ankles. Then she hunkered down. Her fingers found a thick layer of straw at the bottom of the crate, and on afterthought, she tossed it over her head and her back, hoping against hope that she wouldn't be found.

Seconds later a man's voice came upon her, and suddenly her hiding place jerked from side to side. Julianna's neck wrenched painfully, but she dared not make a peep.

"It's full, all right, Mr. Bentley."

"Fine. Fine. Now load 'er up, and ye can have the job."

Neither of the men sounded like Horace, and relief coursed through her. But before she could cry out and make her presence known, a lid clamped down over the top of the tall crate and was hammered into place.

❦

From his position on the poop deck Captain Daniel Sundberg squinted into the sun at the tall, rigged masts of the *Allegiance*. They resembled the spindly fingers of webbed hands, reaching desperately heavenward. They'd remain bare until such time when the *Allegiance* was towed out of London's harbor. Her sails had been neatly folded and stored, awaiting his orders to be hoisted as soon as they set out to sea, bound for New York City.

At last Daniel's gaze fell on the faces of the fifty-seven men who'd signed on as his crew, some newly acquired, others he recognized. They stood broad shoulder to broad shoulder and, together, melded into a motley assortment of fellows. The experienced sailors had clean-shaven jaws and wore neatly pressed uniforms. Duffle bags sat at their booted feet. The others, however, were dressed in various degrees of bedraggled clothing, at least a day's worth of beard covered their jaws, and they stood barefooted on the polished deck.

"Well, sir, what do you think?"

"I think, *Mr. Bentley*," Daniel said with fond but cynical emphasis, "that you must have scrounged up several of these men after the pubs closed this morning."

His first mate chuckled, and Daniel's annoyance mounted. Selecting a crew took careful consideration. After all, he was responsible for both the ship and its cargo, which consisted of several tons of tallow and sundries. But the most precious of it all were several Old Master paintings going to the Metropolitan Museum of Art. Daniel had personally overseen to their safekeeping.

"Need I remind you, Bent, that we've got almost a three-week voyage ahead of us, and it'll seem like a lifetime with the wrong crew aboard."

A hint of a smile still curved Al Bentley's thin lips. "No reminding required, Cap'n. I've been your first officer for a long while now, and I know what you expect." Bent counted on his fingers. "Isaac Cravens has been your second and Billy Lawler your third…"

"I know who my officers are!" Daniel couldn't quell his impatience. "I also know the names of the carpenter, blacksmith, and sailmakers."

"And Dr. Morrison, of course, is sailing with us too," Bent added, much to Daniel's irritation. "Mr. Ramsey wouldn't have it any other way."

"As I'm keenly aware." Daniel rounded his eyes with sarcasm, knowing good and well the requirements that his friend and employer, George Ramsey, put in place for his fleet.

"Jimmy Levins'll be your cabin boy as usual."

"Good, good…" Only a year ago Bent had found Jimmy up on Liverpool's wharf. With nowhere to go, no family, or so he'd sworn, Jimmy had been more than happy to sign on with Ramsey Enterprises.

"As for our crew, I interviewed 'em like ye tol' me, and each sailor proved himself while loading up the *Allegiance*. We're ready to set sail anytime you give the word."

Daniel eyed the men. "I suppose they'll do." Helplessness nipped at him. He didn't have time to be particular. He'd been forced to cut this last visit to London short due to a telegram bearing bad news.

"You won't be sorry, Cap'n. I've a hunch these able-bodied men will serve us well."

Daniel kneaded his chin. "I presume there is a cook on board." He arched a brow before glancing back at his brawny crewmen. Two voyages ago Bent had overlooked that *small detail*.

"Cook's been hired." This time chagrin edged the husky man's reply. "He's been in your employ b'fore. Jeremy Kidwell's his name, and he's presently in the galley, arranging things to his liking."

"Kidwell, eh?" Daniel recalled the young, red-haired man. Other than being somewhat impetuous at times, he filled the position as cook quite adequately.

"Aye, sir, Kidwell's both skillful and resourceful." A hopeful glimmer entered Bent's sea-green eyes.

"Good work." Daniel rarely doled out compliments, but he made a point to do so when they were warranted. He gave Bent a friendly clap on the back.

"Thank you, Cap'n." A smile stretched across the first mate's leathery face, revealing a dark space where a front tooth had once been rooted. "You know, I was sorry to learn this'll likely be our last voyage together."

"Yes, well, it's time for me to move on." Daniel clasped his hands behind his back and widened his stance on the poop. "But before I marry and then step into the role of executor and chief of Ramsey Enterprises, I need to shore up some things from my past."

The news from Wisconsin burned in his memory. *Poppa has taken ill*, his mother, Kristin Sundberg, wrote. *Please come home soon.*

Daniel had been surprised when his mother's telegram arrived from New York City with the rest of his mail. But, of course, *Mor* had no knowledge that he'd spent the last two months in London. It had been seven years since he'd heard from her or any of his family. It had been for the best. He and his parents never saw eye to eye. But now a sense of duty implored him to make certain that his mother and sisters were well provided for once Poppa passed.

"Cap'n?" Bent's voice broke through his troubling thoughts. "It's possible, ye know, that your father'll recover." Bent leaned in close. "My own mother suffered a debilitatin' illness. But now she's back on her feet an' spittin' nails like always."

Daniel wrestled with a grin. "I'll take encouragement from that bit of information."

The warm summer wind brushed over his face, bringing along with it the stench from the Thames. Thank God he wouldn't be docked on this crowded, stinking river for weeks, such as had happened several voyages ago. George Ramsey was not without influence in this city, and he'd pulled some strings all the way from New York. The *Allegiance* was on a short list for a tug, which would see her safely out of London's port.

Arms falling to his side, Daniel turned toward his cabin to finish the paperwork awaiting him on his desk. "All right, Bent. I approve the crew. Carry on."

"Aye, Cap'n!"

Darkness shrouded Julianna so that she couldn't even see her hand in front of her face. Beneath her the sea roiled. Waves crashed rhythmically beyond the walls of her tomblike confines.

A ship. She'd been loaded into the bowels of a ship, for pity's sake!

Julianna gulped back fear and frustration. How could this have happened? She'd tried to cry out. However, her voice hadn't been heard above the din of sliding crates and sailors' shouts. And the language—it had been blue enough to burn the ears of any delicate female. But, of course, Julianna had heard the same foul words, or worse, coming from the pub at which Flora worked. How her sister could abide serving ale every night to those ruffians, Julianna would never know. Of course Flora didn't have much choice, thanks to the young master and his sinful lusts.

It had been a little more than three years ago now that Flora held the stately position of upstairs maid at the Tolbert mansion. But then Olson Junior forced himself on her. Months later Flora couldn't hide the result of that attack, and, of course, the master wouldn't abide an unmarried woman with child working in his house, even if the babe was his own grandchild. He turned Flora out into the streets.

Julianna's heart crimped at the memory. She'd tried to help Flora, but the few coins she made weren't enough for her sister to live on. Sadly, the only help her sister found came from the prostitutes on the wharf. After the baby died at birth, Flora went to work in the Mariner's Pub alongside her new friends. When Julianna tried to see her, Flora turned her away. She had her life now; she had friends. She didn't need her proper little sister infringing on her lifestyle. Had Flora been sober when she'd spouted those words,

Julianna might have believed them. Unfortunately, finding Flora sober hadn't been possible yet.

But now, dear Lord! She'd been loaded onto a ship? Where was it going? How would she get off?

What will I do once I do get off?

Julianna didn't want to return to her job at the Tolberts, not with the young master, that miscreant, home again.

Struggling within her confines, Julianna tried to move her limbs. Prickles of numbness moved from her feet to her ankles. She wiggled, but there wasn't space enough to shift positions.

"Help!" Julianna's voice drowned beneath the noise of the sea and the myriad of cargo. "Help me, please!" When she thought that she might never be found, a sense of panic began to rise. She needed out of here—and now! "Anyone! Please, help!"

CHAPTER 2

*H*OW LONG SHE screamed for help, Julianna couldn't be sure. But now she saw her efforts as sheer folly. Her hoarse voice and parched throat pleaded for even a drop of water. Her strength waned, and like a specter, despair hovered in the darkness surrounding her.

Suddenly she heard a creaking of a door, then a shaft of light appeared. It grew brighter as a door opened farther.

"Help! Please!" She barely croaked out the pleas.

Shuffling boots against the wooden floor brought the lamplight closer. "Well, well…" A man's deep voice filled the cargo space. "What 'ave we 'ere? A stowaway?"

She worked to control the deep and increasing anxiousness inside of her. She didn't trust seafaring men. Before she worked for the Tolberts, she and Flora called the streets of London their home. She'd learned that sailors were all alike, selfish ogres, and yet this one was her only hope. Then again, who had she expected to rescue her, here onboard a ship?

Setting down his lamp, the sailor gave the crate a violent shake, and she cried out. The wood splintered, and then the side of the crate fell open. His thick hand reached in, grabbed hold of her, and pulled her to the floor.

Too stunned to even scream, Julianna lay there while blood flowed to her circulation-starved limbs, causing a million pinpricks under her flesh. Moments later she attempted to stand, but her knees buckled. The iron clamp over her upper arm forced her upright.

"You've done a bad thing, stowin' away on this ship."

"It was a mistake." Julianna stared at the unkempt man, imprisoning her with his meaty fist. His rancid breath caused her stomach to lurch again. She turned away.

"Look at me, you!"

Swallowing hard, she brought her gaze back to the man's grizzled, unshaven face and dark eyes. Sweat stained his faded blue-and-white striped shirt. Julianna shrunk back.

"When the cap'n finds out, he'll make you walk the plank. You're as good as shark bait."

"But it was an accident." Tingles of fear crept up Julianna's spine.

A wicked-looking sneer curled the corners of the man's thick lips. "Maybe it was, an' maybe it wasn't. Either way the cap'n won't like it. He's a mean one, this cap'n."

"Perhaps if I explain—"

"He won't care." The sailor pulled Julianna closer to him. "But I might be persuaded to 'elp you out."

Julianna fought yet another urge to gag. "You sailors are all alike."

"So we are." He snickered. "How 'bout a little kiss for the Grisly Devil?" The feeling returned to Julianna's feet, and she gave the sailor a hard kick in the shin. He yelped and slacked up on his hold around her arm. Julianna wrenched free and ran through the stacks of crates.

He cut her off near the doorway, his eyes squinting in a menacing way. "You ought not 'ave done that to the Grisly Devil."

"You are a devil!" Julianna carefully stepped backward.

"Aye. I've earned this name because of me mean temperament." He inched forward. "An' now you're going to 'ave a little taste of it."

Julianna wetted her parched lips. "A girl has the right to defend herself."

"I suppose she does at that." He produced a wicked laugh. "But ye won't get far from me, girly, although I'm willin' to chase you. And when I get you..."

His muscle-bound arm shot out in her direction, but Julianna successfully dodged it. She turned and ran the way she'd come, then doubled back and nearly made it to the doorway.

That's when the sailor caught her.

He laughed. "I got you, girly. Now how 'bout a kiss?"

Julianna struggled. "You'll get no kiss from me, you brute!"

"Brute, is it? Maybe I'll take more than a kiss."

Julianna swung her palm toward his jaw, but he easily intercepted it and returned the gesture, using his meaty fist. The blow knocked Julianna senseless. When consciousness returned to her, she realized the Grisly Devil had dragged her to a far corner.

"Get your hands off me!"

He pinned her down with one knee on her chest. Both her pinafore and bodice gave way as he ripped the fabric. Panicked, she squirmed and clawed with frantic fervor. He couldn't win this fight. He wouldn't!

With what she knew must be her last breath, she screamed for all she was worth. The Grisly Devil struck her again, this time square in the face. Pain shot across her cheeks and forehead. The back of her throat filled with a thick and salty fluid. She choked but refused to give up. This couldn't be how she'd die—at the hands of this murderous man!

"Stop your flailing. I mean to get what I want."

Her mind screamed against the command. Seeing his arm near her cheek, Julianna turned and bit down hard. Her assailant yelped.

Seconds later his weight lifted from her body, and quietness descended. The ship rolled, and her stomach did the same. Moving onto her side, she retched before gulping in precious air and realizing that she'd survived the ordeal. Julianna blinked. Had the devil vanished?

Clutching the pieces of her torn gown together, she slowly propped herself up on one elbow and saw that, several feet away, a second man just as large as her attacker held a long blade beneath the devil's chin.

"The captain'll hear about this, Griswald."

He sounded like an American.

"Aye, Kidwell, and I'll be a hero for finding that stowaway. 'Tis against the law, ye know."

"So is attacking a helpless female."

Julianna's tension ebbed. It appeared the Yank had come to her aid.

"Bah! She's not so 'elpless, and I've the scratches and bites to prove it."

A long pause.

"I ought to slit your throat right now, Griswald, and spare the captain his time."

The devil lashed out, and Julianna screamed.

"All right. All right. What in the Queen Mother's name is going on in here?"

A third man happened into the cargo hold. An aura of importance encompassed him. His gaze lit on Julianna, and he stopped midstride. His hand moved to the butt of a revolver tucked in between the shiny buttons on his coat.

Griswald struggled until Kidwell set him free. "I 'appened on a stowaway, Mr. Bentley." He pointed a sausage-sized finger at

Julianna. "She gave me a pack of trouble, but I showed her who's boss."

Kidwell came toward Julianna. Locks of thick, curly, red hair fell from his cap and onto his forehead. "Beat her half to death is what it looks like."

He offered his hand. She accepted, and he easily pulled her to her feet, although she nearly lost her balance as the ship tipped slightly to one side before righting again.

Kidwell steadied her. "You'll get your sea legs soon enough."

The man named Mr. Bentley cocked his head, studying Julianna. "What 'appened, Miss?"

"It was an accident." Her nose ran, and she guessed it bled. Kidwell offered his handkerchief and she took it. "I was hiding in the crate to get away from a man like this." She pointed at Griswald. "He tried to…" She clipped her accusation, lest she be the one blamed for the hideous act. The seamen might see her as some sort of hussy.

"We can tell what he tried to do," Kidwell ground out.

"Aye, and wait until the captain 'ears about it." Mr. Bentley said.

Julianna shuddered.

"I'm innocent!" Griswald bellowed. "She's the lawless one."

"I don't think so." Kidwell turned the handle of the knife in his palm. "I think you would have killed this female if I hadn't come in time."

"And so what if I had?" Griswald drawled.

"We'll let the cap'n be the judge. In the meantime"—Bentley focused on Griswald—"it's my duty to place you under this ship's arrest." Pulling out his gun, he aimed the barrel at Griswald's chest. "Let's go." He spoke out of the side of his mouth to Kidwell. "Bring the girl."

"Yes, sir."

Kidwell's approach was easy, and his hold on Julianna's arm felt more like assistance than a policing handgrip.

"Thank you," she whispered.

"You're welcome. But you, Miss"—his voice hardened—"have a lot of explaining to do."

"Yes, sir." She hoped she'd be given a fair opportunity.

Julianna's fingers tightened around the torn fabric of her dress. Surely the captain would understand how she came to be in the bowels of his ship. Wouldn't he?

❦

At the *rat-tat-tat* on his cabin door, Daniel glanced up from the logbook and nodded to Jimmy.

His cabin boy opened the door, revealing a veritable crowd. "Beggin' yer pardon, Cap'n, but we've got a situation here."

Daniel stood. "Come in."

First to enter was a hulking crewman, followed by his first officer, Bentley. Daniel knew it was Cravens's shift at the helm, so he wasn't surprised to see Bentley. But then he glimpsed the old Teat Fire in Bent's hand and guessed the situation was grave at best. "What seems to be the—"

He stopped short when his gaze fell on a dark-headed woman holding together her torn bodice. He quelled an irritable sigh. Judging by her attire, he guessed she worked as some sort of barmaid and that she'd been stealthily brought on board for the crew's entertainment. It seemed that things had already turned out badly for her. The woman's features were obscured by patches of bloodstains, and both eyes were red and puffy.

"What's happened here?" *As if I don't already know.* Daniel rounded his desk and cast a look at Bent. "I didn't realize we had any female passengers."

"We don't, sir. That is...I didn't know we did, until now."

Setting his hands on his hips, Daniel turned his attention back to the woman. She held a bloodied handkerchief to her nose. Her white apron had been ripped from its shoulder seams and lay against her black skirt. The bodice of her black dress too had been torn, and her white cap hung in the knots of her brown tresses.

"I–I can explain, Captain," she said in a timid voice. Her wide gray eyes seemed to beseech him, and to say she looked frightened would be an understatement.

The ship listed to the left, and the woman lost her footing. Daniel caught her arm.

"She's a stowaway," the burly sailor blurted. "I found 'er in a crate in the storeroom."

"That may be," came a voice from the hulk of a man, darkening the cabin doorway, "but you beat her."

Daniel's gaze moved beyond the female and to the man who just spoke. Kidwell. He stood with a butcher knife in his hand.

"You would have done worse," Kidwell continued, "if I hadn't come along."

Daniel clenched his jaw. He didn't tolerate abhorrent behavior on his ship. He peered at the crewman. "Is this true?"

A twisted grin contorted the man's lips. "I was just havin' a bit o' fun is all. I can't help it that the girl fell an' hurt herself."

Daniel's gaze hopped to the woman, and again he noted the extent of her injuries. He released her, stepped back, and glared at the sailor. "Do you take me for a fool? It's quite obvious she didn't fall and *hurt herself.*"

"And that's the truth." The woman's voice shook. "This man, the Grisly Devil, he's responsible for my injuries."

"Grisly Devil, is it?" Daniel arched a brow.

"My nickname, sir." The man had the audacity to raise his chin in a proud fashion.

"His name's Griswald," Bent said. "Devlin Griswald."

"Well, then, *Mr. Griswald,*" Daniel ground out, "let it be known I detest men who abuse women."

"In this case, she's a stowaway, Cap'n."

Daniel noted the disrespectful tone. "Stowaway or not"—he clenched his fists at his side, resisting the urge to pommel this beefy man right into the floorboards. True, men sometimes had to fight it out, but—"a man never has the right to raise his hand to a woman."

"I knew you'd feel that way, sir." Bent lifted the Teat Fire a little higher.

"Besides…" Daniel trained his gaze on the crewman's unshaven face. "I'm master of this ship, and any stowaways are to be reported to *me*."

"Just givin' ye a hand, sir." The sailor puffed out his chest, and Daniel knew the man was trouble.

"I have no use for liars and thugs on board my ship." Daniel looked at Bent. "Take this man below to the prison hold and lock him up."

"Do we have to feed him, sir?" Kidwell's eyes darkened. "I'd prefer to let him starve."

"Might be a good idea." Daniel pulled his handkerchief from his shirt pocket and handed it to the woman. She held it to her bleeding nose.

"A bit harsh, don'cha think?" Defiance glinted in Griswald's murky eyes.

"Perhaps not harsh enough." Daniel set his jaw.

Seconds later the sailor swung his meaty arms upward in a violent thrust and rammed into Bent. The revolver clattered to the floor and discharged. The woman screamed. Jimmy dove under Daniel's desk for cover. Smoke filled the cabin, and through the haze Daniel watched Griswald crumple, cradling his left arm. Kidwell pounced and held his knife to Griswald's throat.

Daniel suddenly recalled the cook's quick temper. "Easy now. I'd prefer that no souls be lost."

Bent inspected the crewman's injury while Griswald bawled

like a newborn calf. Sulfur tinged Daniel's nostrils and stung his eyes, and then he noticed the stowaway huddled in a corner. She appeared all the more frightened but unharmed by the revolver's mishap.

"It's just a surface wound, Cap'n." Bent retrieved his gun, before assisting the crewman to his feet with Kidwell's help. "We'll bandage 'im in the brig."

"Watch yourself," Daniel warned.

"I intend to, sir."

"I've got your back, Mr. Bentley." Kidwell continued to bandy his blade. "And just so we understand each other—" He pointed the tip at Griswald's nose. "I can clean a mackerel in less than thirty seconds."

Daniel heard his stowaway gasp from her corner of the cabin and determined she'd heard quite enough from his crew. "All right. Get Griswald out of here. Patch his wound and lock him up. And Jimmy?"

"Yes, sir?" The shaggy-haired cabin boy climbed out from under the desk.

"Make yourself useful."

"All right, sir."

Daniel watched as the teenage boy followed the men out of his office. Closing the door, he drew in a long breath and finally directed his attention to the injured woman. "And just what do you have to say for yourself?"

CHAPTER 3

*L*IKE I SAID, Captain, I can explain."

Daniel slowly approached the stowaway. She curled her shoulders inward as if in defense.

"You've got nothing to fear from me, Miss."

"You won't make me walk the plank, will you?"

Daniel almost cracked a smile. "I hadn't planned on it, no."

The woman expelled a relieved sigh, although she continued to make good use of his handkerchief. "Glad to hear it. You seem like a reasonable man."

"I suppose I am." Daniel realized introductions had never been made. He gave her a small bow. "Captain Daniel Sundberg at your service."

She unfurled herself and inched up to her full height, which didn't quite meet his chin. "Miss Julianna Wayland...and I'll tell you everything, sir, if I could just have a sip of water."

"Of course. Come and sit down."

"Thank you."

He reached for her elbow and escorted her to an armchair, taking note of her British accent and the graceful way she carried herself.

"You hardly appear to be the usual barmaid who's smuggled aboard or the waif that stows away."

"I'm neither, sir. It was a mistake. Believe me. I was being pursued, so I climbed into an empty crate to hide. Someone nailed it shut, and with all the noise at the wharf, nobody heard me cries."

"I gather you're employed in London?" He filled a cup with water from the pitcher standing on the far table. Crossing the room, he handed it to her.

She drank it down in four swallows. "Oh, thank you, sir."

"You're welcome." He strode across the cabin and fetched an extra shirt from his narrow closet.

"I work for Mr. Olson Tolbert Senior."

"Tolbert?" Daniel knew of the man. "The noted philanthropist."

"I suppose you could call him that, sir. Me sister and I were one of his projects. That's how I came to have me employment."

"Hmm…" Daniel glanced at the shirt in his hand. "Well, um, I don't have any spare female attire"—he couldn't keep a note of sarcasm from his tone—"but this should do nicely until I can get you a needle and some thread."

"Thank you, Captain Sundberg."

She accepted his shirt, and Daniel made his way to the washstand, keeping his back turned while she pulled it over her shoulders. He soaked a cloth in the basin, and when he sensed Miss Wayland had adequately covered herself, he returned.

"Let's have a look at that battered face of yours." He knelt and began removing the dried blood from her cheek. "It's possible that your nose is broken."

"I'll survive. I've suffered worse." Slowly she pulled the wet cloth from his hand. "And, if you don't mind, I can manage on me own."

"All right." Daniel guessed at her general dislike or perhaps distrust of men. Standing, he folded his arms and eyed his stowaway carefully. As more of her features were uncovered, he wondered if he'd seen her before. "I attended Mr. Tolbert's spring charity dinner last month."

"Oh, yes. I was there."

He tipped his head in contemplation and vaguely recollected the petite housemaid with silvery eyes. "I remember you."

"Probably because the master called everyone's attention to me and introduced me as one of his charity's many successes."

"Ah…" Daniel recalled the incident and remembered her being demure and pretty. Of course now she was a bloodied mess.

"Please don't send me back. Please. The young master will ruin me like he did me older sister."

Daniel frowned. "Young master?"

"Tolbert Junior."

Daniel folded his arms. He'd had a couple of run-ins with the wannabe sea captain. "He's not in London."

"On the contrary, sir. He returned yesterday afternoon."

"Really." Daniel tapped his chin in thought. "May I ask how old you are, Miss Wayland?" Not that it mattered, but she appeared awfully young.

She held the cloth against her swollen nose. "I'm nineteen, turning twenty in just three weeks."

Younger than his sister, Adeline. "And you say you were running away from…the younger Tolbert?"

"His manservant Horace, actually. But Cook told me the young master requested"—she ducked her chin as if in shame—"me." A moment's hesitation. "Please don't think badly of me, sir."

Daniel narrowed his gaze. "Why would I think that?"

"On account of me sister, Flora."

"Do I know her?"

"You might, if you frequent the Mariner's Pub. She's one of the more livelier girls there."

"I don't patronize such establishments, Miss Wayland."

"Most seafaring men do."

"Well, not this one." Daniel didn't mean for the edge in his voice to sound quite so sharp, although protecting his reputation against hearsay and assumption was always a perturbing task.

"Glad to hear it, sir."

Daniel massaged the back of his neck. This was really more information than he cared to know, and yet he had somewhat of a vested interest in her circumstance. Not only did he dislike Olson Tolbert Junior, but he also had priceless artwork on board and needed to fully understand just how and why this woman got onto his ship.

He sat down on the corner of his desk. "Why don't you start at the beginning, Miss Wayland."

"Well, all right." She paused in a moment's thought. "I was born in London, and me mum died the day after I was born."

He hadn't meant *that* far back.

"Me older sister Flora and I were raised by me mother's employer and his wife. They weren't mean-spirited, and they didn't beat us, but raising children wasn't something they relished either. Flora was my primary source of love and affection. I adored her. When she was twelve, she got a job at the shoe factory. I was six, and when I wasn't in school, I had to help the Potters with laundering and mending. It wasn't a bad life at all, and I'm not complaining, mind you. But things got worse after the Potters were killed in a freak carriage accident. Flora and I were instantly destitute."

"Miss Wayland—"

"Please allow me to finish, sir. If you understand the whole of me situation, then it helps me defense, doesn't it?"

Impatience pecked at him, but Daniel caved to her request and perched himself on the corner of his darkly varnished desk. "Very well. Go on."

"Thank you." She shifted. "When the Potters died, I was nearly fourteen. Flora was twenty and had already gotten herself into all kinds of trouble. She'd gotten let go at the shoe factory as well as other places of employment because she enjoyed imbibing with friends. To their credit, the Potters didn't throw her out. When they died, however, Flora and I lived at her ne'er-do-well friends' homes. One by one unfortunate situations arose, and Flora and I were on the move again.

"At last we found ourselves on the streets of London. We survived by begging for scraps of food from the upper class. At night Flora made sure no harm came to me—even if it meant she took a beating while I ran and hid."

He didn't believe her. "A woeful tale to be sure, but—"

"Me defense, Captain?"

Daniel held his tongue. He'd give a few more minutes, but nothing more. "Very well."

"Shortly after I had turned sixteen, Mr. Tolbert caught me and Flora rummaging through his garbage." Miss Wayland held the damp cloth against one swelling eyelid, and a lock of hair, the very color of his cabin's dark paneling, fell across her forehead. She pushed it to the side. "After a severe scolding he had mercy on us, philanthropist that he is, and he offered us positions as housemaids—Flora too, in spite of her advanced age of twenty-two."

Daniel couldn't help a grin. Advanced age, indeed! He was the decrepit age of twenty-seven.

"We underwent extensive training and both earned respectable positions, higher than scullery maids. Sometimes I assisted Cook in addition to me regular work and helped serve guests at parties and receptions, like the one you attended."

Daniel inclined his head, sensing he heard the truth now.

"Flora and I were quite content for a while." She kept her gaze averted. "But then we learned how cruel the young master could be." Her voice grew soft. "During one of his visits he took advantage of Flora and ruined her. Months later Mr. Tolbert learned of it and turned Flora out." Miss Wayland's slender shoulders rose and fell as she paused to breathe. "I tried to help me sister, but couldn't. The few coins I earned weren't enough for her to live on, and I only got Sunday afternoons off, so I couldn't care for her." Sadness washed over her features. "The babe died at birth, bless him, and poor Flora was forced to find work as a..." Suddenly Miss Wayland seemed at a loss for words.

"I can fill in the blank." Daniel easily put the pieces together, and it angered him that Olson Junior was held blameless for the ruin of a young woman. "I'm sorry to hear about your sister."

"Thank you, sir." She met his gaze, and he glimpsed her look of relief. "When Cook told me this morning that the young master had designs on me, I ran for me life. I didn't want to end up like Flora." Her breathing accelerated, and she wagged her head. "I just didn't!"

"Easy now, Miss Wayland." Daniel set his hands on her shoulders and felt her muscles tense beneath his palms. She leaned as far back as the chair would allow. He'd only meant to steady her. "Forgive me." He released her and sat back. "I mean you no harm."

After a tenuous smile she pushed to her feet and wandered aimlessly about his office, adjacent to his sleeping quarters—an attempt, perhaps, to put distance between them.

"Rest assured, Miss Wayland, I am nothing like Olson Tolbert Junior."

"It's a relief to hear you say so." She passed the small but functional jail, which Daniel hadn't used in years. In fact, it served as more of a storage room than lockup.

"Is this a portrait of the ship I'm on?" She'd paused at a small oil on canvas, which George had given him as a gift one year.

"Yes. You're aboard the *Allegiance*."

"It's quite large."

"Indeed. She's an elegant clipper, built in eighteen fifty-three." A swell of pride filled Daniel's being. "She'd been around the world three times. In seventy-one, Ramsey Enterprises purchased her, and much of the ship underwent refurbishment. This office area and my sleeping quarters were remodeled to be more spacious. The jail here was installed in case of trouble on the sea and another ship was overtaken. The idea was that officers would find it suitable. Other prisoners are held in the cargo area, where Mr. Griswald will stay." At Miss Wayland's look of interest, he added a tidbit more. "I've served as the *Allegiance*'s commander ever since her recommissioning ceremony in eighteen seventy-four."

"I'm impressed, Captain." She walked to his framed credentials, hanging near the doorway that led to his private quarters.

"Can you read?"

"Yes. I went to school until I was thirteen. But it was the Pigeon Lady who made me practice so that I was any good at it."

"Pigeon Lady?"

"Yes." Miss Wayland smiled fondly. "That was our nickname for an old woman who lived on the streets. She adored those dirty ol' pigeons and often fed them instead of herself."

"Hmm…" Daniel grew weary of all this chatter. He clasped his hands together. "So, you were trying to escape Captain Tolbert's lasciviousness and you came aboard my ship?" He dipped one brow. "Did I hear correctly that Griswald found you in a…*crate*?"

"Yes. I hid there, like I told you. And before I knew it, I was loaded up with all the rest of the cargo."

Daniel gnawed gently on the side of his mouth and narrowed his gaze as he mulled over her explanation. Next thoughts of the Old Master paintings stowed onboard ran across his mind. He'd been warned of the lengths to which thieves would go in order to steal those precious works of art. Could be Miss Wayland's story was just that—some cockamamie tale to get aboard. Perhaps she was in cahoots with Griswald and left her post at the Tolberts in order to steal the priceless artworks. He doubted it, and yet he couldn't be too careful.

He cleared his throat. "Miss Wayland, accident or no, stowing away is a crime punishable by incarceration—unless you have the funds for passage."

She shook her head slightly and her puffy nose began bleeding again. She quickly retrieved his handkerchief, momentarily forgotten on the arm of the chair in which she'd been sitting.

"Normally I'd sentence a stowaway to hard labor so he could work off his passage. But seeing as you're a female, it isn't wise to mix you with my crew and chance another tragic encounter."

"Could you let me off at the next port? Perhaps I can find work in another city."

"I'm afraid that's out of the question. You see, I lost time anchored on the Thames, waiting for the wind to change and a tug, and I cannot make any unplanned stops. I must make New York's harbor in less than three weeks' time, which is pushing my luck unless the wind stays at my back."

"New York?" Miss Wayland stood stock-still, the color in her bruised face drained away. "You mean...?"

"That's right. This ship is bound for America."

❀❀❀

"America!" Julianna gaped at the captain.

"Yes. You heard correctly." His blue eyes darkened with austerity before he turned and walked around his desk. As he lowered himself into the black leather chair, his expression remained grave and pensive. Obviously he wondered what on earth to do with her.

Julianna returned to the matching armchair and sat down. She watched the captain guardedly. Was he a good man or another devil in disguise?

She had to admit he was a handsome fellow. Why, Flora would

have enjoyed plopping herself into his lap and gulping down a few glasses of ale. Perhaps she'd sing one of her bawdy songs and *skoal!* with her thick ale mug.

And yet somehow this man didn't fit Julianna's image of the usual drunken sailor—even one sobered up. The captain's demeanor was calm, sophisticated. And two vertical jags on each side of his mouth indicated the propensity to dimple if only he'd crack a smile.

A bit of grin crept across her own lips as she continued her surreptitious scrutiny of the man. She'd seen anger in those arresting blue eyes of his when he learned of Griswald's abuse. And then to offer his shirt...why, his reaction had been more than she'd hoped for. So far the captain had been almost kind in his treatment of her. But what would he do next?

As he bent his auburn head, cogitating about her fate, Julianna perceived his sense of fairness, and her sore muscles relaxed somewhat.

She straightened his borrowed shirt, buttoned around her torn bodice. It was far too big for her frame but identical to the one the captain wore at present. She couldn't help noticing that his broad shoulders filled it out quite nicely.

He lifted his gaze abruptly, and Julianna sat up with a start. She hadn't meant for him to catch her staring.

"Miss Wayland..."

"Yes?" She'd answered a bit too hastily.

Amusement lit his gaze, and Julianna felt two hot spots rising in her bruised cheeks. Had he figured out she'd been watching him? Oh, who was she kidding? She'd been ogling!

"I believe the thing to do is lock you in the jail here in my office."

"Lock me up? But Captain Sundberg, I thought I explained."

"Indeed, and at great length, I might add." He sat back, his gaze fixed on her face. "But it'll solve all problems, at least temporarily."

"And then what?"

Captain Sundberg stood. "I'm sure I can think up tasks for you to do behind bars once you repair your gown and your bruises heal."

"Such as?" She tipped her head, suspicious.

"I'll consult with my purser, but if you're handy with a needle and thread, I guarantee we can keep your hands busy."

"Yes, I can sew." Her mother had been a seamstress in the Potters' laundering and mending shop. While Flora worked in the shoe factory, Mrs. Potter had taught Julianna the art of washing and repairing garments. "But then what?" Julianna got to her feet as well. "What happens when we dock in America?"

The captain pursed his lips in momentary thought. "You could gain employment and begin a new life. Or, if you wish, you could indenture yourself for a few years and earn your passage back to London."

"A few years?" Julianna wondered what would become of Flora in that time. Who would care for her? Support her?

"In either case, you've got a few weeks to mull over your options." Captain Sundberg sauntered to the jail cell and removed several crates and a large black leather valise. "I'll have the purser bring in a blanket for the berth, and I'll tell Kidwell to bring your meals. As for privacy, you'll have plenty. I don't spend a lot of time in my office during voyages."

Julianna strode slowly toward the hold. All three walls were brick and mortar, the fourth being the barred entryway. The bed hung from one wall by thick chains, and a set of iron shackles dangled menacingly in the far corner. The chamber pot was positioned beside the shackles.

Wheeling around on her heel, Julianna nearly collided with Captain Sundberg's wide chest. She gazed up into his face. "You're not going to chain me up, are you?"

"Not unless you give me good reason."

"I won't, sir. I promise I'll be no trouble."

The captain's features softened. "I believe you."

His breath wafted across her cheek as he replied, and Julianna's heart began to drum in a peculiar beat. *And why not?* She'd lived through quite the ordeal!

She took a step backward into the jail. "I shall be a model prisoner."

Finally a grin! "All right. Now in you go."

After she took another step back, he slid the iron barred doors together until they slammed shut with a finality that gave Julianna a sinking feeling. Her world had suddenly turned upside down. She'd left Flora and London behind and was sailing for...America!

America!

Trepidation gnawed at her every nerve. What fate would befall her in that new land? What if she found an employer just as ruthless as Olson Tolbert?

Or worse?

CHAPTER 4

S o you think the girl's in cahoots with Griswald, Cap'n?"
Bent gave him a stare from beneath busy arched brows.

"I said there is a *chance* she's Griswald's accomplice." In the stately saloon, designated for the *Allegiance*'s captain and officers only, Daniel took a bite of his supper of beef and gravy. He hid a grimace and swallowed. "I don't know anything for sure."

"I think yer mistaken, Cap'n." His first mate shoveled in a bite. "Griswald doesn't 'ave the sense to steal master paintings."

"Maybe, but Miss Wayland lived on the streets of London for a time. There's no telling what sort of tricks she picked up there."

His purser, Jonathan Dinsmore, cleared his throat. "Cap'n, she might be streetwise, but she's mannerly and even a bit naïve, if you ask me."

Daniel had thought so too. He swung his gaze to Dinsmore. The dedicated purser seemed dwarfed sitting between Bent and the second officer, Isaac Cravens. "You spoke with her, then?"

"Aye." Dinsmore inclined his head. "I made up her bunk, and she talked the entire while."

"Ah, yes. She does tend to ramble on, doesn't she?" Daniel sent a gaze upward.

"A reg'lar babbling brook, sir."

Daniel snorted his amusement but then narrowed his gaze. "Did you say you made up her bed, Dinsmore?"

"Used the passenger linens, sir." The man shrugged his narrow shoulders. "Just didn't seem right to allow a lady to sleep on a hard mattress with only a rough blanket for cover up. I also found a cake of scented soap, left behind by a former passenger, and I gave Miss Wayland a needle and thread so she could tend to her torn dress. Just seemed fittin', sir."

All the officers nodded in agreement.

"Fine." Somehow it bothered Daniel that his men were so taken with the stowaway when he still had a shred of suspicion about her. "But in the future, keep in mind that Miss Wayland is a prisoner on this ship. Not a passenger. I will also add that she was accustomed to sleeping on London's cold, cobbled lanes."

"Well, only for a couple of years," Dinsmore corrected. "Since then she's worked at the Tolbert mansion on Bainbury Street."

"So she says." Bent looked at Daniel. "She might be lyin' about that, sir."

"No, I've seen her there. Just last month, in fact." At least Daniel could lay those suspicions to rest.

"Well, you can't blame the girl for wantin' to run away from Cap'n Tolbert." Dinsmore devoured the last of his supper and pushed his plate forward. He rested his long forearms on the scarred tabletop. "I've had me own dealings with the bloke. He swindled me out of a whole day's pay."

Daniel wasn't surprised. "I think it's fair to say he's rogue."

His men murmured their agreements.

"Cap'n," Dinsmore added, "I hope you plan to keep Griswald in the brig the entire voyage for what he's done to poor Miss Wayland."

"I hadn't quite thought that far ahead." Daniel had planned to go below and speak with Griswald in a day or two before making further decisions.

"He shouldn't 'ave ever been hired aboard." Dinsmore's gaze slid in Bent's direction.

The first mate squared his shoulders. "There, now, I interviewed all the men just like the cap'n said. How's I s'posed to know that Griswald is a reviler and abuser of women?"

"He's got a poor reputation on the docks, Mr. Bentley." The purser raised his chin in challenge.

"Mistakes happen." Daniel tapered his gaze at Bent, thinking. Perhaps next time he'd reclaim the job of hiring a crew. Bent didn't seem to have the knack. "What's done is done."

And then Daniel remembered this would likely be his last voyage. He'd inform his crew once the *Allegiance* dropped anchor in New York. Certainly he'd miss mastering a ship, but becoming George's executive appealed to him so much more.

Standing from where he'd been seated on the padded bench, Daniel nodded to his men. "I have work in my office to complete, but I'll take the helm at dawn unless you need me beforehand."

They gave him respectful nods.

Leaving the saloon, Daniel made his way to his cabin and its adjoining office. He knocked hard at the door, so as not to catch Miss Wayland in a state of undress. He heard a murmured reply.

He opened the door slowly. "May I come in?"

"Yes, Captain."

Pushing the door wider, he entered his office and lit the wall sconces. A golden glow filled his paneled quarters. He glanced toward the jail and noticed Miss Wayland had repaired her gown and apron. She stood behind the iron bars looking every bit the parlor maid—well, except for no cap on her head and her battered face. But that too appeared cleaned up, and her nut-brown hair had been repinned.

"I trust you've eaten your supper."

"Yes, thank you, Captain." She hesitated. "And I've repaired my dress and pinafore, so I can return your shirt. Nary a drop of blood on it either."

"Good news." He strode to the jail, and she handed it back to him between the iron bars. He caught a faint whiff of the floral-scented soap Dinsmore had given to her. She'd obviously used it.

He gave her a speculative glance. Most of her face was hidden in the shadows, which for some odd reason fueled his suspicions.

Crossing the room, Daniel hung up his shirt and then sat down in one of the two leather armchairs that were bolted to the floor. "Miss Wayland, when did you first meet Mr. Griswald?" He figured he might as well come right out and question her.

"Meet him?" Fingers of her right hand curled around the iron bars. "It was in the storage room, Captain. Just today."

"And you were never acquainted with him in any way up until that time?"

"No, sir."

Daniel gauged her response.

"Why do you ask?"

He pushed out his bottom lip in a moment's pensiveness. "I want to be sure I have all the facts for my logbook." And part of him—most of him, in fact—wanted to believe the young woman. But he had priceless paintings to look after. "I turn the logbook into my superiors after our voyage." That was a bit of an exaggeration, yet truthful.

"Ah…makes sense." She leaned her slender frame against the cell bars.

"I seem to recall that you mentioned coming across Griswald's ilk in the pub where your sister works."

"Yes, unfortunately, I have. Barbaric is what they are."

Was that apprehension in her voice?

"As you're aware, I agree with you, Miss Wayland, and won't tolerate that sort of barbarianism on my ship."

"And lucky for me that you do, Captain." She shifted. "You're not what I expected in a sailor, sea captain or otherwise."

Daniel arched a brow. "Is that a compliment?"

"Yes. You see, the only sailors I've met are drunken louts."

"Hmm, well...I don't imbibe. As for being a 'lout,' you may want to reserve your opinion for after our voyage."

"I've already determined that you're no lout, Captain." Her voice softened, and for some odd reason it touched Daniel like a caress.

But what had he expected from a streetwise scamp? She'd no doubt honed her wiles.

"You're a smart man to refrain from strong drink."

"Hmm, well, I must confess that I went through a time where I enjoyed a brandy or two too many. Found out it's no way to live—especially if one hopes to be successful." He thought he sounded a bit like his benefactor. Then, again, George had ground that concept into Daniel's brain.

And what would George have to say about Daniel returning to his family's farm in Wisconsin? After that last disastrous visit there, George discouraged him from ever setting foot on his parents' acreage again. George cited the fact that *Mor* and Poppa refused to accept Daniel's educational and career choices.

But that had been seven years ago. At the time he'd hated college and didn't know what the future held for him. Now he did. Daniel wondered if his parents would see him differently. They hadn't thought he'd amount to much, but George and Eliza always believed in him.

Would his parents—especially *Mor*—finally admit how wrong they'd been? Would they finally be proud of him and all his accomplishments?

Pushing to his feet, he crossed his office and unlocked the door to his adjoining cabin. Without a word he stepped inside and shrugged out of his dark blue captain's jacket with its brass buttons and gold bars. He'd worked hard for each one of them, worked his way up from a mere deckhand and then an apprentice—

And it was thanks to George Ramsey that he'd gotten those opportunities.

Thoughts of the man filled his mind. George had been like a second father. He and his wife, Eliza, took Daniel in, although once they discovered he was a runaway, they wired his parents in Wisconsin to let them know he was unharmed. Daniel had fumed for days afterward. Finally George coaxed the truth out of him—Daniel didn't want to return to Wisconsin and take over his family's farm. He wanted adventure, and that's why he'd run away from home at age fifteen to try to join the Union Army. Daniel had wound up in New York City, and that's where George found him, exhausted, bedraggled, and hungry.

"Captain?"

Miss Wayland's voice jarred him from his thoughts. "Yes, what is it?" The reply came out sharper than he intended.

"I hate to trouble you again, sir, but I wondered if I could have a cup of water."

He strode to the pitcher on the stand in his office and filled a tin cup. "Hands out in front of you, where I can see them." Daniel wasn't about to be bushwhacked by this female.

He made his way to the cell. Miss Wayland did as he bid her, and he unlocked the door.

Accepting the tin cup, she drank down its contents in two blinks of his eyes.

"I've been parched all day."

"Would you like another?"

"No, sir. I'm happy to report that my thirst has been satisfied."

"Good." Daniel reclaimed the cup, and his fingers collided with hers. He felt how cold they were. He glanced around. "Didn't my purser, Mr. Dinsmore, give you a blanket?"

"Oh, yes, Captain. It's in me bunk."

"You may want to use it. It's cold and damp on the high seas." Daniel stepped back and closed the jail cell door. The iron clanged together. The lock clicked tight. He noticed Miss Wayland didn't move, and her gray eyes seemed to beckon to him from amidst their swelling and bruising. "Is there something else?"

"No, sir. It's just…well, I'm glad you're not a drunkard." Her hands gripped the cell bars. "I thought all sailors were. To tell you the truth, I've been worrying since suppertime because…well, fighting off that devil, Griswald, this afternoon took everything out of me. I don't have much strength left." She clung to the iron bars as if for support.

Daniel felt rooted in place. Had she been assuming that he'd return to his office, drink his fill of liquor, and then take advantage of her?

A noble sense ignited deep within his core. He'd been reared to be a gentleman from birth—one thing his parents had done correctly. The Ramseys further instilled that quality in him.

He squared his shoulders and straightened to his full height. "Miss Wayland, you have my word, as the captain of the *Allegiance*, that no harm will come to you while you're in my custody."

The tip of her pink tongue ran over her fattened lips. "I've never known a man to keep his word before."

Daniel grinned. "Then I'd say it's your good fortune to meet one now."

❦

Julianna's knees weakened, and not from fright or the rolling of the ship. But this man. As handsome as he was commanding. And she'd been correct about the twin dimples. She wondered if Captain

Sundberg had this effect on every woman. A perfect charmer, that's what he was. Julianna had met his kind before. However, his blue eyes sparked with a light of sincerity that made her believe he meant what he said.

She was safe.

Safe. Had she ever really experienced the true meaning of the word?

"May I suggest you get some rest now, Miss Wayland?"

"Oh, yes, sir. Thank you, sir." She curtsied, and every muscle in her body screamed from her beating this afternoon.

She noticed the captain watched her. "You're quite mannered for a young woman who has resided on London's streets." He raised a brow, appearing suspicious. And why wouldn't he be? He didn't know her.

Julianna hurried to explain. "In addition to Mr. Tolbert's training, I have Molly Stanton, the upstairs maid, to thank for me manners." She smiled, remembering the meek young woman. "Molly had grown up with wealth until her father got himself thrown into debtor's prison. Poor Molly ended up employed by Mr. Tolbert, which worked to my advantage. She taught me how to be a lady. Worked on me every time the housekeeper turned her head. Then I practiced in the evenings on me own."

"Well, thank you, Miss Wayland. I'd been hoping for a . . . *bedtime story.*"

Cynicism flashed in his blue eyes, and Julianna guessed the reason. "I've been told that I chatter like a magpie. But it only happens when I'm under duress. I'll do my best to hold my tongue in the future, Captain." She didn't want this man to be angry with her. She'd fare better on this voyage if he liked her, even a little.

Pausing, Captain Sundberg glanced at her from over one broad shoulder. "Under duress?"

"Yes, sir."

With deliberate steps he turned and walked toward her again. "Yes, I suppose you have suffered a goodly amount of hardship today. Would you like me to ask Kidwell to make you a tonic? It'll mute your pain and help you sleep."

His offer touched Julianna. "Yes, sir, I'd like that very much."

"Fine. I'll return shortly."

After the captain left, Julianna moved toward her bunk, realizing her head was beginning to throb. Dried blood had clotted in her nasal cavity, and it, combined with the swelling, made breathing through her nose nearly impossible. When she lay down, the pressure in the middle of her forehead became a pulsating ache.

She carefully sat on the narrow bed and waited. Mr. Kidwell entered just minutes later.

"The captain said you requested a tonic, Miss Wayland." She heard the eagerness in his voice, and it made her wary. Would he demand some sort of repayment for this service? He'd already brought up her dinner, unappealing as it was.

But the captain had said she was safe.

Deciding she had no choice but to trust Captain Sundberg and his discernment, Julianna stood. "The captain thought a tonic might help me feel better."

"I've got it right here." The man slid off his cap and strode forward. Setting the cup he held onto a nearby tabletop, he fished in his jacket pocket and pulled out a ring of keys. Next he proceeded to unlock Julianna's cell. Opening the door, he lifted the cup of gurgling brew and handed it to her. "I'm famous for my medicinal tonics. You'll see."

She tried to give it a whiff but couldn't make out a single ingredient.

"Is your nose working, Miss Wayland?"

"I should say it's not!"

"Probably best you can't smell it then. Just drink up."

"Well, all right." Julianna stared at the tin cup in her hand. "Down the 'atch, as me sister would say."

Daniel turned his ring of keys in his palm as he strode to his quarters. He'd been detained by Bent, who had a bit of a situation over a card game in the galley after supper. But the disagreement wasn't serious and the matter quickly solved. Opening the door, he stepped into his office and found Kidwell sputtering and hopping from side to side as he bent over Miss Wayland's sleeping form.

Daniel stopped short. "What on earth are you doing?"

"It's Miss Wayland, sir."

"She's resting peacefully. Let her be."

"She's having trouble breathing, Captain. I think she needs to be upright. Could you give me a hand?"

Daniel unfastened a wall sconce and made quick strides into the cell. "How much tonic did you give her?"

"Same as always." Kidwell's voice echoed in a mix of pride and innocence.

"Your usual dose could fell a two-hundred-and-fifty-pound man."

"I gave her too much, then?"

"I'd say so." Hanging the sconce on a nail above the bunk, Daniel knelt and carefully pulled Miss Wayland into a sitting position. A throaty, gurgling groan escaped her, and her eyes rolled back inside her head. But her facial injuries appeared worse than Daniel had realized.

How could a man do this to a woman?

Daniel turned his gaze to Kidwell. "Definitely too much tonic. And you'd best go fetch Dr. Morrison. The swelling around her nose has increased."

"Right away, sir."

Kidwell jogged from the cell, and Daniel worked to fix the

blanket behind Miss Wayland's head. Just above her ear his fingers found a swollen bump, and he chided himself for being so cavalier about her injuries. He was accustomed to men pummeling each other, and he often turned an indifferent shoulder as they usually got what they deserved. But in this case he'd been altogether neglectful. Of course, he'd reasoned, she'd stood in the shadows of her cell this evening and he hadn't gotten a good look at her face. Still…

As he moved Miss Wayland's shoulders, her head dropped into the crook of his elbow. He gave up trying to position her and gathered her into his arms. She felt lighter than he'd anticipated. He thought she'd be strong and sturdy from her work as a maid.

Strands of silky hair fell across the back of his hand, and a hint of lilac reached his nose. The lamp above them rained a glow that illuminated Miss Wayland's features, and he was reminded of the way she'd looked at the dinner party. Lovely—in a pure and simple way. Dark-winged brows and feathery lashes framed almond-shaped eyelids. A pert little turn to the end of her nose hinted at a similar personality, and wide, pink lips looked fat and bruised. He had a hunch that when they weren't so swollen, they'd look ripe for kissing. Daniel could well imagine why Captain Tolbert desired to make this woman his own—which made Daniel wonder over her virtues. How could a woman with Miss Wayland's beauty survive on the streets of London untarnished? Perhaps in her early teens she was less comely and men ignored her.

Of course, *Mor* would say God's hand of protection was that far-reaching, and all at once Daniel recalled a passage of Scripture he'd learned as a boy. He couldn't recall the psalm verbatim, but King David had penned something about being in hell and God being right there with him.

A wave of surprise caught him up. How amazing that he'd remembered anything about his parents' religion. He never used to pay attention in church or when Poppa read the Bible. Instead Daniel's thoughts were consumed by wild adventures on the high seas or heroics on the battlefield. After his uncle Jack fell at Gettysburg, Daniel decided to join the Union Army and take on the Rebs single-handedly. To his disappointment, by the time he calculated his plans, collected some funds, and actually worked up the nerve to leave home, the war came to an end. At fifteen Daniel found himself in New York City alone, hungry, and with his dreams dashed at his feet.

That's when George Ramsey entered his life. He owed George everything; his family in Wisconsin, nothing. Poppa had given into *Mor* and set aside his political career in order to farm, a fact that disappointed Daniel greatly. Then his mother tried to convince Daniel to follow in his father's footsteps. Daniel rebelled. There was no way he'd farm.

The woman in his arms convulsed as if struggling for air. Daniel pulled her upright even more and turned her slightly so her head rested against his chest. She choked, coughed. "That's right. Breathe, Miss Wayland." Reaching around, he cupped her small chin. "In and out." Why did the thought of her dying seem overwhelming?

And here he'd been so concerned about the souls in his cabin when the Teat Fire went off—all his men's souls and not this petite maid who'd survived Griswald's beating. *God forgive me.* Well, he wouldn't let it happen! He held her body so that she was nearly leaning forward. Her congestion eased, and she sucked in a clearer-sounding breath. "That's right, little one. In and out."

Dr. Morrison marched into the office, followed by Kidwell.

"I understand there's an injured woman on board?" The spindly physician adjusted his spectacles before bending over Miss Wayland. "Good heavens! How'd this happen?"

Kidwell hurried to explain. "Toppin' things off, I gave her one o' my tonics."

"Of all the cotton bloomin' things!" Dr. Morrison stood. "You might have left the medicinal side of things to me, you know."

"Sorry 'bout that, sir." Kidwell sent an apologetic look to Daniel.

"I authorized it." He took full responsibility. "I knew you'd been occupied with Griswald's gunshot wound, and Kidwell, being the cook, knows how to concoct quite the elixir. It's worked for crewmen in the past."

"But this is a woman." The physician's intelligent brown eyes rested on Daniel.

"So I've noticed, thank you." He'd become increasingly aware that Miss Wayland possessed curves in all the right places.

Dr. Morrison leaned in for a closer inspection. "She's badly hurt, all right. Bring her to the sick bay."

CHAPTER 5

*J*ULIANNA'S EYES SLOWLY opened to see the pinched features of a skinny old man hovering over her. Sunlight spilled into the room, causing her to squint. She realized she sat in an upright position but tried to move. The clamoring in her head gave her pause. The man stretched out his bony hand.

"Just rest."

Her head sank into a soft pillow.

"Where am I?" she croaked, inching the single sheet up over her chemise. Why, she'd been undressed!

"You're recovering in my infirmary, Miss."

He sounded like another Yank. Then Julianna spied the stethoscope around the gent's long neck.

"I'm Dr. Morrison."

"Julianna Wayland, sir." She realized she'd been stripped of her dress, corset, crinoline, and camisole. "Where are my clothes?"

"Hangin' up in the closet, Miss."

"You had no right to take them off of me." She couldn't help her indignant tone.

The doctor glanced her way as a grandfatherly smile stretched across his face. "I've been a physician for thirty years. I saw to it that your modesty was never compromised, but I had to check for other bruises and any broken bones."

She relaxed. "I suppose a doctor has to do his job." At least she still wore her stockings, drawers, and chemise.

From out of the corner of her eye she glimpsed movement. Turning her head to one side, she saw Captain Sundberg striding across the room. He appeared a tad disheveled, with whiskers darkening his jaw and one flap of his white shirt hung over the belt of his black britches.

Julianna brought the sheet up to her chin and attempted to rise once again. But the captain's strong hand on her shoulder held her in place.

"Easy there, Miss Wayland. You gave us quite the scare." The captain ran his fingers through his thick reddish-brown hair.

"I did?" She felt transfixed by his attention.

The captain replied with a single nod. "Kidwell gave you too much of his tonic and that, combined with the injuries you sustained two days ago—"

"Two days ago?" In spite of her pounding head, Julianna propped herself up on the berth. She clung to a fistful of the starched white linen covering her. "But didn't it just happen...yesterday, judging by the way the sun's shining?"

The captain lifted his gaze and met the physician's stare. "You, um..." He looked back at Julianna and expelled a sigh of resignation. "Miss Wayland, I'm afraid Griswald injured you worse than I had originally thought. I must apologize for my insensitivity in that regard."

At the sound of his soft voice, Julianna experienced a wave of dizziness that she was certain had nothing to do with her injuries. A rush of heat spread across her face. How could she so easily fall for such charm?

She averted her gaze. "You don't have to apologize to me, Captain. I'm just a lowly maid."

"Your station in life has nothing to do with it, Miss Wayland. You see, as this ship's captain, I am responsible for every soul onboard, stowaways included." His blue eyes darkened, but his steady gaze never left her face, for which Julianna was grateful. It proved the captain was a gentleman, just like he claimed. "I should not have allowed your injuries to go unattended as I did."

"Apology accepted." She thought the captain could probably charm even the old cook out of her kitchen at Mr. Tolbert's mansion.

He dipped his head and then turned to the physician. "Now that Miss Wayland has regained consciousness, I will leave you to your work."

"Very good, Captain."

He swung his broad shoulders toward the door. "Oh, and one more thing…"

The doctor's graying brows arched in expectancy.

"Miss Wayland is not to leave this sick bay without my prior authorization." His gaze darted her way before he looked back at the aging doctor. "Is that clear?"

"Clear as the Thames, sir."

Julianna pressed her swollen lips together, staving off a grin. The good doctor was being rather flip.

The captain scowled before making strides across the infirmary's polished floor. He gave the paneled door a good slam as he left.

The doctor chuckled.

"We might be walking the plank together, if you're not careful." Julianna smiled then suddenly winced as pain spread across her face.

"As you can see, I'm not worried." The doctor held out a cup of water.

Taking it, Julianna swallowed it in two gulps. "May I have more?"

"Of course, but drink it slowly this time."

"I will, I promise." Her face heated with chagrin. "I'm used to having to see to me needs in quick order so Mr. Tolbert wouldn't get angry."

"Well, Mr. Tolbert's not here."

"Thank goodness for that!" She accepted the proffered cup of water again and forced herself to sip as curiosity continued its annoying jab. "So you and Captain Sundberg don't see eye to eye?"

"Sure we do. But I've known Daniel Sundberg ever since he was a smart-mouthed pup. I've known George Ramsey at least twice as long."

"Is Mr. Ramsey some relation to the captain?"

"In a manner of speaking. He had a hand in Daniel's upbringing, and now our prince is the heir to Ramsey Enterprises."

"Prince?"

The doctor gave her a half shrug. "He's earned the title of Prince of Sea Captains because he doesn't mistreat his crew like some ship's masters do. Sailors get in line to sign on with him."

"Prince of Sea Captains..." Julianna knew that name. She'd overhead sailors in the Mariner's Pub referring to him when she visited her sister there on a Sunday afternoon. She only wished she could recall what those drunken sailors had said. Nothing awful, if her memory served her well. "The captain must be a very important man."

"I s'pose he is, although Daniel has had to work for every bit of it."

Julianna took another sip of water. The captain was a puzzle to her, so she enjoyed getting this tidbit of information on him.

"Apparently this is his last voyage," the aging physician continued. "Must be time for our prince to trade in his helm for the Ramsey crown."

"Hmm..." Julianna wondered what would happen to her once

she set foot on American soil. What sort of employment would she find? "I don't suppose Mr. Ramsey would be needing a new maid?"

"You?

Julianna nodded. "I didn't stowaway on purpose."

"Yes, I heard something to that effect."

"And I'll need to find a way to pay for me passage back to London."

Dr. Morrison narrowed his gaze. "What do you want to go back there for? Sounds like you've never had it very good. I'd look at this accidental stowaway as a gift from God above."

"I would, except…"

"Except what?"

"I can't help but think of me poor sister. She's living a terrible life on the wharf, and I'm trying to save me money so I can buy us a house in the country someday." She thought of her jar of coins, stashed away in her bedroom. No doubt her meager savings was lost now.

"How old is your sister?" The doctor planted a hand on one narrow hip.

"Twenty-six."

"Is she handicapped?"

"In a manner of speaking, I guess." Julianna handed back the cup. "She's stricken with inebriety."

"You've tried to help her?"

"Of course! And I did help her when I could—but she refuses my help."

"So are you certain you want to return to London—and to that? A drunken sister who doesn't want your help?"

Julianna shook her head. "I don't want to end up like me sister."

"Well, then, there's a new life waiting for you, Missy." The doctor tucked away his stethoscope and reached for a wad of white bandages and a bottle of antiseptic. "You've been given a second chance.

Make this one count." He paused, bending over her once more. "Now let's take another look at your injuries."

⊛⊚⊛

The Atlantic stretched out before Daniel like a sea of blue-green ice. The *Allegiance* gently rose and fell as it sliced through it unencumbered. The wind caused Daniel's coattails to flap, and on deck his crewmen sang a call-and-response chantey as they pulled and hoisted, adjusting the billowing sails.

"Boney was a warrior—"

"Away—a-yah!"

"A warrior and a terrier—"

"Jean Francois!"

Daniel grinned.

"The men are in good spirits this afternoon." Bent stepped in beside him.

"And they should be." At the helm, Daniel maintained his steady grip. He stood a head taller than the poop deck and had a clear view of the masts. He'd call orders to his second mate, standing on the poop, and he, in turn, hollered orders to the crew on the main deck below. "There's not a cloud in the sky and the wind is abaft."

"Aye, sir." Bent regarded him askance. "But maybe you should see about getting some shut-eye."

"I feel fine."

"Aye, but I've got a feelin' the weather'll turn soon."

Daniel eyed his first mate. "Oh?" Bent had a knack for predicting tempests.

"It's me knees. They never lie."

"So I've come to know." Daniel stepped aside and allowed Bent to take the helm.

"And now you can check on our pretty stowaway too."

Daniel heard the goading in his tone. "That's not funny, Bent."

"Not a bit, sir." He smirked anyhow. "Why, any man in his right mind can see she's a lovely lit'le thing in spite of the pounding she took from Griswald."

Daniel couldn't deny it—and more's the reason he wanted to keep her whereabouts guarded from a majority of the crewmen. He'd likely have mutiny on his hands if he didn't.

"And she's strong, for a woman. Courageous too, I'd say, seein' how she stood up to the Grisly Devil." The older man gave a sorrowful wag of his head. "She's kind-hearted. She wanted to take care of her drunken older sister who fell to ruin."

"Bent, I don't need you to list Miss Wayland's virtues." A moment's hesitation, and then he admitted, "I realize now she's telling the truth. She's not involved in any conspiracy to steal those paintings. She came aboard by accident."

"You're a wise man, Cap'n."

Daniel sensed a pinch of sarcasm, but coming from Bent, he'd let it go. "Griswald, on the other hand, can stay in the hold for the remainder of the voyage. I don't trust him and suspect he'll be a poor influence on the other men."

"Good call, sir, although the brute won't be pleased to learn his sentence."

Daniel raised a shoulder of indifference. "So be it. I plan to alert port authorities as soon as we dock too. An animal like Griswald shouldn't be allowed to roam the same streets as decent citizens."

"I agree, sir."

"Thank you, Bent." Daniel inclined his head. "Carry on."

"Aye, Cap'n."

Daniel went below and, as his first mate suggested, checked in at the infirmary before heading to his bunk. He walked in to find Miss Wayland asleep.

He swung his gaze to the physician. "How is she?"

"Comin' along. I don't think her nose is broken after all, although

I removed a large blood clot from her nasal cavity. I suspect she'll be breathing easier from here on in."

"Good news."

Dr. Morrison tossed him a glance. "She took quite a beating, and I suspect her wrist is sprained and a rib is cracked."

Daniel grimaced. However, this latest information cemented his decision to keep Griswald behind bars.

"Keep her here, then." Removing his jacket, he folded it over one forearm. "Bent senses foul weather in our future." He kept his voice low so as not to disturb Miss Wayland. "You may acquire more patients. Be sure she remains safe. Don't let her out of your sight."

"I will, Captain."

"I'm going to get some rest. If you need me, you know where to find me."

Morrison sent him an affirming nod.

The ship rocked to and fro. Julianna sat in the corner of the infirmary and braced herself for the next violent wave. It had taken a good twenty-four hours after waking from the tonic before she felt like herself again. But then, just as she'd gotten up and dressed, a terrible storm hit. She glanced at Dr. Morrison, so calm and collected. He didn't appear the least bit worried the tempest might reduce the *Allegiance* to mere driftwood.

Thunder clapped, and the ship rose and dipped. Julianna's stomach turned. She could hear men's shouts over the gale.

"We're going to die, aren't we?" She couldn't imagine having escaped the young master and then the Grisly Devil, only to die in the middle of the ocean.

"Bah!" The doctor snorted. "It's just a squall."

"A squall, you say?"

"I've been through worse. But don't fear. The prince is at the helm.

Besides," he added, struggling to keep his medical supplies from spilling from the built-in cabinet, "God controls life and death. If it's our time, then we've got no say about it."

"If that's true, Doctor, then where was God when I lived in the dirty streets of London, begging for someone kind to take me sister and me into their large, warm home?"

"He was right there with you, Miss."

Julianna had to concede that God answered her prayers when Mr. Tolbert took her and Flora in. But any happiness was short-lived after the young master ruined Flora. Perhaps the devil had had his way and not the Lord at all.

"God is here with us now, saying, 'Peace, be still.'"

"I wish I could believe that, Doctor."

Another wave came, another lurch of the ship, more thunder, followed closely by a brilliant flash of lightning. Julianna could hear men calling to each other and their footfalls as they ran across the deck above.

The ship dipped to one side. Sliding across the cabin on her backside, Julianna tried to grab onto anything nailed down. For all her life she couldn't fathom how God was in this storm.

All at once two men burst through the door of the sick bay, half carrying and half dragging an injured man. They were drenched to the bone in spite of their oilskins, and they soaked the bedding on which they set the man.

"We think he broke his leg, Doc," said one of the men.

"Thank you, Mr. Cravens; I'll attend to it."

The patient moaned.

The crewmen took their leave just as another crack of thunder shook the ship. Despite the roiling ship, Dr. Morrison expertly slit open the sailor's pant leg.

"Yes, this leg is broken all right." He glanced at Julianna. "I'm going to need your help. Are you up to it? Your wrist? Your ribs?"

"I'm up to it." Julianna wasn't in any pain. Perhaps her fear of the storm had numbed it. Either way, helping the physician might keep her mind busy.

Her gaze fell on their patient, a wide-shouldered, middle-aged blond.

"You're not afraid of a mean sailor like me, are you?" He narrowed hazel eyes at Julianna while the physician removed his wet clothes.

"I might be if your leg weren't broken."

He ground out a grin at her quip—or was it an audible wince?

Julianna scrutinized the man's injured leg, twisted into an odd angle. She tried not to let her grimace show. Dr. Morrison called for a blanket. She fetched it—which proved no simple feat with the boat listing from side to side.

At last she found the dry covering and handed it off. Dr. Morrison placed it over the groaning man.

"Give him a spoonful of this." Dr. Morrison shoved a small brown bottle and metal utensil at Julianna. "Careful not to drop it."

"Yes, Doctor." She braced herself, but her hand shook too badly to pour some of the liquid onto the spoon.

The sailor growled, took the bottle, and took a hearty swig.

"That should do it. Not too much." Dr. Morrison pulled the medicine from the sailor's lips. "Lie down now, boy."

He did as directed.

"Let him bite on this while I set his leg." Dr. Morrison put a leather strap in Julianna's palm. "Let him keep biting and tell him to holler as loud as he wants to."

For the first time in her life Julianna felt compassion and not contempt for a seafaring man. She pitied him for what was about to take place.

"This is going to hurt, son."

"I'm ready, you old salty piece of pork."

Julianna put the strap between the man's jaws.

"UUUUHHHHHHHH!" He let out a yell.

Julianna tensed but managed to keep his forehead down and the leather between his clenched teeth. "You'll be all right. You'll see. You're going to survive this and be all the stronger for it." They were words she often murmured to herself as a girl.

The sailor bellowed again. Beads of sweat began dotting his brow. Finally he lost consciousness.

Julianna moved back. "Did he die?"

The doctor glanced over his shoulder. "No, no..." With his arms around the man's log-sized leg, the doctor tugged and turned. "His name's Whitley, and he's far too stubborn to die. He merely succumbed to the pain and laudanum. Better for him that he did too."

Once satisfied that the bones were aligned, Dr. Morrison splinted their patient's leg. "That's all we can do for now."

Exhaustion weighed heavily on Julianna's limbs. She collapsed on the cabin floor. It was then she noticed that the storm had quieted. The ship steadied. It appeared that Mr. Whitley wasn't the only survivor in the room.

CHAPTER 6

*T*HE STORM PASSED, and Julianna spent the next day helping Dr. Morrison with both his patient and righting his office. That evening Mr. Kidwell escorted her back to her jail cell, where she remained for another two days. Both the cabin boy, Jimmy, and Mr. Kidwell brought up her meals, and Mr. Kidwell often sat and conversed with her or read aloud from a book while she ate. Julianna supposed she liked him all right. He seemed like a kind-hearted fellow, until it came to dealing with men like the Grisly Devil—and a good thing for her too.

"I've got plans to cross America and settle in the untamed west," he said one night.

"Sounds exciting."

"It will be."

She gave Mr. Kidwell a polite smile. She didn't mind listening to the man's dreams. After all, he had saved her life. It was the least she could do. Besides, his conversation and the tales he read to her helped to pass the time.

"I see you're finished eating." Mr. Kidwell rose from where he'd been sitting in one of the captain's black leather chairs. "I'll take your supper tray back to the galley."

"You're most kind, Mr. Kidwell. Thank you."

"Call me Jeremy." He gave her a smile and purposely caught her gaze. "It's my given name."

"It's a fine one." With a measure of uncertainty Julianna held out the tray to him. He accepted it. He'd left the cell door open, an indication that he trusted her, and Julianna was most grateful for it.

"Are you ready to listen to me read?"

"Sure."

"All right, then. I'll drop off your tray in the galley, fetch my book, and be back."

He left, and Julianna strode to her berth and sat down, leaning her back up against the cold brick wall. If she wasn't mistaken, Mr. Kidwell—Jeremy—was beginning to take a shine to her. She could see it in his face, the way his eyes darkened whenever she spoke, and how his gaze lingered on her mouth when she replied. The very idea caused her insides to knot with trepidation. Anytime a man had been interested in her, they'd had nothing but lasciviousness on their minds.

Would Jeremy be different from the others?

Captain Sundberg entered the cabin and proceeded to shrug out of his impressive blue jacket with all its brass trimmings. Since setting out to sea, he and the rest of his crew didn't bother with a razor, so now a reddish-brown beard shadowed the captain's jaw and chin. The same colored mustache covered his upper lip. If the captain looked ruggedly handsome before, he was tenfold now.

He glanced her way and caught her gaze. Julianna quickly ducked her head, hoping she hadn't been caught ogling the captain like some floozy. Although, if he was like most men, he enjoyed women's appreciative stares. Perhaps the captain even expected them.

"Why is this cell door open?"

Julianna quickly lifted her head. "Oh, Jeremy left it open. He's coming back with a storybook."

"Jeremy, is it?" The captain slammed shut the jail door with more force than seemed necessary.

Julianna jumped up from the bunk. "Sir, surely you know by now that I'm not a danger to you or anyone else."

"Miss Wayland," he began in a mocking tone that she was beginning to detest, "I have left explicit orders that you're to be locked behind bars at all times. Your recuperation and duty in the infirmary were exceptions, of course. Nevertheless, I will not abide my instruction being ignored."

"As I said, Captain, Jeremy is coming back. I'm sure he didn't mean to—"

"Miss Wayland, I have more than fifty men onboard this ship. Many I've employed before, and I trust them. But others, I suspect, are as uncouth and abusive as Mr. Griswald. Therefore, my insisting your cell door be kept locked at all times is more for your protection than mine or my crew."

At his implication Julianna felt the blood seep from her face. "I understand, Captain, and from now on I'll make sure your orders are followed."

His blue eyes searched her face before he answered with a curt dip of his head. Turning, he made long-legged strides toward his quarters. Julianna set her head against the cold iron bars. How grateful she was for this man's protection.

Minutes later Jeremy returned with a leather-bound volume under his arm. "I purchased a collection of Hans Christian Andersen's work. I'll read 'The Great Sea Serpent' to you."

"Oh, I don't think I'd like to hear about sea serpents."

"Sure you would. This is a wonderful story. I've read it before." He stared at the closed jail cell door, only just now realizing it had been shut. His brow furrowed.

"The captain's here," Julianna whispered. She pointed toward his quarters.

"Ah…" Jeremy looked hesitant, glanced over one broad shoulder, then shrugged. "Shall I begin?"

"If you insist." Julianna strolled to her berth and sat down.

Jeremy lowered himself onto the floor and leaned against the cell door. Opening the book, he began to read. "'There was a little fish—a salt-water fish—of good family: I don't recall the name—you will have to get that from the learned people.'"

He read on. But when he reached a part in the story where the little fish finds a woman and her child dead in a sunken ship, Julianna halted him. "I can't bear it. I'll have nightmares, for pity's sake!" She shuddered and thought of that terrible storm a couple of days ago.

"But the dead woman and child are symbolic. Keep listening."

She groaned. From the corner of her eye Julianna glimpsed the captain standing in the doorway of his private quarters with his arms folded across his broad chest. She guessed that he'd paused in his undressing because his shirt had been partially unbuttoned and one side lay open, revealing a mat of hair that matched his beard.

But how could she notice such things? Julianna tore her gaze away, and an odd feeling betwixt a chill and a wave of heat stole over her.

Jeremy continued with his story, and she forced herself to pay attention. At last she got the gist of the tale.

"So it's a telegraph cable that has all these fish in a tizzy? What absurd, little fish."

"You're missing the point, Miss Wayland. Please, allow me to finish."

She released an audible sigh before catching the captain's grin. A pity those dimples were hidden by his whiskers now.

Finally Jeremy read the end of the story. "'Men's thoughts in all languages course through it noiselessly. "The serpent of science for good and evil, Midgard's snake, the most wonderful of all the ocean's wonders, our—GREAT SEA-SERPENT!"'"

Julianna yawned.

"Which reminds me"—Captain Sundberg unfolded his muscular arms and straightened—"I must send a wire when we reach New York."

Jeremy's expression said he wasn't amused. "That's not the point, sir. Our modern technology and conveniences are far-reaching, from mountaintops to the ocean depths."

"Why not say so plainly? Besides, Kidwell, there's no such thing as mermaids."

Julianna stared at the captain. Was he goading the poor man?

"It's a fairy tale, sir." Exasperation waxed thick in Jeremy's voice.

"Well, just so you know," Julianna put in, "real or not, referring to her as a sea cow is most insulting. No woman wants a man to call her a cow. I don't care if she's a mermaid or a chamber maid."

After casting her a curious glance, the captain dropped his head back and laughed so that his shoulders shook. The deep, rich timbre of his *hah, hah* chuckles reverberated like welcomed thunder after a long, dry spell.

Jeremy grinned.

Julianna bristled. "I don't think it's so funny."

"Miss Wayland"—the captain gave her a bow—"you have lifted my spirits with your candid opinions."

"I'm glad you find them so amusing," she quipped. "A lady doesn't like being laughed at either."

"No insult intended. Right, Kidwell?"

Jeremy hastened to wipe the smile off his face with the sleeve of his shirt. "Right, Captain." He tucked his book under his arm. "I should be on my way." He turned. "Good night, Miss Wayland."

She leveled a gaze at both of them for having fun at her expense.

Jeremy almost ran from the room.

The captain chuckled again. "He'll take on a brute like Griswald, but a stern look from the woman he cares about sends him running away like a frightened boy." Captain Sundberg folded his arms again, a grin lingering on his lips. "Do you scare off all your suitors, Miss Wayland?"

"I can't really say." She squared her shoulders, wondering if she'd really *scared* Jeremy. "I never had a proper suitor before."

"Ah…" He sniffed, but the twinkle in his eye never dimmed.

Julianna had to admit she liked seeing amusement dance in his blue eyes. "I never cared for being the butt of any jokes."

"My apologies, although I wasn't laughing at you."

Was he serious? Julianna tipped her head, scrutinizing his expression. Or was he goading her too?

Either way, it wasn't like she could do anything about it. She returned to her berth and pulled the blanket around her shoulders. Without another word the captain extinguished the lamps, entered his quarters, and closed the door behind him.

Julianna lay in the darkness, wondering about him. Handsome as the day was long—and the days certainly were long on the ship.

But soon the voyage would end. She was headed for America!

The idea still stunned Julianna.

More thoughts crowded in. What would she do when she arrived in a new country? Where would she go? For whom would she end up working?

Julianna's mind flitted to Jeremy. His romantic interest in her was obvious, and she was grateful to the man for rescuing her from Griswald's clutches. She always would be. But the idea of marrying him, if things escalated to that point, frightened her. She'd seen the poundings several sailors gave Flora. Twice Julianna had gotten in the middle of such frays and had gotten pummeled herself. Fortunately nothing worse had befallen her.

Sailors. They were scoundrels, every one!

Would Jeremy be that sort as a husband?

Would the captain?

Julianna shook herself, wondering how Captain Sundberg had suddenly entered the equation.

Around her sounds of the ship groaning and straining indicated its perseverance across the sea. Waves licked at the outer side of her cell, and Julianna pushed away thoughts of Jeremy's story about the dead woman and her child pickled inside a sunken vessel. Instead she allowed herself a moment's wonder about the kind of woman the captain would pursue.

She'd be a beauty, that's for certain, and one with a proper upbringing. She'd be educated and well-read so she could banter with him over those silly stories about telegraph cables and little fish. And the captain? Julianna imagined he'd treat his woman with a gentle hand. Some men did, she supposed. Perhaps once sailors became captains, they lost some of their fiery temperament. She hoped so—for the sake of that woman fortunate enough to win the captain's heart, of course.

❦

Daniel couldn't sleep. Why, he couldn't figure. He was physically tired enough, but thoughts of Kidwell courting Miss Wayland in her jail cell irked him beyond measure.

Turning, he plumped his down-filled pillow and tried to get comfortable. He shouldn't allow such a trivial thing to bother him. After all, Kidwell might be the answer to his question of what to do with Miss Wayland once they reached New York. He could instruct Dinsmore to dock Kidwell's pay and apply it to Miss Wayland's passage. That would set the books straight and ensure Miss Wayland possessed the right paperwork. He supposed Kidwell would make an adequate husband for Miss Wayland—

That is, if he intended to marry her.

With an irritable groan Daniel rolled onto his back again. He shouldn't care, but he did. The young lady deserved a decent chance at life. She had already lived an arduous existence with loveless caretakers and then on London's streets. She'd watched her sister's fall to ruin, fearing it was only a matter of time before the same thing happened to her. She was vulnerable. She needed a man's protection.

Fine, but why did he feel so blasted responsible to provide it? He certainly wasn't about to marry her.

Thoughts of a pale-skinned countess flitted across his mind. He could still feel Reagan's voluptuous body pressed against his as they danced at the spring ball. And her kiss—Daniel had enjoyed it. He grinned into the darkness of his quarters. George would be pleased to know that he intended to marry Reagan, although Daniel had not officially proposed marriage yet. After all, she was only eight months into mourning her late husband's death, not that she'd ever loved the man. It had been an arranged marriage, and the earl had been an elderly fellow. Reagan said she was ready to marry a man her own age and enjoy the pleasures of matrimony at long last. Then she'd kissed him again, whispering that Daniel was "the one."

His smile grew. Once they were wed, Ramsey Enterprises would merge with one of England's largest merchant fleets, a company Reagan inherited from her late father. The merger would produce more wealth than Daniel could imagine.

But love?

He grunted out a laugh. *Love.* Such a useless sentiment. Whoever got rich falling in love?

As for Kidwell, he would learn that soon enough, after he nursed his broken heart. In the meantime he was succumbing, the fool. Julianna didn't love him. Probably never would. She needed guidance and direction, yet soft words and a gentle hand—and Kidwell didn't seem like the sort to deliver.

Oh, but why should I care?

With an irritable sigh Daniel rolled again, this time onto his other side. His future was mapped out with the best-laid plans that his and George Ramsey's vast experience offered, so he'd best annihilate thoughts and concerns of Miss Wayland soon—*now!*

CHAPTER 7

"CAPTAIN, WOULD YOU possibly have a Bible that I can borrow?"
Daniel paused in midstride. "A...*Bible*?" He turned to
stare at Miss Wayland. After more than a week since Griswald's
beating, she began looking more like the pretty maid Daniel
recalled seeing at Tolbert's spring affair—which proved more of a
distraction to Daniel. Earlier as she'd brushed out her mahogany
tresses, he'd barely been able to concentrate on his daily log.

"Yes, a Bible. You see, Dr. Morrison mentioned something about
God knowing everything and about His being able to protect people.
Well..." A mix of sorrow and terror rounded her smoky eyes. "I
can't help thinking about the story Jeremy read. The one where the
woman and her child were—"

"Yes, I know the one to which you're referring." Daniel quelled the
impatient sigh making its way out of his throat. Miss Wayland had
only mentioned this matter three or four times already. Obviously
that part of the tale had disturbed her. "Miss Wayland..." He
stepped in her direction. "You must realize that Hans Christian
Andersen's story was a product of his imagination, and interpreta-
tion of it varies."

"But ships can really sink."

"I'm well aware of that." Daniel gave her a confident grin. "If you're worried about this vessel, I can tell you she's seaworthy, and I have a capable crew onboard."

"But what if God decides to sink her like a stone?" Miss Wayland clutched the cell bars on either side of her oval-shaped face. "What then, Captain?"

"Do you know how to swim?"

She shook her head.

"Ah...well, then, swimming is easy." Perhaps getting her to think she could learn to survive might quell her fears. "First, you put your head back as far as you can and allow yourself to float on your back. Like so." With arms spread out he lolled his head back. "When a wave washes over you, you hold your breath." Again he demonstrated. "Once it passes, you breathe again." Daniel righted himself, setting his hands on his hips. "Now you've had your first swimming lesson."

The pucker in her brow said she wasn't appeased in the least, and Daniel felt like tossing Kidwell overboard for frightening her with that ridiculous tale.

He clasped the jail bars, covering Miss Wayland's hands with his own. How soft and fragile they felt beneath his palms. "We will not go down."

"How can you be certain?"

"I am experienced. I've made this run between London and New York City plenty of times without incident. Except for that last storm, we've had smooth sailing. I expect the mild weather to hold."

"And if it doesn't?" She rested her forehead in between the bars.

Daniel resisted the urge to place a kiss on it. "Trust me. Everything will be all right. I promise." As the last word tumbled from his tongue, a sense of utter powerlessness enveloped him. He had no right to vow such a thing. He had no control over the wind or the waves or life and death.

Or falling in love…

He shook himself.

"Thank you, Captain." She lifted her head. "I feel better now because you're a man of your word."

"That I am." *Dear God, don't let me be a liar.*

Lifting his hands from hers, Daniel turned on his heel and strode across the office area and into his adjacent chamber. His mind played tricks on him—again. Of course that explained his confounded emotions of late.

Daniel peered over his shoulder at Julianna. He was keenly aware that his attraction to her might prove his downfall—something George had warned him about over and over. Lust was a trap. Leave the ladies alone, particularly those with little or no means.

Well, he wasn't about to jeopardize his future. He had a ship to command—a ship as well as his own life!

"What about the Bible, Captain?" Her sweet voice wafted over from the cell.

"Yes, I'll get you one." He kept one onboard as something of a good luck charm. His father had given it to him for his confirmation.

⊛⊛⊛

Hours later, Julianna sat on the edge of her bunk and leafed through the delicate pages of Captain Sundberg's Bible. Questions pummeled her like Griswald's fists. She'd never had much religious training—she'd only attended those long and inexplicable church services as ordered by Mr. Tolbert. In her nearly two years on the street she'd seen the well-attired church people as they went to and fro from the monstrous cathedral. She begged for a coin or two. They shooed her away like a repulsive insect.

Was God like those church people? Did He speak another language that she didn't know?

Julianna pushed aside strands of her damp hair. Her dry mouth yearned for a cup of cool water. It had been hours since Jeremy brought her supper, and she'd begged off another bedtime story, so he wouldn't likely be returning anytime soon.

Moisture collected around her forehead, ears, and neck. Lifting the hem of her pinafore, she dabbed it away. The temperature had risen in her jail cell today, and the air felt suffocatingly thick. If only she had a little round window in her cell like the one in Dr. Morrison's infirmary.

Minutes later the cabin door opened, and Captain Sundberg entered. Julianna smiled. A knight in shining armor if she'd ever seen one.

"Captain?"

"What is it?" His curt tone caught her off guard. Only this afternoon he'd been kind and sensitive.

Hadn't he? Or had she imagined it?

"I don't mean to trouble you, but I wondered…would it be possible for me to get some fresh air?"

He shrugged out of his uniformed jacket without giving her so much as a flick of a glance. "I've told you several times now why I must keep you behind bars."

"Yes, I know, but…" Carefully setting the Bible aside, Julianna rose from the berth and walked the few steps to the secured door. "It's quite stuffy in here, wouldn't you agree? I wondered if I could spend a few minutes in the infirmary, beneath the open window there."

"I'll open the porthole in my quarters. That may help."

"Thank you, sir." Julianna fought to keep the disappointment from her voice. But perhaps a bit of wind would indeed reach her cell.

She watched the captain make long-legged strides across the office area and into his private quarters. She heard the creaking of the window as he opened it. Seconds later he returned to his desk and sat down.

Leaning on the barred doorway, Julianna watched him open his logbook. He was a man she could watch for hours. She especially liked the way his eyelids narrowed and creased at the outer edges while he contemplated the pages before him. And, speaking of eyes—with that reddish-brown beard covering half of his face, the blue of them seemed ever so much brighter.

"Captain, are you a married man?"

"Excuse me?" He looked her way, eyes wide with surprise. "Married?"

"No." He looked back at his desktop. "I'm of the opinion that a sea captain doesn't make a good husband."

"I might agree, but why do you say so?"

"Because he's never at home."

She lifted a shoulder. "I would think that's what's good about him."

The captain raised his head, looking surprised again.

"I've been told that me father was a seafaring man. A no-good scoundrel, I suspect."

"Hmm..." The captain reclined in his chair and lifted his booted feet up onto the desk.

"I believe you're the only decent mariner in all creation."

"I appreciate the compliment, Miss Wayland." The corner of his mouth twitched as if he fought a smile.

"Oh, and speaking of creation..." Julianna glanced toward the Bible on her bunk. "I read today about how God created the world in just six days. Is that true, or is it another fairy tale?"

"I'm a sea captain"—he stretched and brought his hands to the back of his head—"not a theologian."

Whatever that is. "A simple true or false will do."

"The truth is, Miss Wayland, it matters little what I think. It's what *you* think that's important."

"Me? But I never went to school like you did."

"I'm talking about what you believe in here." He thumped his chest. "Deep inside."

"Do you believe in God?"

"Yes. A sea captain would be a fool not to believe in Him. But I also believe in myself. The decisions I made as a boy have no bearing on me as a man." He sat forward and dropped his legs off the desk. "So there you have it. And now, Miss Wayland, I suggest you go and think about it. I have work to finish."

Julianna paced the small cell. "I suppose it is true, then."

"Fine."

"I mean, when a person tells you to swear on the Bible, he's insisting you tell the truth...*or else.*"

"Right."

The captain's indifference annoyed her, although Julianna couldn't say why, exactly. Perhaps the heat had frayed her nerves.

"Captain, could I trouble you for a cup of water?"

"Why not?" He pushed to his feet. "You have troubled me for everything else."

"Well, excuse you me, Captain, but I'm not the one who locked me in this hot and smelly jail." Julianna's arms dropped to her sides, and she clenched her fists. But then she realized getting lathered over the situation would only make her feel hotter.

The captain said nothing as he filled a cup with water. However, as he turned from the pitcher and neared, she saw the muscle flex in his jaw. Oh, she'd angered him with her outburst, all right. Now what? Would he strike her?

Julianna stepped back as Captain Sundberg's keys connected with the cell door's lock. "Forgive me please, Captain. I'll watch me tongue from now on."

He silently held out the cup of water to her, his gaze locked on her face.

She reached for it, her senses on alert. But only when he walked away after she'd taken hold of the cup, leaving the cell door wide open, did Julianna sag in relief—at least for the moment.

She watched him leave the cabin. Was he off to fetch his whip? She'd heard a sailor in the pub talk of the flogging he'd gotten aboard for refusing to do what he'd been told. Another time she'd seen—no, *heard*—the young master whipping a stable hand. The boy couldn't have been more than ten years old. His screams still lingered in Julianna's memory.

Captain Sundberg returned, donned his jacket, and motioned her toward the door. Julianna set down her now empty cup and stepped cautiously toward him.

He put his forefinger to his lips. "Not a word."

With a slight bob of her head Julianna agreed. However, she wanted to ask where they were going.

Moments later her mind slammed into a terrifying conclusion.

Taking hold of the captain's elbow, she halted him before he stepped from the cabin. "You're not putting me in with the Grisly Devil, are you?" She whispered the question, but her senses screamed in terror. The brute would kill her for sure!

The captain gave her a glare. "I told you that I'm an honorable man and that you needn't fear while I'm in command of this ship. Which part of that statement, Miss Wayland, didn't you understand?"

"It's not a question of misunderstanding, sir." She swallowed her nerve and pressed on. "More of disbelief, I'd say."

The flesh around his blue eyes slacked. His broad shoulders eased downward beneath his blue jacket. "Yes, well, given your background, I can't blame you for being suspicious of me and men in general."

Incredulity rooted her to the plank flooring. Had she heard

correctly? Here stood a man whom sailors feared and obeyed, and yet he, so far, proved himself a gentleman in her lowliest of company. "You're hardly honor-bound, Captain," she stated tenuously, "given me social status."

She read the speculation in his sapphire eyes.

"Who would know if you mistreated me or not? Who would care?"

"I would." He arched a brow. "And that, Miss Wayland, separates the honorable from the despicable."

"You know, you're absolutely right." Julianna blinked. "It does."

He gave her a gentle smile. "Now, come along. I have a surprise for you."

"In general I don't care for surprises."

"Shh…no more talking. My officers are asleep in the next cabin. They're on duty in a few hours."

Julianna dipped her chin, indicating she understood. She gnawed her lower lip, grateful that he'd again diminished her fears. But a surprise?

The captain's strong hand folded around hers, and he led her through a narrow hallway, one that looked vaguely familiar, then up several stairs, and they reached a door. The captain opened it and indicated that she should walk outside before him. She did, and two steps forward, Julianna froze. She faced the stern of the ship and saw Mr. Bentley, off to her right, standing at a large wheel with protruding spokes. Behind him the rolling, bluish-gray water melded into a dusky sky for as far as Julianna's eyes could see.

The captain coaxed onward, and she realized his hand now gently gripped her upper arm. The rush of evening air felt exhilarating after being holed up in that sun-cooked cell. She could breathe again!

"Come along. You won't fall. I've got you."

Still, her steps faltered. "What about my being seen by your crew?"

A sigh escaped him. "They all know you're aboard, thanks to the night of the storm when Whitley broke his leg. He claims you're another Florence Nightingale—"

"Really?" Julianna had heard the woman's name but wasn't certain of her position.

"A compassionate nurse."

"Oh." Had the captain divined her thoughts? Still, she supposed it was quite the compliment.

"It seems you've earned the respect of my crew. Even so, we need to be careful. As I've said before, a number of these men are newcomers on the *Allegiance*. For all I know, they could conduct themselves as poorly around women as Mr. Griswald. Therefore I want you to remain behind bars unless one of my officers, Kidwell, or I am nearby."

"Say no more, Captain. I shan't complain."

"How refreshing."

Julianna bristled. Did he have to be so cynical?

"Well, good evening, Miss." Mr. Bentley gave her a welcoming smile. "It's a fine evening for a stroll."

Julianna inhaled deeply once again. "That it is." But as they neared the wheel, she nearly lost her balance on the slick deck. The captain's hold kept her upright.

"Perhaps if you hang on to the rail…" Captain Sundberg placed her hand on the sturdy brass fixture.

"I won't fall overboard, will I?" Ironic how only minutes before she'd been dreaming of a cool bath—but not one of the sea's magnitude. Besides, she didn't want to end up like that pickled woman and her poor child at the bottom of the ocean.

"You worry too much, Miss Wayland."

Had he read her thoughts again?

Mr. Bentley's jovial chuckle reached her ears. "Oh, don't be too hard on the girl, Cap'n. This is likely her first voyage."

"First and last," Julianna quipped.

"In that case, you'll 'ave to give her the grand tour, Cap'n."

Julianna felt as unsure about a look-about as Captain Sundberg appeared.

Moments later an expression of resignation crept into his blue eyes. "All right. Let's begin here. This is the stern, or the back of the ship."

She'd learned that much from listening to the sailors' banter on given Sunday afternoons in the Mariner's Pub.

"Mr. Bentley, here, is at the helm. He's steering the ship."

"And doing a fine job, if I say so m'self." He raised a proud chin, and Julianna laughed at his antics.

Captain Sundberg even grinned. "Now, Miss Wayland, if you'll step this way." He strode across the deck, and she tentatively followed. But as the ship rose and fell with another wave, she slid over the slippery, wet planks.

"Oh! Oh, my!" Her arms flailed as she fought to keep her balance. Seconds later she slammed into the captain. She clutched his blue coat until she found her footing. "So sorry, Captain."

Mr. Bentley's chuckles wafted to her ears. "Haven't found yer sea legs yet, eh, Miss?"

"Apparently not." And what would the captain think of the near mishap?

Clinging to him, her gaze traveled up the front of his wool coat. She determined a chance look into his eyes. But instead of finding the annoyance she expected, she saw a familiar tenderness in his gaze, one that she'd been sure she only imagined before.

He planted his hands on her waist. "Perhaps you are in danger of going overboard after all. I'd best keep a hold on you."

She swallowed. "Thank you, sir." She wondered if his beard felt soft or coarse. If she stretched out her fingers, they'd brush against his chin and she'd likely find out.

But she didn't dare be that bold.

My, oh, my, but he looked even more handsome in dusk with the distant sunset accentuating the gold strands of his coppery hair.

"Miss Wayland?"

She blinked. "Beg your pardon, sir." A flush of heat entered her cheeks.

The captain said nothing but carefully threaded her arm around his elbow. "There now, hang on to my arm." He raised his other one and took her hand. "I think you're secure now."

"I think so too." She didn't mind holding on to him for dear life. Not a bit.

He directed her attention toward the bow.

Julianna refocused. As she stared toward the front of the ship, complete amazement filled her being. The vessel looked as long as a city block. Sails billowed, appearing like puffy clouds against the sky.

"What an incredible sight!" Julianna had only seen the skeletal-like masts of ships in London's harbor.

"Ah, please allow me to show you the best view."

They climbed some stairs, and then the captain led her to the edge of the deck.

"We're standing on what is referred to as the poop deck," he said. "A portion of it runs over the top of my office quarters, along with a dining saloon, used when special guests are on board, and the officers' quarters. Straight ahead, then, you'll note the three towering poles, known as the mizzenmast, then the mainmast, and the foremast. All the ropes and chains, dangling from the masts, are known as the rigging."

"How fascinating."

Several sailors called greetings. The captain respectfully replied. Julianna noticed how well the crew responded to him. They tried to show off, in fact. One man took time to wave and salute while climbing what the captain called "the ratlines." The sailor resembled a daring acrobat.

"Give them sight of a pretty face," the captain muttered, "and the wisest men become fools."

Surely he didn't mean these men put on a show for her benefit. Just in case Julianna lifted her hand and returned the gesture.

"Please ignore them before someone gets himself killed."

"Yes, Captain." She slid her gaze to him. His bearded face made a far more appealing sight anyway.

"Now, you see those smaller boats there?"

She followed his line of vision.

"One's the lifeboat, and the other is the jollyboat. Beyond them is the doorway to the galley, the carpenter's shop, and the main saloon. This ship was also designed with passenger cabins below, along with the sick bay, which you're already familiar with."

"Passengers?" Julianna's mind had anchored on that word. Why anyone in their right mind would willingly sail the high seas, she couldn't fathom.

"We entertain passengers from time to time, yes. But we're transporting cargo on this particular run. Now then, continuing on, the crew's quarters are near the bow, called the forecastle."

"How terribly interesting." Julianna shivered. "And I can't tell you how relieved I am that so much distance lay between me quarters and your sailors'."

"I'm sure."

She noted the understanding in his tone. "Is...is the Grisly Devil nearby?" She stepped closer to the captain.

"No. You needn't worry about him. He'll remain locked up in the hold for the remainder of this voyage." He unloosed his arm and shrugged out of his coat. "Here. You'll be warmer with this around your shoulders."

"Oh, but, sir..."

"You're more likely to catch your death out here than you are to fall overboard."

"Thank you—and I didn't mean to seem ungrateful."

"Regarding which? Griswald's imprisonment or wearing a coat that's ten times too large?"

A giggle erupted. "Both, Captain." It felt so good to laugh. Julianna hadn't felt so lighthearted since…she couldn't even remember when.

Her smile lingering, she glanced up at the captain. He met her gaze before his eyes wandered to her mouth. She felt suddenly quite self-conscious. "I must look a sight. My hair unpinned. No cap on my head."

He didn't reply but returned his gaze out toward the deck. "You have a beautiful smile."

"Thank you, sir. Your smile is quite becoming too, if I may say so."

"You may."

She glimpsed one of those alluring dimples, which attempted to hide beneath his whiskers. Oh, he was a heartbreaker, this one. Even so, she felt a particular draw to him.

His eyes drifted back to her, and he stared as if memorizing her every feature. Did he like what he saw? Why did she hope he did?

He put his arm about her waist again. "Don't worry. You're safe."

"I feel safe…with you."

"Good."

He inched toward her, his lips slightly parted. She held her breath. Did he mean to kiss her? Oh, but she knew she'd enjoy it if he did.

He turned his head as if realizing how very unwise such an action would be. Here they both stood in front of all his crew to see. Disappointment assailed her, and in the next moment she wondered if she were in more danger now than she'd been in on the streets of London.

CHAPTER 8

*D*ARKNESS CAME DOWN fast, and the captain guided her back toward Mr. Bentley and to a short, nearby bench. She sat down. Any magic she'd felt moments ago had been whisked away on the night's sea wind, which was just fine with Julianna. She had no business falling for the captain's charm, although his masculine scent emanated from his jacket she wore about her shoulders. She had to admit that she found it quite appealing.

But she wasn't about to end up like Flora or Mum. She'd not fall in love or give herself over to a sailing man.

As an inward show of defiance, Julianna shrugged off the captain's jacket and handed it back to him. Better that she freeze to death if need be.

He gave her a curious look.

"I'm warm enough now, thank you." She lifted her gaze to the sky, longing to set her mind on other things than one handsome sea captain. Stars were sprinkled throughout its inky depths.

"Well, now," Mr. Bentley drawled, "I can see the fresh air has lifted both your spirits. We've had fine weather on this voyage, not that I'm jinxing it."

"Please don't." The captain folded his coat over his forearm. How he could stand on the deck without holding on for dear life amazed her. He looked her way. "I think we'd best get you back inside, Miss Wayland."

"Oh, no, please, Captain. Just a while longer?" Salty sea spray sprinkled over her as the ship dipped, then rose again, and Julianna decided it felt far more refreshing here than locked inside her cell.

"All right. A few more minutes."

She smiled and glanced upward. The stars mesmerized her. "I see black velvet and a million diamond buttons—a gown fit for a queen."

"I wouldn't know about such lavish apparel." Mr. Bentley snorted a laugh that claimed Julianna's attention. "But I'll bet the captain's countess does."

"A countess?" She turned and strained to see the captain's expression in the dark. "You have a countess?"

"One doesn't *have a countess* like one has a hound, Miss Wayland."

The retort stung. "Begging your pardon, sir. I didn't mean any insult. I was merely curious."

He exhaled audibly. "I shouldn't have been so gruff."

She relaxed a bit and looked heavenward again, mentally arranging the pieces she'd learned about the captain into a picture of what kind of man he really was. And, of course, he'd consort with countesses and other important people. Hadn't he said he'd attended Mr. Tolbert's dinner affair?

Her mind conjured up memories of that night. Julianna wondered why she hadn't noticed the dashing captain, Perhaps because she'd been working so hard to make sure her actions were perfect for Mr. Tolbert's fine guests. Only the wealthy and privileged had been invited.

"The captain has a countess, all right." Mr. Bentley's voice sang with amusement. "She's a beauty." Hands firmly on the ship's wheel, he stepped nearer to where Julianna sat. "Best of all, she's rich."

"Yes, so I'd assumed."

"That's enough, Bent. I'm sure Miss Wayland doesn't want to be bored with the details of my private life."

"On the contrary, Captain. I find it a hundred times more interesting than the tales that Jeremy reads to me."

She heard his soft chuckle in reply.

"Well, our cap'n 'ere is truly amazing. I know he won't mind me bragging on him."

"Must you?"

"If you don't mind, sir." The first mate didn't wait for an answer. "The master is from humble beginnings, proving that we Yanks can rise up through the social ranks." He dipped one eye. "But more likely is that he charmed his countess senseless."

Julianna grinned while Captain Sundberg expelled a weary-sounding sigh. "What kind of humble beginnings—if you don't mind me asking."

"He's from a farm in the middle of America," Bently rushed on before the captain could answer. "In a state called Wisconsin."

She had no idea where in the world that was. "A farm, you say? I've always dreamed of living in the country meself."

"Cows, goats, pigs, and the like," Mr. Bentley added.

"I'd prefer them to men any day—present company excluded, of course."

"Of course," the captain said.

She heard his amused tone, and it made her smile.

"Mind if I continue, sir?" Mr. Bentley eyed the captain.

"Why not? You've already told her most of my life's story." The captain strode to the side of the deck and peered out over the water.

"Wisconsin is where his parents and sisters still live."

Julianna felt pangs of jealousy. "You have a family, Captain?" That's all she'd ever wanted in her whole life.

"Two families, I guess you might say. Isn't that right, sir?" Again,

Mr. Bentley barreled on before the captain could get a word in. "He left the farm at age fifteen, thinking he'd fight in America's Civil War. But Mr. Ramsey found him before the army did and raised him up the rest of the way. Like his own son. Soon our beloved captain will be running Mr. Ramsey's shipping company from New York City." He chortled. "But try as you might, Cap'n, you'll never persuade me to leave the love of m'life—the sea."

Typical sailor. Julianna rolled her eyes.

The captain turned back around and grinned. "I know better than to ask you to become a landlubber." A long moment's pause ensued. "You may as well know right now, I plan to make you the master of the *Allegiance* on her voyage back to London."

"Thank you, sir."

Julianna noted the tone of gratitude in Mr. Bentley's voice. Being promoted to sea captain must certainly be an honor—and how thoughtful of the captain to bestow it on his trusty first mate. But that Captain Sundberg had left his family behind to sail the seas was beyond her level of comprehension.

Unless that family consisted of an evil lot.

"May I be so bold to inquire why you left your family and the farm, Captain?"

"He wanted adventure, Miss."

Captain Sundberg cleared his throat. "You are not the master of this ship yet, Bent."

"My apologies, sir."

Julianna found herself enjoying the banter. She could hear in the captain's voice that he was only mildly annoyed with his first mate. "Did your first family mistreat you, Captain? Is that what prompted you to flee?"

"I was never mistreated, no."

"Hmm…" Julianna still couldn't understand why someone would

leave his home and family for anything short of self-preservation. "Adventure comes at a high price, doesn't it?"

"And that means?"

Beneath the light of a slivered moon Julianna saw the captain step toward her. "Family is of great price, is it not? And a home?" She lowered her gaze. "I never had either, although I've always had me sister, Flora. I guess I should consider her me family."

"Some 'ave it better than others," Mr. Bentley remarked. "Just the way o' the world."

"I suppose you're right." Sadness gripped her when she thought she might never see Flora again. Despite her position of ill repute and her imbibing, Flora was still her sister. Julianna's gaze returned to the captain. "I'm ready to go inside now, sir."

Two nights later Daniel sat at his desk, logging the *Allegiance*'s progress. He felt pleased. The wind had remained in their favor, so each night he logged three hundred—sometimes four hundred—miles. The only exceptions were those days during the storm in which he'd been blown slightly off course. The rough waters afterward made it difficult to get back on the navigational track. But the *Allegiance* and her crew had done it—and more. At this rate Daniel wouldn't be surprised if they made New York City in eighteen days, certainly one of this ship's better records. George would be pleased.

Setting down his pen, he sat back. An unusual quiet came from the jail. After the night he'd taken Julianna on deck for air, she'd been reticent, speaking only when spoken to, and he couldn't keep from pondering over her change in behavior.

Had she sensed the strange and powerful attraction between them? How could she not? Perhaps it had frightened her. It had certainly put him on high alert—again. Why he allowed himself to be in the least distracted by her, Daniel couldn't figure. A mistake.

George would have a conniption if he learned Daniel felt such an attraction to a serving girl. So, as a counterbalance of sorts, he made a point these past two days to send Kidwell in here to deliver her meals. The young man hadn't objected. In fact, Kidwell spent every free minute in Julianna's company.

But, again, why did he care? He shouldn't!

Which brought Daniel to a matter of great importance that warranted discussion.

"Miss Wayland?" In spite of the late hour he sensed she wasn't asleep.

"Yes, sir?"

He stood. Kidwell had been visiting just an hour before, and Daniel had allowed the jail cell to remain open.

"Can you come out into my office so I might have a few words with you?"

She didn't reply, but Daniel heard the wood creak ever so slightly as she rose from her berth. Moments later she stepped into his office. She'd taken to wearing her long, brown tresses in a knot that hung between her shoulder blades. She'd removed her white apron, so now she stood before him in only her black uniform dress. The bruises on her face were healing nicely; only yellow shadows existed where Griswald's fists had struck her.

"Julianna..." Chagrin exploded in his gut. He'd played her name on his tongue many times the past forty-eight hours, but always in private whispers. He hadn't meant to allow formalities to slip. He cleared the discomfort from his throat. "May I call you by your given name?"

"Of course." She looked at him askance without a trace of suspicion in her gray eyes.

Daniel came around and sat on the corner of his desk. "I'm estimating that in about four days we'll reach New York's harbor, and we have yet to decide on a plan for you."

Her gaze fell to the floor.

Daniel regretted the news he had to tell her. But perhaps she'd be ecstatic. "Kidwell has offered to pay your passage. He's got plans to go west once we reach America. He'd like to take you with him."

"Yes, sir, I know."

Daniel raised his brows in surprise. "You know? So Kidwell proposed marriage?"

She looked up. "No. He just told me he needs a woman to accompany him on his journey."

"And you accepted?"

She hesitated. "No, sir, I didn't. That is, I didn't give him an answer. Jeremy was quick to point out that I've no other options. But..."

"But?" Daniel glimpsed the hopefulness in her eyes and tried to ignore it. "He's right. You have no other options."

She quickly dropped her gaze again. Her shoulders drooped slightly forward as if in defeat. Remorse knifed him. But what could he do?

"Kidwell has been in my employ a couple of times now, Julianna, and I'm confident that he won't mistreat you."

Still peering at the tips of her black boots, she moved her head in a submissive nod.

Daniel wrestled with a mutiny of emotions, telling himself this seemed the most logical solution. "Take Kidwell's offer. Perhaps you'll get that family you've always wanted."

"With Jeremy?" Her head swung up and she stared at him. "Quite unlikely, Captain."

"Why?"

She swallowed obvious discomfort, although her eyes held his gaze captive. "There's only one man I'll ever love. I realize that now. It's a curse, you see, handed down by me mother. She fell for a seafaring man herself."

Daniel folded his arms. Why did he feel so insanely jealous all of a sudden? "Where is this seafaring man that you love? Any idea?"

"Oh, I know where he is." Julianna turned her back to him. "But he's well above my grasp. Still, I'll never marry anyone else." On a sigh she whirled around to face him again. "So...I suppose I'll go with Jeremy if that's my only choice." Her voice grew softer, although the determination in her tone still remained. "Except I shan't marry him."

"Hmm...well, I admire your faithfulness to your heart, although it doesn't behoove you to play the martyr or become a hopeless romantic." Daniel pushed to his feet and walked to where she stood. He gently cupped her face. Her eyes reminded him of a balmy sea at dusk. "You're a beautiful woman, Julianna."

She seemed to warm to his compliment for only seconds before her gray eyes darkened. "What's beauty got to do with it?"

"And sassy." He smiled into her gaze. "Did I mention that you're sassy?"

She pulled back and stepped beyond his reach.

"I'm sorry to tease you." He wiped the grin from his lips. "All humor aside, Julianna, you deserve to be happy. Forget that sailing man." Daniel wagged his head. "Whoever he is, he's not worthy of your affection."

She just stared up at him in...in *adoration*?

He laughed inwardly and retreated into the center of his office. Clearly he imagined her shining esteem just now. Didn't he?

"The man I love is more than worthy of someone like me. It's just..." She paused, and Daniel felt her presence just behind his left elbow. "Well, isn't there any other way, Captain? What about the nuns? Does America have convents? Wouldn't they take me?"

"A nun?" Daniel turned slowly back around, and he might have laughed, except for the austerity scribed across her face.

"I've been reading your Bible, and I know I love God. Each word speaks to me in a special way."

"That doesn't mean you're called to be a nun. My mother is a godly woman, and she's not a nun, obviously."

"But what else can I do?"

Daniel grappled for an answer. Far be it for him to persuade her from her divine calling. However, the idea just didn't sit well in his gut. "Don't you want children, Julianna?"

"Not if it means begetting them with Jeremy Kidwell."

A chuckle escaped him. She was honest if nothing else. But why Daniel felt encouraged was most peculiar and quite unreasonable.

He drew in a slow, thoughtful breath. He wouldn't insist, even though it went against every grain of logic he possessed. But perhaps he merely pitied her. After all, he knew what it was like to be young, alone, and scared. Fortunately for him he'd found a trusted friend in George Ramsey. Daniel couldn't be 100 percent sure Kidwell would be as good, even honorable, to Julianna.

"Well, I suppose…" He ran a hand along his whiskered jaw. "In all good conscience I can't force you to accept Kidwell's offer."

"Oh, thank you, Captain." The tension disappeared from her features, and she closed the distance between them. "It's true what they say about you." She clasped her hands over her heart. "You are the prince of sea captains."

"Now, now…" He wanted to be humble, although her remark pleased him.

But seconds later he felt pinned by her gaze. In it he saw a mix of vulnerability and tenacity. Her pouty lips challenged him to kiss, and he wanted to in the worst way.

He brushed silky strands of hair from her face and traced the side of her cheek with his finger. She didn't move or swat his hand away. Could it be she felt the same intense stirrings?

He lowered his head. She lifted her chin. Suddenly their lips met, and he drank in the delicate sweetness she so willingly gave. A desire, fierce and intoxicating, swept through him, and he knew he had to fight against it, lest he be helplessly and forever caught in its snare.

He pulled away, but then hugged Julianna to him. He closed his eyes, trying to catch his breath. He felt like he'd run a mile. This was wrong. He knew it. Still, he didn't want to let her go.

Her hands slowly slid up his back, and another dizzying wave washed over him. However, in that very moment, he sensed a scheme. Could it be he'd fallen for an age-old trick?

Taking her by her shoulders, he pushed her away and held her at arm's length. "What are you doing?" Playing the temptress is what he presumed.

"I–I don't know."

She looked a bit dazed and Daniel instantly knew he'd misjudged her.

"What am I doing? That's a good question." Julianna stepped back into his embrace. She rested her head on his chest. "I should be terrified, but I'm not. You're the most decent, honest, warm, and…and loving man I've ever met. I'll never forget you, Captain Daniel Sundberg."

He held her again, one arm around her waist, the other cupping her head. He immediately understood. He'd shown kindness to a young woman who'd never known kindness from a man before. Now she fancied herself in love with him.

So then he ought to set her straight.

Right now.

She should go with Kidwell and find happiness.

Why did he keep his mouth shut?

Julianna could hear the captain's heart drumming out a rapid but steady beat. He was the man she loved—and she would love him forever. Since that starry night when they stood on the deck, she'd known it. She hadn't wanted to love him. Nothing would come of it.

And she was wrong to cling to him this way.

She strained back, and he let up on his hold. Julianna touched his reddish-brown beard, marveling at its softness. His lips found her fingertips.

"Will you kiss me one last time?"

He obliged her, and Julianna was stunned by his gentleness. He trailed kisses down her jaw and neck, and a soft moan escaped her.

Then, abruptly, he pushed her away.

"Enough, Julianna. This dallying isn't good for either one of us. What's more, if one of my men should happen to walk through that door—"

"You're right." She smoothed down the front of her dress. "And please believe me when I say that I'm no hussy, even if I did enjoy meself just now."

He smiled, and his blue eyes twinkled. "I guess that proves you're no nun."

Julianna saw no humor in his remark. "God won't have me now?" Disappointment dropped like an anvil inside of her.

"From what I remember as a boy, God will always want you. But the convent is a different story altogether." The captain walked around to the other side of his desk and sat down. Leaning forward, he clasped his hands and stared at them.

Julianna slowly sank into the leather chair poised in front of his desk. Her gaze darted around the richly paneled room. Another solution. Dear God, but there had to be one! "Please don't make me go with Jeremy. I beg of you."

He said nothing, appearing deep in thought.

"If the convent is out of the question, what about a paying job? Surely someone in New York needs a maid. I could work off my passage."

"You're coming with me."

"What?" Julianna didn't think she'd heard him correctly.

"I'm taking you with me." His gaze finally met hers. "That will solve everything."

"But...but you're marrying a countess." Indignation brewed inside of her. "I'll fling meself overboard before I'll be your mistress! I love you. There. I said it. It's true. But what you're asking is far more than I'm willing to give."

Captain Sundberg held up a forestalling hand. "Did you hear me make such a request of you, *Miss Wayland*?"

She squeezed her shoulders back at his cynical tone. "No. But just in case you're thinking it—"

"I am not. And I wonder if you really think so highly of me after all."

"I do. I swear I do. It's just"—she rolled a shoulder—"you're a man, so I'm sure that you can't help certain things."

"Like being a complete rogue, I presume."

"Rogue might be too strong a word...*sir*."

The captain narrowed his gaze. "You're one plucky female. I must be crazy."

Julianna decided to change her tone lest the captain have a change in heart—that is, if he'd thought up a suitable plan. "Will you tell me what you have in mind?"

His features softened. "Let's look at the globe over there in the corner."

She stood and followed him across the office to where a round, multicolored orb stood suspended by both ends in a gleaming brass fixture.

The captain gave it a spin. "This is the world, perhaps as God sees it. The blue is the sea, brown is land. Here's where we are right now."

She peered at where the captain pointed. "In the middle of the ocean."

"Sort of. Now, here's London, from where we set sail, here's New York, and here is ... *Wisconsin*."

"Wisconsin." It looked a long way from London.

"If you agree, you may accompany me to Manitowoc, Wisconsin. If I know my mother, she'll take you in without question. You can help her on the farm. She's going to need extra hands with my father so gravely ill." The captain released a long breath that carried a note of sadness. "Maybe he's even dead by now, I don't know. But in any case, you'll be safe there, and you can rebuild your life. Start anew."

"On a farm?" Julianna considered it. "I've never worked on a farm, but I could learn."

"I have no doubt." The captain folded his arms. "Now, then, you'll need suitable attire. I'll lend you the money and keep a tab, which will include your passage."

"Sounds more than fair. I'll work hard. I promise."

"I know you will."

She saw him smile before he stared back at the colorful world.

"I'll have no qualms about leaving you in Manitowoc."

Leaving her ... to return to New York and continue his sailing ventures at the helm of a shipping company. Leaving her to marry his countess.

Julianna hadn't dared to dream otherwise. Nevertheless, his offer seemed too good to be true.

"I wholeheartedly accept." She gave the captain a smile that reached in and took hold of her heart. "My future doesn't seem so glum after all."

He chuckled. "You might reserve judgment until after you've mucked out a few stalls."

She wrinkled her nose then shrugged. "I'll get along. Thank you, Captain." She put her hands on his forearms. "Thank you for not forcing me to go with Jeremy."

He gently ran his rough knuckles across her still-bruised cheek. "You're welcome." His voice was as soft as his caress, and then that certain spark reentered his eyes. Would he kiss her again? She wouldn't mind. She even hoped. Except...

Julianna spun around on her heel. It had taken all her will to do so. "We shouldn't...since nothing good can come of it anyway."

"I agree. We need to keep as much distance between us as possible."

As sad as the idea made her feel, Julianna knew in her heart of hearts it was the right thing to do. "I'll keep my distance, Captain."

"You do that, Miss Wayland. And I'll keep mine."

CHAPTER 9

*F*OUR DAYS AND eight hours later Julianna brushed out her hair and stared into the wood-framed looking glass. The rhythmic motion proved both a luxury and a chore. Her entire body ached from the fatigue of the voyage combined with today's disembarking and subsequent events. She'd been scrubbed, rubbed, measured, and fitted for more than a suitable new wardrobe. The captain had ordered her attired from "stem to stern."

She still bristled. How very like a seaman to use such demeaning verbiage.

Seconds later she softened. More than miffed, she felt grateful.

And puzzled. How did wealthy women survive such grueling attempts at beauty?

And she was worried too. What about her tab? How would she ever repay the captain for the dresses, pinnings, and accessories, which the maids insisted she possess? Every protest she'd made this afternoon went ignored—and she planned to speak with the captain about the matter when the opportunity presented itself. Perhaps something could be returned to the department store.

Julianna's mind wandered back over the entirety of her day. Hours after they'd dropped anchor in New York's harbor, a primly dressed, mature woman came aboard the ship to fetch her. Within minutes she introduced herself as Mrs. Cookson, member of Mr. George Ramsey's household staff. Today she'd been employed by Captain Sundberg to see her home, bathed, and then taken to an enormous store to be fitted and dressed. The captain had ordered that everything be placed on his account. Later Mrs. Cookson saw her safely to the Ramsey's elegant mansion.

And now here she was.

A leafy tree branch scraped the window pane, and a cool breeze wafted inside. She resumed her hair brushing. How good it felt to leave that hot and muggy cell and have clean hair once more. And her bath this afternoon felt positively delicious.

When she'd arrived here at the Ramseys, she'd been immediately shown to one of the opulent guest bedrooms. Bertha informed her that Mrs. Ramsey had taken ill with a headache and that Mr. Ramsey and Captain Sundberg were conducting business. Therefore a formal dinner was out of the question. However, all three would expect her for breakfast in the morning.

A light supper of sliced fresh fruit, cheese, cold meats, and a fat, buttered roll was delivered to her bedroom a short time ago. After weeks of Jeremy's overcooked beef, scalded potatoes, and canned beans, the meal tasted like sheer delight. When Julianna finished eating, Laurabetha helped her dress for bed. Never in Julianna's life had she been pampered in such a way. In fact, she was accustomed to doing the pampering.

Laying aside the gleaming, silver-handled brush, Julianna rose from the polished oak vanity and once more took in the room's elegance. A wide, plump bed occupied most of the center of the room. A bureau and chest of drawers stood adjacent to the vanity, along with two velvet-padded chairs. Green silk drapes framed the long windows, and a rose-on-the-vine paper covered the walls. Why, none of the rooms in Mr. Tolbert's mansion could compare to the

warmth and richness of this one. Just wait until she wrote and told
Flora!

Julianna frowned. Or maybe she shouldn't contact her sister. She
nibbled the side of her lip. Perhaps she'd speak to the captain about
that too.

Padding to the bedside table, Julianna extinguished the lamp
before crawling beneath the covers. She sighed as she sank into its
softness.

Her eyelids grew heavy, and she snuggled deeper into the freshly
scented linens. They felt like the finest silk against her skin. She
wondered if this is what heaven felt like as her lids slowly fluttered
closed.

❦

The next morning Mrs. Cookson helped Julianna dress. She
resigned herself to the service, concluding she'd not receive such
special treatment on the captain's family's farm.

Besides, today was a special day, marking her twentieth birthday.
She doubted the captain remembered.

With her new, dusky-blue blouse buttoned and her fawn-colored
skirt fastened, Julianna watched in the mirror as Mrs. Cookson duti-
fully styled her hair and smoothed some cover-up onto Julianna's
yellowish bruises.

"Thank you." She gave the older woman a smile.

Her stoic expression never changed. "You're welcome, Miss."

Julianna gave her appearance a last look in the mirror. She
scarcely recognized the reflection staring back at her. Gone was that
pitiful girl with the sad, soulful, and sometimes frightened eyes. In
her place stood a fashionable... *woman*. When had the transforma-
tion taken place?

"You'd best hurry," the maid said. "Breakfast is being served."

Julianna heeded the warning.

Feeling a bit bemused, she descended the winding stairwell. She tried to recall everything Molly had taught her about being a lady. It wouldn't do if her behavior didn't match her new appearance. She was, after all, about to meet the Ramseys.

The toes of one kid slipper touched down on the polished floor of the airy foyer, and she nearly slipped when she saw Captain Sundberg standing with his back to her near the front door. So much for grace and dignity—except she wasn't accustomed to wearing such fine footwear, either.

He heard her arrival and turned. The expression on his face resembled Julianna's surprise when she'd first glimpsed her own reflection this morning.

"Good morning, Captain." She smiled, feeling shy for some odd reason. "I look a bit different, don't I?"

He recovered quickly. "You look lovely, Miss Wayland." His tone was starched and formal, reminding Julianna of their agreement.

Even so, she couldn't help noticing how dashing he was—like the first time she'd seen him. He'd shaved his weeks' worth of beard, revealing those alluring indents on either side of his mouth.

He cleared his throat, and Julianna blinked to attention, realizing she'd been openly appreciating the man. Dropping her gaze, she stared at her hands, clasped in front of her. "I hope I haven't kept you and the Ramseys waiting."

"No. You're right on time."

Hearing him come forward, she looked up, and he offered his arm. Carefully threading her hand around his elbow, she felt the superior quality of his pressed white dress shirt, and then she noticed the gold timepiece peeking from a pocket in his ivory waistcoat.

"I've told the Ramseys nothing of our departure to Wisconsin."

His voice was a husky whisper, and as he leaned toward her, Julianna caught the enticingly sweet scents of sandalwood and myrrh.

"I've only said that you were a last-minute passenger—"

She forced herself to pay attention.

"—that you're from London, and that you're leaving New York tomorrow."

Julianna understood. He'd given a partial truth for now. "Yes, Captain."

He led her through the sitting room and down a hallway. Julianna noticed the lavish furnishings.

"We'll eat our breakfast on the terrace this morning."

"That sounds quite pleasant. Thank you."

They walked through the opened white, glass-paned double doors and onto a cement porch that looked out over a lush green lawn. Beyond it was the blue of the ocean. A tepid summer breeze washed over her, and Julianna wondered if God had given her this beautiful day, beautiful clothes, and beautiful people with whom to celebrate as a special birthday gift. She knew she'd never forget it.

An older gentleman with neatly trimmed graying brown whiskers stood from his seat at the round, wrought-iron table.

The captain made the introductions. "George and Eliza, allow me to present Miss Julianna Wayland."

"How nice to meet you, dear," Mrs. Ramsey said.

"Likewise." Julianna's gaze flitted to the pudgy woman with soft brown curls, clad in a blue velvet housecoat. Was the woman still ill?

"You'll have to forgive my informal attire," Mrs. Ramsey said as if divining Julianna's thoughts. "My sick headache is lingering."

"So sorry to hear it, ma'am." Julianna looked to the well-dressed gentleman again.

"A pleasure to mee—" He faltered and his polite smile waned. His hazel eyes darkened with familiarity. "Have we met?"

"I don't believe so." The captain held her chair and Julianna sat down.

"Wayland." Mr. Ramsey murmured her last name then appeared immersed in thought.

Julianna sent a glance the captain's way as he seated himself across from her. His gaze narrowed in a momentary frown. However, he seemed to shake off any concerns quickly enough.

Still, Mr. Ramsey looked pensive and perplexed too, as he lowered himself back into his chair. "Where in London are you from, Miss Wayland?"

"Oh, I've lived all over the city, really." She hoped the vague reply would suffice. At least she thought the captain looked pacified.

Another maid, dressed in the traditional black and white uniform, came over and filled a small crystal glass in front of Julianna with fresh orange juice.

"Thank you." She would always remember to thank the help.

"What does your, um, father do for a living?" Mr. Ramsey asked.

"I'm afraid I don't have a father. He was never a part of my life on account of his sailing background."

The captain feigned a little cough, and Julianna realized she'd said too much. She sipped her orange juice. She would have to be more careful.

"How sad that you didn't know your father," Mrs. Ramsey said. "But it's true that a sailor's first love is the sea."

"Maybe for some sailors," the captain said. "I personally am looking forward to trading the helm for office space." He gave the older man a smirk. "And I'd like a nice view of New York too."

"Of course. As my executive you may work wherever you please." Mr. Ramsey seemed distracted, even disturbed. He peered at Julianna again. "Miss Wayland, do you...remember anything about your father?"

"Not a thing." That was a fib. Mr. Potter occasionally talked about what he recalled of Julianna's father. Rugged, yet refined. Another womanizing, seafaring man who believed his lofty ideas for the future. Ideas that never came true. Mum had been one of the women who'd fallen for him.

Julianna's gaze settled on the captain, a man with lofty ideas of his own.

His eyes drifted to hers and locked. Julianna thought she could stare into those warm blue eyes of his all day long.

"So, Miss Wayland—"

She snapped to attention. "Yes, Mr. Ramsey?" She forced herself to look at the man as she spoke.

"Daniel mentioned you were a last-minute passenger on the *Allegiance*." He sipped his coffee. "What made you want to leave London so hastily? Surely other passenger ships were setting sail that day as well."

"George, it just worked out that way. I thought you'd be happy to earn the extra fare."

"I am, indeed, but I'd still like to hear from Miss Wayland."

She decided on another half truth. "Well, you see, I'm an acquaintance of Mr. Olson Tolbert Senior..."

"Tolbert?" Mr. Ramsey set down his porcelain cup and stroked his beard. "Why do I know that name?"

Captain Sundberg groaned.

"And I don't recall it with particular fondness."

"You're most likely thinking of Captain Tolbert, or the young master, as he's known in his father's house."

"Ah, yes...Captain Tolbert. Flogs his crew on a daily basis, or so I hear."

Mrs. Ramsey clucked her tongue. "Such abuse is despicable."

"I agree." Captain Sundberg took a drink of coffee then dabbed his lips with his linen napkin. "But his father, Mr. Tolbert the senior, is a popular philanthropist in London and quite respectable."

"I see." Mr. Ramsey's frown diminished slightly—until he regarded Julianna again. "And you're acquainted with him?"

"Yes...well, the both of them, really, father and son." Julianna ignored the captain's wide-eyed stare. "And let me say, Olson Junior is rude and overbearing and I refused his...advances."

Mrs. Ramsey gasped but seemed intrigued all the same.

Captain Sundberg's face reddened. Was he angry?

"Well, being an unmarried woman without a man's protection, such as I am..." Had she been too descriptive? Best she wrap it up. "I decided to leave London and begin my life anew in America."

A long moment passed in silence.

"I see." Mr. Ramsey drank the rest of his coffee, and the captain quickly poured him another cup. "What about your family in London. Surely they'll miss you."

"I don't have family, per se. Just an older sister, and she's—"

Julianna dropped her gaze to the napkin in her lap. Would Flora miss her? Would she even know Julianna was gone?

"Well, long story short, me sister won't care that I'm gone." Sorrow clipped her heart.

She looked up then, and decided Mr. Ramsey's expression was a mix of shock and irritation.

"An older sister?"

"Yes. Her name is Flora."

Another impregnated moment of silence ticked by, and Julianna prayed it was the end of the questioning.

"What about your...your mother?" Mr. Ramsey honed his gaze in on her.

Julianna wanted to squirm. "Sadly, she died shortly after giving birth to me. I never knew her either."

"Oh, you poor thing." Mrs. Ramsey reached over and patted Julianna's hand. "Raised in an orphanage?"

"No." *Unfortunately*, she added silently.

Mr. Ramsey removed his handkerchief and dabbed it across his perspiring forehead.

"George?" The captain leaned toward him. "Are you all right?"

"Yes, George..." Mrs. Ramsey peered at him with concern etched alongside the corners of her eyes. "You do look a bit ashen."

"I'm fine." He waved off further attention. "A bit of a sour stomach. Eating breakfast should help."

"The maid will bring it out shortly, dear." Mrs. Ramsey sent him a weak smile then turned to Julianna. "So you were raised by your older sister then?"

"No, ma'am. Mr. and Mrs. Bartholomew Potter raised me and Flora. They're the ones who owned the store Mum worked in. When she died, the Potters took us in."

"What kind of shop?" Mrs. Ramsey sipped her coffee.

"Mending and laundering. Mum was a seamstress, and Mrs. Potter said I got me gift of sewing from her."

"How nice." Mrs. Ramsey set down her delicate porcelain cup. "It's just a pity you never met a trustworthy man in London." She smiled. "But I imagine our Daniel was a gentleman during your voyage."

"Oh, yes. A true gentleman in every sense of the word."

Mrs. Ramsey beamed with motherly pride, and Julianna coveted the fact that the captain had two families. She'd never had a one. The Potters, as good as they'd been to take her and Flora in, were never nurturing, caring parents. They were more like loyal employers, and together, the four of them hardly resembled a family—not like the ones Julianna had observed while growing up.

But it was too late for that now anyway. A family wasn't in her future. She loved a man she could never marry—the one sitting across from her at this most appealing breakfast table on this gorgeous morning. And she accepted the painful truth. All she hoped for was a lasting job on the captain's family farm—his other family. She hoped for a place at which she could work respectably the rest of her days.

"Oh, Daniel, you must bring Julianna to Mabel Brunning's home tonight. We're all invited to celebrate the twentieth anniversary of her contributing to *Scientific American* magazine." Mrs. Ramsey leaned over to Julianna. "Mabel is quite liberated for a woman."

"Rebellious is what she is," Mr. Ramsey sputtered.

His wife pulled her shoulders back. "Nevertheless, George, it's an honor to be invited." Mrs. Ramsey shifted her gaze to the captain. "When Mabel learned your ship arrived, she extended the invitation to you, Daniel, and it's just assumed you'll bring a guest." Mrs. Ramsey's eyes lit on Julianna.

Mr. Ramsey's hand shook slightly as he brought his cup to his lips.

"I think, perhaps, Miss Wayland might be too exhausted from her journey to go out tonight." Captain Sundberg gave Julianna a pointed stare.

"Yes, I am a tired." Disappointment welled up inside of her.

"You can take a nap this afternoon." Mrs. Ramsey smiled at her own suggestion. "And I'll do the same. With some rest we'll both feel refreshed for our evening out."

Julianna couldn't help but match the gesture. "I'd actually enjoy an outing. Today is my birthday."

"Your birthday?" The captain's features puckered, but then softened as his memory obviously served him correctly. "That's right. You mentioned something about it at the onset of our voyage."

Mr. Ramsey eyed Julianna with suspicion. "Today...the twenty-second day of June...is your birthday?"

"Yes, sir."

Mr. Ramsey drew in his bottom lip, looking thoughtful for several long moments. "Let me guess...you're...twenty?"

"Why, yes!" She felt awed. "Most people can't guess me age. Since I'm rather small in stature, they guess I'm younger than I really am."

Julianna noticed the man's sudden sickly pallor. "Mr. Ramsey, are you feeling all right?"

He stood and slapped his linen napkin on the table. "Daniel, I want to speak with you in my study."

Mrs. Ramsey sucked in a surprised breath.

"Now!"

Daniel paced the fine Persian rug in George's richly paneled study. Bookshelves lined one wall. He wondered what had gone so terribly wrong just now. True, Julianna liked to chatter, but she hadn't lied. She hadn't divulged the whole truth, but she hadn't told any falsehoods.

"This can't be happening," George muttered.

Daniel paused and cast a curious glance at his benefactor. "What can't be happening?"

"That young woman..." George held his hand over his heart and dropped into one of two black leather chairs near the hearth. "Has she made any demands?"

"Demands?"

"Money? Property?"

"What in the world are you talking about?" Daniel crossed the room and slowly seated himself in the other chair. He deemed it reckoning time. "Look, George, I'll be honest. Julianna got on board the *Allegiance* totally by accident."

"Bah! Some accident."

With a sigh Daniel leaned back in his chair and relayed the specifics to George. How Julianna arrived in his office, a stowaway and badly beaten. She'd been in the elderly Tolbert's employ but had been running from his son, who undoubtedly had dubious plans for her, and hid in a crate, which had been loaded onto the ship.

"And you believed that tripe?" George's face reddened.

"Not at first." He recalled his fear that she might be there to steal the Old Master paintings. But yesterday he'd delivered them safely to the museum in New York, and now in retrospect his concerns seemed ludicrous.

"Oh?" George tipped his head.

"I found no reason *not* to believe her. What's more, my officers and our cook found her truthful, even delightful." He recalled Kidwell's moon eyes whenever he gazed at Julianna. Days ago Kidwell's disappointment had been evident after Daniel told him the news that she'd be coming with him to Manitowoc, where she'd work off her passage.

But of course Daniel wanted Julianna to start off with the best of everything she'd need to begin a new life. She'd endured enough hardship in her young life. She deserved a chance at a comfortable future, although he suspected it wouldn't be long before she had a proposal of marriage that suited her.

Envy nipped at him, and he recalled the way she looked minutes ago in her new clothes. She was lovelier than he'd ever seen or imagined—and she seldom left his thoughts for long.

"Daniel?"

He jerked from his musing. "I beg your pardon, George. As you were saying?"

"No, son, as *you* were saying." He eyed him speculatively. "Don't tell me you're smitten."

"Smitten?" Daniel grinned. "I should say not." *Obsessed might be the better word.* But he dared not convey his true feelings to George. "Oh, and by the way, you'll be pleased to know that Countess Reagan Carghill and I got along famously. We'll make a suitable match." A piece of his heart withered as he spoke the words.

"Don't change the subject, Daniel."

He narrowed his gaze. "I thought you'd be glad to hear it."

"Under different circumstances, I would be." George leaned forward. "We have a crisis on our hands!"

Daniel shook his head. "I don't understand."

"That Wayland girl!" George stood and resumed the pacing that Daniel left off. "When she walked onto the terrace this morning, I felt like I was seeing a ghost. A ghost from my past."

Prickles of unease moved up Daniel's spine. "Your past, George?"

"She looks just like her mother, Phoebe. Phoebe Wayland." An expression of wistfulness fell over his features. "And her first name, Julianna...it was my mother's name. Phoebe knew that. She knew everything about me. I loved her with all my heart, but my father..." George shook his head as he gazed at the carpet. "He would have never approved of a match between us."

Daniel sprang to his feet. "What are you saying?" He thought back to all the times this father figure of a man had warned him about getting involved with the "wrong kind of woman" and how his actions could lead to scandal and catastrophe. But it never occurred to him that George might have warned him from his own personal experience.

Slowly George faced him. "From what she has said, I have good reason to believe that...that Julianna Wayland is my daughter."

CHAPTER 10

*A*ND THIS ENTIRE thing smacks of an extortion plot!"

Daniel slowly sank back into his chair. Did it? Could he have been that fooled?

Not a chance!

"Maybe that insolent Captain Tolbert put her up to it."

"I don't believe the man has the intelligence, let alone the motive. His father has plenty of money."

"Then her sister...even at five years old that girl was a lot of trouble, as I recall. Once she stole coins from me while I napped, the little scamp—took them right out of my pocket. Perhaps Flora put Julianna up to it."

Daniel felt too stunned to let the idea sink in. "Flora? She knew you, George? Knew your name?"

"I'm not sure." Additional drops of perspiration spotted George's forehead as he continued pacing. "Phoebe had a nickname for me. Christopher Columbus. It was the name of my ship. Flora always used it to address me."

"The only problem is—"

"Yes?" George paused.

"If Flora knew that you're Julianna's father, why didn't she try this trick sooner? After their guardians were killed, both Julianna and Flora wound up living on the streets of London before gaining meaningful employment. For nearly two years they begged for each coin they had and every meal they ate."

"That's about the last thing I want to hear. Don't you think I feel guilty enough?"

Daniel eyed him. "How would I know that, George?" He felt like he didn't know this man at all.

George blotted his forehead with his handkerchief. "Phoebe suspected she was with child when I last saw her that gloomy November day. I promised I'd be back come springtime." He shook his head. "But I never made it. My father had arranged my marriage to a wealthy ship-builder's daughter."

"Eliza?"

"Yes, and I was to take over Ramsey Enterprises, which I did. Years later I found myself back in London. I went to the shop where Phoebe had worked as a seamstress, but ownership had changed and no one knew her. I wanted to ask at the pubs along the wharf that we frequented. However, by then I couldn't risk my good name by entering such establishments."

"It would have been worth the risk, George." Disappointment knotted in Daniel's gut. "Your daughter nearly starved on the streets of London. God only knows what could have happened to her. She was but sixteen years old."

"Stop it, Daniel!"

He refused. "It's a wonder Julianna survived with any semblance of moral decency—and, yes, I have found her to be morally decent in more ways than one."

"Hmm…" George arched a brow. "If she's telling the truth."

He made a good point. Still, Daniel felt sure he would have seen through any charade by now.

He stood. "Julianna is on the up and up, George. What's more, I highly doubt Flora put her up to something even resembling extortion. I've sailed in and out of London many times in years past. There are enough ruffians on the wharf who are willing to hold a sea captain for ransom. Flora could have easily gone that route if money had been her objective."

"True enough." George sounded defeated.

But Daniel wasn't through. "I don't think Julianna is even aware that you could be her father." He walked to the window and opened it wider, reveling in the gentle breeze that greeted him. "She's rather naïve for her twenty years." She so obviously needed someone to watch over her, protect her.

"Bah!" George squared his shoulders. "A street-wise imp? Naïve? I can't believe it."

Daniel stepped farther into the room. "She's been working hard to rescue her sister from an unseemly lifestyle. I doubt Julianna would have ever left her had she not been accidentally loaded into the *Allegiance* that fateful day." He reclaimed his leather chair, preparing himself to heap another weighty truth on George. "I convinced her not to return to London."

"What?" George gave that hawkish stare that bespoke of his displeasure. "Why?"

Daniel wasn't deterred. "Julianna can make a fresh start here in America. I've decided to take her to Wisconsin. I received word that my father is ill. My mother can probably use Julianna's help."

"Wisconsin?" George looked stunned for a moment, and then a smile broke through. "Good, good..."

"Good?" Daniel's brows shot up. He'd expected to have more of a tussle on his hands.

"Actually, it's a brilliant plan, my boy!" George's countenance brightened. "Wisconsin is a safe distance from New York City. We may, in fact, avoid a scandal."

"Only if she knows she's your daughter and talks."

"You mustn't tell her."

"All right." He could, at least, temporarily agree to it.

"Meanwhile I'll hire the best detectives that London has to offer. I'll get to the bottom of this."

"We'll leave Monday morning, George."

"The sooner the better."

⁂

Thirty minutes later Daniel walked back onto the terrace to find Julianna sitting alone at the table. She picked at the food on her plate.

"Please forgive George and me for our hasty exits." He shrugged. "Business."

"Oh." She visibly relaxed. "Here I thought maybe I'd said something wrong."

"No." *If she only knew!*

Julianna's gaze slid to Eliza's empty chair. "Mrs. Ramsey went upstairs to lie down, but she's determined to attend the party tonight."

"How do you feel about that—the party, I mean?" As a housemaid from London she might be intimidated around some of New York City's more prominent citizens.

"I feel fine. Excited, actually." She leaned forward conspiratorially. "I know how to behave too, because I've watched Mr. Tolbert's guests and mimicked their behavior in jest. I can do it for real tonight."

Her answer surprised him—although it shouldn't have. He grinned.

She returned his smile. "Besides, Mrs. Ramsey said Mabel Brunning is quite unconventional."

Daniel raised his brows. "Indeed." He'd met the older woman several times in the past and had even succumbed to one of her interminable interviews.

"Mrs. Brunning will likely accept me despite me lowly background. But, you know…" Julianna shook her head, threatening her carefully pinned curls. "We really don't have to go. I guess I got a bit overenthusiastic."

"Nonsense. It's your birthday." He sat down. "Have you ever had a birthday party?"

"Well wishes, mostly." She rolled a shoulder. "Although since Flora began working at the Mariner's Pub, there's always been some drunken sailor willing to lift another glass of ale in m' behalf."

"Tonight there will be none of that." Daniel felt indignant for her. "Tonight I'll show you a proper celebration. I highly doubt Mrs. Brunning will mind if we use her auspicious occasion to celebrate yours as well." He grinned. "How does that sound?"

"Proper? I can only imagine how that'll be." Julianna's cheeks turned a pretty shade of pink. "Once more, I'm grateful to you, Captain. Thank you."

"It's entirely my pleasure." Daniel forced his attention away from her sweet, smiling face. "I'm sure you'll do just fine tonight. You, um, seem to have adequate table manners despite your upbringing."

"If I do it's because of Cook—that's what everyone in the Tolbert household called her. I don't even know her first name." A little laugh bubbled out, causing Daniel to grin. "She was full of starch and vinegar, that one! But if we wanted our supper, we had to use the correct utensils. Why, Cook would slap her wooden spoon against our knuckles if she caught us using our fingers."

Daniel arched a brow. "I take it you were a quick study."

"Extremely."

His grin widening, he stared out over the terrace. "Beautiful morning."

"Oh, it is. It's the most beautiful I've ever seen." Julianna set down her fork. "Me birthday has already been a special one."

"*My* birthday," he corrected. "You're going to need to practice talking like we Americans do."

"I'll try."

He glanced over in time to see her gray eyes shining with gratitude even before the next words came from her mouth.

"How will I ever repay you, Captain?"

"None is required." How could he think to charge her? He took a peculiar delight in seeing her fashionably attired and happy.

"But—"

Daniel reached over and pressed his finger against her soft lips. "Never mind such talk of repayment on your birthday. It's a day of gifts, is it not?"

Smiling, she clasped his hand in both of hers. Her expression resembled a childlike joy.

There's no way she's got extortion on her mind.

Julianna released his hand just as the maid appeared with another plate of eggs, potatoes, and a thick piece of ham. Spreading his napkin across his lap, he began eating and noticed that Julianna picked less and ate more since he'd sat down with her. He thought it would do her some good to get a little meat on her too-thin frame.

"This certainly beats Kidwell's cooking any day," Daniel joked.

Julianna laughed again, a light, fluttery sound so infectious it made Daniel smile. "You're right about Jeremy's cooking. To his credit, he tried hard, and I'm sure the meals could have been worse, eh?"

"Far worse." He swallowed then dabbed the corners of his mouth with his napkin. "Once I hired a man who thought he'd save money by ordering meat from an inferior butcher. In a few days' time the kitchen was vermin-infested."

At once Daniel regretted the gaffe, but Julianna didn't even flinch.

"I recall a man known to us on the street as Fang because of the way his teeth hung off his lower lip. He always said a little vermin never killed a man, especially if he's starving to death." Amusement danced in her eyes.

But Daniel failed to find the humor in it. Instead his chest constricted with anguish. The horrors this young woman must have known as a girl…and yet she smiled as she recollected such a one.

He watched Julianna fork a bite of fried potatoes into her mouth. She amazed him again. No swooning. No loss of appetite due to this most *distasteful* discussion. It told Daniel of her courage. She'd probably overcome anything.

And he hadn't forgotten how she'd assisted Dr. Morrison on board with Whitley's broken leg only days after suffering a brutal attack herself.

"Captain, is something wrong?"

"I beg your pardon?" He pried himself from his thoughts.

"You're staring at me." She touched her face, and then the neckline of her blouse. "Is anything amiss with me attire—I mean, *my* attire?"

He gave her a gentle grin. "No, and I do apologize. I was just deep in thought."

"Oh, I know what you're thinking." She lifted a brow. "It's about your countess, isn't it?"

His smile ebbed. "Actually, no." He hadn't thought much about Reagan since leaving London. "I, um, thought that perhaps you'll need another dress for the party tonight. Something more formal."

"Oh, no, Captain, really…"

"I insist. It will be a birthday gift."

"Another one?" She gave her head a wag in protest. "A formal gown is far too impractical for me."

"Eliza will insist you're dressed appropriately."

That quelled her protests, and Daniel felt a tad ashamed for the manipulative ploy.

"You're a wonderful man." Julianna lowered her gaze and ran the tongs of her fork aimlessly around her plate, but Daniel caught sight of the pretty blush creeping into her cheeks. "You're honorable in the highest sense of the word."

"Not that honorable." Now he felt downright guilty.

"Well, you can't change me mind. I'm stubborn that way."

"You don't say?" He grinned when her gaze popped up to meet his.

When she saw he teased her, she rolled her eyes just as saucy-as-you-please. Daniel chuckled. She was adorable—and quite the temptation.

Too much so, perhaps.

Daniel watched as she sipped her juice. He'd been a fool to think he could resist her all the way to Wisconsin.

He sat back in his chair, thinking, wondering over his own poor judgment in that regard. But there was still time to correct it. Perhaps he'd bring a couple of the Ramseys' staff along for chaperoning. He'd talk to George about it. It only made sense. A lady's maid for Julianna and a valet for himself while they journeyed. There would be little time for Julianna and him to be alone and tempted. Daniel had known for quite some time that she was his weakness. One wrong move too far, and he'd be forever haunted just as George was now.

He folded his arms and looked on as Julianna smiled and stared out over the terrace.

"Such a beautiful day," she murmured again.

The light breeze toyed with the wisps of hair coiling at her temples. What a lovely and innocent picture she made—

And if she proved to be a liar and extortionist, then she was the finest actress in all the world!

That night only a sliver of a moon hung in the dusky sky as Julianna boarded the carriage for Mrs. Brunning's party. The weather was pleasant enough, not too hot and not too cool. *Perfect.* The enchanting off-the-shoulder pink silk gown with its black trim and white lace made her feel like a princess. In fact, this entire day had made her feel like royalty. She'd ambled through the flower gardens, poked around in the Ramseys' library—with their consent, of course—and then she'd taken a nap. Right in the middle of the afternoon! The maid awoke her after her gown arrived in its colorfully wrapped paper. The captain had purchased it for her, and it was unlike any other that Julianna had ever seen. This gown was elegance *perfected.* For her *perfect* birthday.

The captain sat across the way from her, next to Mr. Ramsey. "You look lovely, Miss Wayland—as do you, Eliza," he quickly added.

Julianna blushed. He'd told her how lovely she looked twice already.

"You're so kind, Daniel." Sitting beside her, Mrs. Ramsey smiled. "And, George, do try to at least pretend you're enjoying yourself once we arrive at Mabel's home."

"I shall do my best." He grumbled the reply. "I have no use for bold and independent women."

"Or so he thinks," Mrs. Ramsey whispered near Julianna's ear.

"I heard that, and it proves my point." Mr. Ramsey's tone increased. "Mabel Brunning is a terrible influence on the genteel women in New York."

Julianna decided she liked the woman already.

Her gaze flitted across the carriage, where she met the captain's blue eyes and amused-looking wink. Had he guessed her thoughts?

"Oh, George, don't start in again." Mrs. Ramsey huffed softly.

"Eliza, you know I can't abide Mabel Brunning. Next time ask me before you accept an invitation for the both of us."

"Now, George, there's no need for harsh replies and poor attitudes. Strong, outspoken women like Mrs. Brunning fill the corners of the world."

The captain's broad shoulders moved quickly up and down. "Sometimes they say important things. You might try listening."

"Thank you, Daniel." A satisfied sigh passed Mrs. Ramsey's lips.

Mr. Ramsey snorted and stared out the carriage's window, his expression pinched and terse.

The captain chuckled.

Concealing her grin, Julianna realized that Captain Sundberg was the only one who could take Mr. Ramsey down a few pegs. The older man cowed everyone else.

The carriage rolled to a stop in front of a tall, square, brick building with lamps already lit in most windows. Formally dressed men and women strolled up the walk to the door. It amazed Julianna to think that tonight she'd be among them—and not as a housemaid.

Captain Sundberg helped the ladies alight and then escorted Julianna into the elegant foyer of the home. Framed artwork in gilded frames adorned the papered walls, and the golden floor tiles gleamed from a thorough waxing.

"Why, Captain Sundberg, it's a pleasure to see you again." A rotund woman wearing folds of deep green silk extended her hand.

He placed a perfunctory kiss on her gloved fingers. "Mrs. Brunning, the pleasure is all mine. You also have my congratulations on your many years of publishing articles."

"Thank you, dear man." Musical strains from an ensemble played from somewhere in the house. Mrs. Brunning turned to George Ramsey. "How good of you to come, George."

Julianna resisted the urge to roll her eyes as he greeted their hostess just as the captain had, the phony.

Next Mrs. Ramsey said hello and gave Mrs. Brunning quick kisses on both cheeks. "You look divine in that emerald dress, Mabel."

"Why, thank you. And who might this little darling be?" Mrs. Brunning's intelligent brown eyes zeroed in on Julianna.

The captain made the introductions. "Mrs. Mabel Brunning, may I present Miss Julianna Wayland. She's from London and a guest of the Ramseys." He then whispered something more.

"Her birthday!" Mrs. Brunning's face lit with surprise. "How noteworthy! Well, then, Miss Wayland, I'll expect Captain Sundberg to show you an exceptionally delightful time at my home tonight."

"Thank you, ma'am." Julianna glanced at the captain and thought the reply wasn't quite what he'd expected.

He took her elbow and glided her out of the queue of guests waiting to greet Mrs. Brunning.

"Is something wrong?"

The captain paused near the doorway of another expensively decorated room. "With my luck, Mrs. Brunning will extend her writing skills to the *New York Times*, and Reagan will read about my escorting you here. I hadn't thought about it until minutes ago."

"Your countess?" Julianna hoped she'd read about it—and more. "May I have some punch, please?"

Captain Sundberg arched a brow. "Anything else, m'lady?"

His sarcasm made laughter bubble up inside of Julianna. "I'll let you know the moment I think of something."

The evening progressed, and Julianna was introduced to scores of interesting people. She noted the respect Captain Sundberg garnered, and she learned of some of his voyages. In the past years he'd been to Asia, South America, and all of Europe, loading up cargo there, from tea and produce to iron ore and lumber, then transporting it back to New York.

Julianna found herself in awe of this seafaring man. He certainly wasn't like any other she'd met, but she'd known that already.

Eliza approached them. "I'm famished. Let's find a table and fix ourselves plates with some of those delectable hors d'oeuvres."

Julianna's stomach rumbled with anticipation. She'd been too excited to eat any dinner tonight. She followed the Ramseys through the ornately decorated ballroom.

"Allow me to fix your plate, m'lady." Captain Sundberg spoke so near to Julianna's ear that his warm breath caused delightful shivers to run down her neck.

She smiled and nodded. Mr. Ramsey left to fix his wife's plate also.

"Isn't this fun?" Mrs. Ramsey glanced around the room. "We're participating in history tonight."

"I'd say so."

The ensemble played a stirring melody, and Julianna rocked slightly to the beat. Soon the captain and Mr. Ramsey returned with the food. It looked scrumptious. Julianna couldn't wait to try everything on her plate.

As the men seated themselves, Julianna glanced around the room again. During her years on London's streets she'd only hoped to eat the scraps from a party like this, but here she was actually a guest.

She wanted to pinch herself.

"Well, now, Miss Wayland," Mr. Ramsey began, "suppose you tell us more about yourself as we eat."

Julianna could barely hear him above the din of chatting and music.

"George, let's not put Miss Wayland on the spot." The captain gave her what appeared like a forced smile.

"Come now, Daniel. Allow Miss Wayland a chance to speak."

She slid a gaze to the captain, who gave her a subtle nod. Did he want her to be completely honest?

"Not much to tell, really," she murmured.

"Everyone has a story," Mrs. Ramsey remarked before she ate caviar on a small, crisp biscuit. "Are you acquainted with any of London's clothing designers?"

"No." Julianna brightened. "But Mum was a seamstress."

Mr. Ramsey groaned, and the captain muttered something to him in that cynical tone of his.

"But as I said, I never knew her."

"You poor dear. I was very close to my mother. She passed years ago, but I still miss her terribly." Mrs. Ramsey's expression oozed with empathy. "It had to be difficult, being raised by an older sister."

"Flora did her best. She was only a child herself. And Mrs. Potter had good intentions." Disquiet began to plume inside of her. "I'd prefer not to speak about me childhood years anymore."

"But how shall we get to know you better?" Again that exaggerated condescension from Mr. Ramsey. Julianna couldn't figure him out. Was she an imposition?

"I told you about meself this morning, Mr. Ramsey."

"Yes, but surely you remember more about your, um, father." He shook out the white linen napkin and set it across his lap. "Perhaps I can help you locate him."

The idea struck Julianna as ludicrous. "Why would I want to locate the man?"

"I thought he was dead." Puzzlement drizzled across Mrs. Ramsey's features as she turned to Julianna for explanation.

"He's been dead to me all me life, the rotten scoundrel." Glimpsing the look of shock on the other woman's face, Julianna quickly adjusted her tone. "Beggin' your pardon, ma'am. I guess I got carried away with me sentiments—that is, *my* sentiments." She looked at the captain and saw a muscle work in his jaw. Was she doing all right?

"Fret not, my dear." Mrs. Ramsey reached across the way and touched Julianna's forearm. "I get carried away at times too."

"How do you know your father's a..." Mr. Ramsey paused. "A scoundrel?" Something like chagrin reddened his face.

Julianna wished her knight would speak up and save her from this interrogation. What if she embarrassed him?

She glanced about. It seemed no one was within earshot. Candlelight glowed all around them.

"Please, Mr. Ramsey, I would prefer to change the subject, although"—Julianna ran a gloved finger along the starched edge of her napkin—"with all the talk this morning, I managed to recall something amusing. You see, Flora said she never knew me father's real name. She and Mum called him by a nickname. *Christopher Columbus*."

As Julianna giggled over the name, Mr. Ramsey began to hack as though he'd gotten something caught in his throat. He held his napkin to his lips.

"Goodness, George, what's wrong with you?" Mrs. Ramsey leaned forward. "Have you caught yourself a cold?"

"No, no..." *Cough. Cough.*

A few heads turned. The captain assured onlookers that the situation was under control.

Julianna sobered, sensing the reason for Mr. Ramsey's reaction. "I'm completely aware that it's shameful how he never married Mum, but it's not me fault. I didn't ask to be born."

"Of course you didn't, you poor thing." Mrs. Ramsey patted her hand.

Meanwhile, the captain clapped Mr. Ramsey between the shoulder blades.

"A similar circumstance happened to a girlhood friend of mine,"

Mrs. Ramsey whispered. "She fell in with a notorious rake, and he didn't do right by her either."

"A very good description, Mrs. Ramsey. Such men are rakes." Julianna gave a nod.

Mr. Ramsey continued to clear his throat.

Julianna sent the captain a curious look.

He met her gaze. "Not to worry. I believe George's coughing fits are brought on by his own doing." Captain Sundberg cast a dark glance at the older man.

"You've been smoking those awful cigars again, haven't you, dear?" Mrs. Ramsey jerked her chin. "I told you they were bad for your health."

Captain Sundberg took a turn at clearing his throat. "If you, George, and Eliza will excuse me, I believe I shall dance with Miss Wayland. It is, after all, her birthday."

Julianna held up a hand in protest. "You think that's a good idea?" What about keeping their distance?

He stood and took her hand. As if reading her thoughts, he said, "I assure you, all proprieties will be observed."

"Yes, yes, go and dance," Mrs. Ramsey encouraged. "Enjoy yourselves."

The captain helped Julianna to her feet, and Julianna's heart picked up its pace. He bowed regally. "May I have this dance, Miss Wayland?"

Oh! But how could she refuse? He looked so handsome in his dark suit. The blue of his eyes shimmered beneath the golden radiance of the chandeliers. "Yes…"

He led her away from the table. Other couples swayed to the melodious waltz. He made a smooth pivot and locked his arm around her waist then brought her up as close as proper etiquette allowed.

"Just follow my lead." Like a feather, his breath softly brushed against her temple.

"Oh, I've waltzed before, but not with a man."

His amused chuckle reached her ears. "By yourself, then?"

"No, Flora taught me the basics."

"Well, you're doing fine." He spoke the words for her ears only.

How utterly natural it felt to glide across the floor in his arms. Julianna never wanted their dance to end.

"This has been the best day of me life."

He smiled.

They made a turn around the room, and Julianna's confidence grew. When at last the melody ended, she felt rather proud of her accomplishment. At the same time she knew it was only because of the captain's arm holding her so tightly that she'd achieved it.

"Don't move!" a man shouted.

She and the captain froze. He groaned. Moments later a bright light exploded, and Julianna saw white spots in front of her eyes.

Mabel Brunning rushed up to them and took Julianna's hand. "My gift to you, my dear. A photograph so you can remember this birthday forever."

"Thank you." Julianna had never been photographed before. She blinked, and the spots began to fade.

Julianna smiled all the way to their corner table. As Captain Sundberg held the chair for her, she felt a dizzying happiness flood her being.

"Why, my dear, you're positively glowing." The corners of Mrs. Ramsey's mouth went up in a knowing sort of way.

"It's not every day a girl gets to dance with the prince of sea captains." *I feel like a princess at that.*

"You flatter me, Miss Wayland." The captain's short chuckle sounded more embarrassed than amused.

Mrs. Ramsey's pleased-looking smile grew.

Mr. Ramsey, on the other hand, sat ramrod-straight and appeared none too pleased. But why? Whatever was the matter with him?

Julianna found herself praying that the older man wouldn't ruin the rest of this incredible night. But to her relief she found that the evening passed in a delightful blur of dancing and conversation and delicious food.

It neared the midnight hour when the carriage stopped at the Ramseys' front door. Mr. Ramsey let himself out and called instructions to his driver. The captain climbed out the opposite doorway and extended his hand first to Mrs. Ramsey and then Julianna.

"Did you enjoy your birthday, little one?" He held onto her hand as he waited for a reply.

She heard the endearment, and it only made this night all the more special. "It was perfect." It was the only word she knew to describe it.

A satisfied smile worked its way into the captain's handsome face, and beneath the far-reaching glow of the front porch lamps Julianna saw those irresistible dimples winking at her.

He closed the carriage door and took her arm. Julianna lifted her hems with her other hand and felt as though she didn't walk but instead floated to the massive double-door entrance.

In the grand front hallway Mrs. Ramsey bid them all a goodnight and took to the stairs. Her husband entered the house just seconds after the captain and Julianna.

"Join me in the study, Daniel?" Mr. Ramsey glanced at Julianna, although he didn't meet her gaze. "Goodnight, Miss Wayland."

She was obviously dismissed. "Goodnight. Thank you for a lovely evening—and for everything."

As she headed for the stairwell, she heard the captain murmur, "Sleep well."

Glancing over her shoulder, Julianna watched him disappear into the study. Mr. Ramsey followed, and then the door closed firmly behind them.

CHAPTER 11

*O*N MONDAY MORNING Julianna pulled back the curtains to see another glorious day. The weekend's weather had been fine, although Saturday was much less eventful than her birthday. Then yesterday they'd ridden to church in the morning and attended a formal mass, spoken in Latin. More affirmation that a convent wasn't her destiny.

"Miss, the train leaves soon. Captain Sundberg detests tardiness."

Turning from the window, Julianna smiled at the stern-faced maid and allowed her to assist with her morning toilette, although she was tired of being pampered. As she slipped into the comely beige skirt and pulled on the multicolor printed blouse, flutters of anticipation filled her insides. Would she enjoy farm life? Thoughts of living beyond the clutches of the city certainly appealed to her.

Finally dressed, Julianna gazed at herself in the looking glass. She was getting accustomed to seeing the pretty, well-groomed young woman who stared back at her. Scrutinizing her traveling outfit, Julianna enjoyed the way the bodice of her dress formed a V where it adjoined with the full skirt, which bustled in the back. The many colors complemented her dark hair, and—Julianna moved forward—only a slight trace of bruising under her left eye was visible, mostly because she stood in a pool of bright sunshine that streamed through the bedroom window.

With her primping completed, Julianna made her way downstairs. The sweet aroma of fresh bread caught her nose, and she began making her way to the dining room. But then she heard her name and turned on her heel. The captain, dressed handsomely once again, stood in the doorway of Mr. Ramsey's study. With his hand palm-side up, he motioned for her to come forward. She did.

"George and I would like a word with you before breakfast."

"All right." Julianna smiled, although she thought he seemed rather abrupt.

The stench of tobacco lingered in the darkened room, and Julianna was reminded of Mr. Tolbert's den.

"Good morning, Miss Wayland." Mr. Ramsey, also impeccably dressed, stood behind his large desk. "Please come in. It's about time we discussed business, don't you think?"

"Of course." Her passage and new wardrobe. She needed to promise to repay all but the birthday gift from the captain.

"Please be seated, Julianna." Captain Sundberg's tone was more cordial now. "Would you care for a cup of tea?"

"Yes, please."

A half smile moved across his mouth. "I figured as much and took the liberty of pouring out."

"Why, thank you." She accepted the dainty porcelain cup and saucer. "How very thoughtful of you."

He sat on the corner of Mr. Ramsey's mahogany desk. "I wanted to tell you that Devlin Griswald, also known as the Grisly Devil, will never harm you again. He's been ordered to return to London and stand trial on charges of attempted murder and insubordination at sea, as well as mutinous behavior. "

"What will happen to him if he's found guilty?" And he was. Julianna hoped he'd hang from a short rope.

"My guess is that he'll be sentenced to a life of hard labor or institutionalized in an insane asylum. I believe he's mad."

Julianna didn't doubt it for a moment.

"But you're not to give the man another thought, all right? He's out of your life forever." The captain's steady gaze held a promise that touched Julianna's core.

"I'm more than happy to never think of that man again." She sipped her tea and noticed Mr. Ramsey eyed her with an odd expression.

"You look lovely today. Are you rested for our journey?"

Mr. Ramsey cleared his throat in what sounded to Julianna like disapproval, but the captain didn't appear to pay the man much mind.

"Thank you." Her gaze returned to the captain. "And, yes, I believe I'm ready."

"Let's begin, shall we?" An impatient note sounded in Mr. Ramsey's request. "Now, Miss Wayland…"

Again, she sipped from the cup. Mmm, just the way she liked her black tea, good and strong in the morning.

"…let's get right to the point here. What is it, exactly, that you want from me?"

Julianna frowned. "Sir?"

"What do you want? The deed to my home in Virginia, perhaps?"

Noting the derision in Mr. Ramsey's tone, she quickly looked to the captain. "But I thought I was going to a place called Wisconsin."

He said nothing but studied the cufflink on his ivory-colored shirt.

"So you want money, is that it?" Mr. Ramsey's voice raised several decibels. "How much money?"

The teacup in Julianna's hand clattered against the saucer. She didn't like this man. Not a single bit. What was he talking about?

Leaning forward, she set the cup and saucer on the edge of Mr.

Ramsey's desk. "I want nothing more from you, sir. You've been most generous. In fact, I thought we were going to discuss me passage and wardrobe."

The captain still didn't acknowledge her with a glance.

Julianna felt suddenly very alone. She rose from the chair.

"So you want more clothes and money for passage, is that right?" Mr. Ramsey demanded.

Julianna gaped at Mr. Ramsey.

"For heaven's sake, name your price!"

"But I..." Julianna didn't understand what was happening. Her hackles went up. She looked over her shoulder at the closed door. Should she make a run for it?

A hand clamped over her forearm, and she startled. But then she saw the captain beside her.

"That's enough, George. Now we do this my way."

Wearing a scowl, Mr. Ramsey reclined in his chair.

"Julianna?"

She gave him a wary regard.

"The new clothes are a gift. From me. I want you to have everything you need to start a new life in Wisconsin."

"So I'm still going there?" She blinked, confused.

Before the captain could reply, Mr. Ramsey erupted again. "Where else did you have in mind, Miss Wayland? The south of France, perhaps? Paris?"

"George!"

Julianna pulled out of the captain's grasp. "Are you both mad? What's wrong with you?" She leaned closer to the captain and inhaled. He didn't smell like he'd been drinking.

Mr. Ramsey clambered to his feet and drew back until he peered down his nose at her. "Be warned, Miss Wayland—if that's really your name—I have notified Scotland Yard. I'll find out the truth."

"The truth? But my name is really Julianna Wayland. I never lied about it." Suspicious, she tilted her head. "And why have you contacted London's finest?" She swung her line of vision back to the captain. "I'm not going back to London with the Grisly Devil, am I?"

"No, of course not."

"Then you're sending me back to Mr. Tolbert and the young master?" Even as she spoke those words, her mind screamed against the idea.

"No, never. I would never do something like that to you." He spoke in that commanding tone of his, and Julianna believed him. "Your wardrobe and accessories are a gift from me. You have a job in Wisconsin if that's what you want."

She felt suddenly so unsure of everything. Did she have other options? But where would she go?

She gazed into the captain's blue eyes, trying to discern his thoughts. "You said you would take me to Wisconsin to help your mother on the farm."

"Is that agreeable to you?"

Julianna thought he asked sincerely. She replied with a timid nod.

"Fine," Mr. Ramsey said. "Then let's make an agreement. We'll exchange your passage from London to New York and your fares from here to Wisconsin for your signature stating you expect nothing more from our shipping company or from Daniel and me personally. Is that fair enough?"

She didn't know what to say. How was it fair? Seemed to Julianna like she'd gotten the better end of the bargain.

Looking at the captain, she caught a flash of his pained expression. "I never expected all the kindness and generosity in the first place."

"This is business. Daniel and I must ensure the safety of his investments."

"Oh, well, all right." If this was the way men conducted business, then it was little wonder they ended up shooting each other.

"So, do we have an agreement, Miss Wayland?" Mr. Ramsey's voice sounded constrained, as if he still wanted to shout at her.

"I suppose so." Julianna still sensed something was amiss. "And you're really not sending me back to Mr. Tolbert?" She moved toward the captain. "Are you?"

"Have I ever lied to you?"

She shook her head.

The crinkles around the captain's eyes softened just before his gaze moved to Mr. Ramsey. "Add a line into the agreement that states Miss Wayland is in no way obligated to return to Mr. Tolbert's employ. In return, she will forgive any wages he owes her up to the date of her leave." He looked at Julianna again. "The latter will most likely silence Tolbert or his son if they have a mind to track you down. However, I highly doubt his influence is as far-reaching as America."

"If you say so." The captain hadn't betrayed her trust so far.

Mr. Ramsey sat down and penned the addition across the pre-written agreement. "There." He handed it to the captain.

"Allow me to read this in its entirety, Julianna."

She gave a single nod, glad she didn't have to read it herself. She managed well enough with printed words, but not hand-scribed documents.

The captain read from the paper in his hand. It listed the sum of her travel expenses, a dizzying amount. In exchange for it, Julianna would not ask or require anything more from Ramsey Enterprises, the Ramsey family, or Captain Daniel Sundberg. Then he read the lines about not being required to return to the Tolbert residence.

"So, what do you think?" The captain set the agreement on the desktop once more.

She scrutinized the captain's expression. "This is awfully kind of you, Captain. No one's ever done anything nice for me before—not like this, anyway."

His jaw muscle worked. Was he angry?

When no further comment came forth, she stared at the agreement. "I guess I'd be a fool not to sign the paper, wouldn't I?" Julianna walked closer to the desk. "Just one more thing."

"What is it?" Mr. Ramsey's face reddened.

Julianna longed to get this over with and leave this place forever. "May I borrow your pen—or is that asking too much?"

From the corner of her eye she saw the captain rub his neck. He seemed to stave off a grin. She hadn't meant to be funny or sassy.

Mr. Ramsey thrust the ink pen at her. "Sign, and be quick about it."

❦

Daniel watched as Julianna printed her name. He sensed George's impatience and aggravation but cast him a frowning innuendo to hold his temper. He'd warned George to tread lightly if he wanted the agreement signed. Daniel knew Julianna didn't trust many people, and he'd won her over. She thought of him as honorable, and yet here he stood, watching this young woman innocently sign away her rightful inheritance.

His conscience pressed in on him, but he held his tongue. George was sure their futures were at stake.

At last Julianna set down the pen. "Is there anything else, sir?"

"No. That'll be all, Miss Wayland."

Daniel winced at George's tone. He sounded as though he spoke to one of his hirelings, not his own flesh and blood.

Julianna glanced at Daniel. Questions still pooled in her eyes.

"We'll leave for the train station in about an hour."

"I'm ready to go whenever you say."

He replied with a single nod.

She whirled around and practically ran to the door.

When it closed behind her, something in Daniel's gut twisted.

He felt like a hypocrite. If he was any kind of an honorable man, he'd go to her and tell her the truth right now. Instead he remained silently loyal to George.

"Well, it's done. I'll get this document over to my attorney's office."

"You ought to tear it up this minute. She's your daughter!"

"Now, Daniel, think of the consequences—for both of us. She can't learn the truth. If news of this got out, it would result in a scandalous firestorm that would never go away." George slowly circled Daniel. "I'd never be able to face my friends or the public. Why, Eliza would never forgive me. What's more, you could forget all about marrying a countess anytime soon. Instead, you'd be forced to share your inheritance with that... *scamp*." George stepped closer. "Consider everything you've worked so hard to accomplish in the last twelve years. Are you willing to give away a portion to... to *her*?" He extended his manicured forefinger toward the closed door.

Daniel narrowed his gaze and swallowed a retort.

"That's right, think about it, son. Think hard!"

George made some inarguable points. Daniel couldn't deny it.

With a smile he clapped his hand on Daniel's shoulder. "And while you cogitate, let's eat some breakfast, shall we?"

Daniel had lost his appetite, but he walked alongside George as they left the study. A busy maid scurried through the wide foyer, stopping only for a quick curtsey when she saw them coming.

Daniel nodded politely and then remembered his request. "That reminds me, George. Did Eliza speak with you about two of your staff accompanying me to Wisconsin?"

"Yes, and I made the arrangements. A neighbor hired a lady's maid and valet, but it's not working out, so she's sending them back to Chicago. I have agreed to pay half their fare, provided they accompany you and, um, Miss Wayland."

Daniel didn't care. At this point he wasn't selective. Any two hirelings would be better than none at all.

"Oh, and I almost forgot..."

George pulled a folded piece of paper from his waistcoat's pocket. "A telegram arrived this morning around the same time as the written agreement from my attorney."

Daniel opened it and saw that it came from his mother—a reply to his telegram the day they'd dropped anchor in New York. He read, *Poppa lives. Please come home soon.*

Relief coursed through him. His father was still alive. There was still time for Daniel to see him.

"Good news?"

"Yes." He refolded the message. "My father is still alive."

"Your biological father?"

"Correct." Daniel pushed out a grin.

"Well, do what you must, son, to sever any remaining ties in Wisconsin. And, for heaven's sake, deposit that Wayland girl and hurry back. We have a trip to London to make. You'll propose marriage to the countess and then there will be a seemingly endless string of parties and balls to attend."

They stopped to finish their conversation.

"Of course, the countess will be eager to get that ring on your finger." George elbowed him and laughed. "She'll have captured the elusive prince of the sea captains, eh?"

Daniel forced an amused grin. He disliked his husbandly role being equated to captivity.

"You and the countess will make a fine couple, and a very wealthy one at that."

Wealth overrode captivity, didn't it?

He caught sight of Julianna entering the foyer, and his heart squeezed with some inexplicable emotion.

"Mrs. Ramsey asked me to fetch the two of you. She says breakfast is on the table and getting cold." Her gaze fixed on Daniel as she spoke. "Apparently our train leaves soon."

"Then we'd best eat a hot, tasty meal while we can." Stepping forward, he offered his arm to Julianna, but she evidently didn't see the gesture in time and strode back to the dining room.

George's voice came from just behind him. "And she's an ill-mannered scamp to boot!"

CHAPTER 12

TWO DAYS LATER Julianna sat alone at a table in the Trackside Inn's eatery. Only eight more hours to go before the train would arrive at Chicago's dockside depot, where they'd board a steamship for Manitowoc.

She'd been practicing the city's pronunciation whenever possible. Man-it-tow-wok.

Sipping her tea, Julianna decided she'd be glad to leave the railroad behind. The passenger car had been stifling, and the collective smell of human perspiration and tobacco, nauseating. If the windows were opened and the wind blew in the wrong direction, thick black smoke from the locomotive wafted into the car on the hot summer air. The sleeper car had been just as warm and uncomfortable, so it had been an enormous relief when the captain announced they'd take the layover stop. While the Trackside Inn had been noisy, it was a far sight better than some places she'd slept, and since she'd been able to enjoy a cool bath before bed, Julianna hadn't a single complaint.

Unlike Priscilla, the woman hired as her lady's maid. Julianna sighed. Poor Priscilla was sorely lacking in the area of service, and she complained continually after their departure from New York's busy station. But that the captain hired a lady's maid to accompany *her* amazed Julianna once more, especially since his odd behavior in Mr. Ramsey's study. She still didn't know what to make of the incident.

"Deep in thought, are you?"

Julianna started and looked up to see Captain Sundberg.

"Or are you still sleepy?"

She smiled. "You were correct the first time."

"May I join you?"

"Of course." Why would he ask? Then, again, the captain was ever the gentleman. Even now, wearing his crisp ivory shirt and waistcoat and light brown dress coat, he appeared every bit the groomed and educated man, even when the other men around him appeared slightly bedraggled.

Removing his hat, he sat down, hailed the serving gent, and then ordered a cup of coffee. Next he glanced around the eatery. "I see Priscilla and Tubs are nowhere to be found—as usual."

"I knocked on their door. The couple is just waking up."

"Hmm...well, I dislike it that you were sitting here by yourself."

"I didn't sense any danger, Captain, and I can take care of meself." She'd survived the twenty years before she'd met him.

He leaned forward. "The word is *myself*, remember?" He spoke softly.

"My apologies."

He smiled in a way that warmed Julianna's insides better than a swallow of hot tea.

"Since we're both here, Captain, may I ask you a question?" In the passenger car he'd sat beside Mr. Tubs while she'd been pinned to Priscilla, whose oversized waistline and broad hips made it impossible to even squirm.

"Of course."

"It's about Mr. Ramsey. I've been wondering what I did to make him dislike me."

The captain shook his head. "Don't worry your pretty head about it a moment longer. George has a lot on his mind."

"I'm sure he does." Except things still didn't sit right with Julianna. She'd made a million speculations in the last forty-eight hours but came to only one conclusion. Mr. Ramsey feared she'd somehow corrupt Captain Sundberg. However, Julianna knew the captain had his own plans. Besides, he was socially her superior.

His coffee arrived, and the captain insisted they eat breakfast. Julianna made her choice from the menu, and the captain ordered the same thing. Afterward he requested a newspaper.

Julianna had already noted he read quite a bit. Upon leaving New York, he'd given her the society page of daily news, and it had taken her an entire afternoon to look it over. She wasn't a fast reader. Further slowing her process was Priscilla, who wanted to know each detail from Julianna, upon which she added her own editorials. Julianna had finally met a woman who talked more than she did. But at least the conversations passed the time.

She chanced a look at the captain. "I overheard you and Mr. Ramsey making mention of your wedding plans. I'm sure that will be very exciting. Are you returning to England for your marriage?"

The captain looked momentarily pensive before answering. "It's a business arrangement, Julianna, nothing more."

"You don't love her in the least bit?"

He took a sip of coffee. "Perhaps love will come later."

"What if it doesn't?"

"Then we'll be very rich," he whispered, "and that'll be enough for the both of us."

"Money can do that, hmm?" She supposed it explained a lot. She thought of the precious coins she'd hidden in her room at Mr. Tolbert's home. Surely someone else had found them by now. She'd been saving for that little cottage somewhere—somewhere safe, where Flora wouldn't have to sell herself and where drunken sailors were nonexistent.

"You look troubled. What's on your mind?"

"Oh, nothing really. I'm just beginning to miss Flora. In fact…" She ran her finger along a scar on the tabletop. "I'm worried about her."

The captain set down his cup. "I'm sure she's fine."

Julianna frowned. She hoped so.

More people entered the eatery, but Priscilla and her spouse weren't among them. Bowls of porridge and plates containing slices of bread slathered with honey arrived. She and the captain began to eat.

"Cook always made us say grace before we ate."

"Say it then, if it makes you feel better."

Julianna bowed her head and whispered a memorized prayer of thanks. She lifted her head. The captain had buried himself in his newspaper.

Minutes passed. Finally the captain dabbed the sides of his mouth with his napkin. "If your lady's maid and my valet aren't here soon, they'll miss breakfast."

"Odd for them to miss a meal."

"Especially since I'm paying the bill." A sardonic smile curved his lips.

In that regard Julianna thought it downright shameful that Priscilla and her spouse proved little assistance on this journey. Having been a maid herself, Julianna was, perhaps, more critical than most, although she fancied herself more gracious too. The fact was, Priscilla and her husband weren't cut out for the service industry.

"Little wonder they didn't work out for George and Eliza's neighbors," the captain muttered.

"I wish them better in Chicago."

He drained his cup of coffee, then waved to the serving gent and pointed to his cup.

Julianna marveled at his confidence. In fact, she never tired of watching the man.

He caught her gaze and smiled. "You'd best eat your breakfast. There's no guarantee the boxed lunches on the train today will be acceptable, and supper in the dining car is hours away."

"All right."

The captain's features relaxed. "Just think, this evening we'll board a steamship, and we'll be on the water again"—he widened his eyes for emphasis—"where it's safe." He shook his head, and Julianna glimpsed the way his auburn hair curled at his shirt's collar. "I would have much preferred sailing through the Erie Canal and up around the Great Lakes."

"Why didn't you get your way?"

"I'm afraid George is enamored with the railroad. He wants to expand Ramsey Enterprises to perhaps include a large investment in the rail line that runs this express train."

"Ah…another business arrangement." She sipped her tea. "Is that all men think about?"

"Hardly." The captain added an indiscernible little grin while his blue eyes searched her face. Then he went back to reading his newspaper.

At the mention of Mr. Ramsey's name and future ambitions, a knot of uncertainty grew inside of her. Would her new position on the Sundberg farm work out favorably for her? What if she didn't enjoy working with animals?

Swirling the spoon around her porridge, she looked askance at the captain. "Do you think that, perhaps, this wasn't such a good idea?"

Captain Sundberg's gaze met hers. "In what way?"

"Well, um..." How did she say this without sounding ungrateful? "America is so very far away from England. Perhaps I won't fit in here. Would you consider taking me back? I won't be any trouble. I promise. Maybe your countess needs a maid."

"I'm afraid that's out of the question, Julianna." His blue eyes darkened, and she wasn't sure if she'd angered him with her request.

She sunk her gaze into her porridge.

"But I understand how anxious you must feel. You're in a strange new country where everyone speaks and behaves differently. You've left behind your sister, although it seems to me like she didn't have your best interest at heart."

"But you obviously do." She lifted her gaze and moistened her lips. "I still find it hard to believe that I'm here. I owe you my life."

"Nonsense. But let's continue this conversation later. This establishment is getting far too crowded for my comfort."

"Of course." She hadn't meant to get so personal in public.

An older man in dark trousers and a white shirt with a black bowtie approached their table. By his uniform, Julianna guessed he worked at the hotel.

"Are you Captain Sundberg?"

He nodded. "I am."

"I have a message for you from Mr. and Mrs. Tubs." He held out a small piece of paper.

The captain opened it and quickly read its contents. "Fine, thank you. But make note that, as of now, the bill is to be put in Tubs' name."

"Yes, sir."

The man walked away, and Julianna's gaze trailed him as far as the front desk. Then she gave the captain a curious glance.

"Apparently the Tubses aren't up to traveling today. But we're not waiting for them. I would like to see my father before he passes into eternity."

"Do you believe in the hereafter?"

The captain arched a brow. "Do you?"

"I'm not sure. Do you?"

He sighed, and a weary expression shadowed his rugged features. "Eat your breakfast. We have a train to board."

She bristled, feeling as though he spoke down to her just now. She leaned forward so as not to be overheard. "I'm not a child, Captain."

"Yes." He opened his newspaper again. "I am very much aware of that fact, thank you."

***

Despite his occasional cynicism, traveling in the company of Captain Sundberg proved ever so much more pleasant than Priscilla's companionship. He pointed out various articles of importance in the newspaper and explained more about the American culture. Women were rapidly becoming part of the workforce. They taught school and wrote books on various subjects, even if they weren't aristocratic or wealthy. Women like Louisa May Alcott, who worked as a servant, a seamstress, and then a nurse during America's Civil War. And Susan Brownell Anthony, who was well-known in New York circles for her work with the American Anti-Slavery Society during the war and, more recently, the women's suffrage movement.

Julianna became intrigued. Maybe now that she was in America, she could do something important with her life, like the women the captain mentioned.

When evening arrived, Captain Sundberg escorted her to the dining car, where they ate a light supper. Afterward he requested a pen and piece of stationary.

"I've been thinking about what you said this morning, about missing your sister. I rudely dismissed your concerns. I apologize."

"No need, but thank you."

"Well, we may not get another chance at privacy, and I thought perhaps you'd like to write to Flora and let her know you're all right. I'll post the letter when we arrive at the station tonight. There's always a clerk on duty."

"Thanks for the offer, but me penmanship is lacking." She quickly amended her statement. "*My* penmanship." And with the methodical rocking of the train, Julianna was sure she wouldn't accomplish anything except making herself look like a simpleton. She hated for the captain to watch her struggle with something he accomplished routinely.

"Then allow me to be at your service. You can tell me what you'd like to say to Flora, and I'll write it."

"You'd do that for me?"

"Of course. You know I'll help you any way that I'm able. I sensed all day that you're feeling a bit…*homesick*." His lips thinned with momentary disdain. "I can't imagine why."

"Life in London is all I've ever known. Working on a farm frightens me."

"You'll do just fine."

"How do you know?"

"The chores will be easy for you to learn, and you'll get along with my mother and sisters very well."

She regarded him askance. "That doesn't mean much, coming from a man who's traveled the world. New places and people aren't frightening for you."

"Not frightening. Exciting. And be assured that a far better life awaits you here in America than in London."

"You've been right about everything so far." Julianna smiled. "I believe you, Captain. And…" She paused, thinking back on Monday morning. "If I said something wrong last Monday I'm terribly sorry."

"It's nothing like that, Julianna."

"Please know that I trust you completely. I don't always understand you, but I trust you."

He didn't answer but shifted in his cushioned leather seat beneath an opened window. The smoke, thank God, wasn't blowing inside the car. Instead Julianna caught the sweetest of scents and glanced outside in time to see a field of blooming wildflowers. America was certainly a picturesque place.

The writing supplies came, and the stationery boasted the railroad's embossed initials. Flora would be impressed when she saw the missive. Why, she'd likely show everyone at the Mariner's Pub, and they'd all know that Julianna resided in a better place.

"Now be sure to write with large letters so it's easy for me sister— I mean, *my* sister—to read."

"As you wish."

Julianna again was amazed that this commanding, highly regarded sea captain would deign to write a simple letter—and post it, no less. "Dearest Flora," she began, "by some miracle I've arrived in America. It's too long a story to write, but I'm alive and healthy. I'll soon reside on a farm in Manitowoc, Wisconsin."

The captain hesitated. "Let's refrain from giving her your exact location until we get my mother's permission. Besides, you may decide you don't want Flora in your life anymore. She's part of the old one—the one you left behind."

Julianna wasn't sure she concurred, but she saw the wisdom in his suggestion. "Once I'm settled, I'll write more. The important thing is for you to know I'm safe and very much alive." With her elbow on the table, Julianna set her chin in her hand and waited for the captain to catch up with her.

He wrote quickly.

"I'm accompanied by a brave, strong, and courageous man. He's been very good to me. A true gentleman."

Captain Sundberg's eyed her. "I'm not the only gentleman in the world, you know." A frown wrinkled his brow. "Sometimes I'm not even a gentleman."

"Yes, I know." Julianna recalled their kiss, and just the memory of it had a dizzying effect on her.

He arched an eyebrow. "On with your letter, *Miss Wayland.*"

"Very well." She smiled, still finding her own quip just now rather amusing. "I hope this letter finds you well." She paused. "Please sign it, 'Your loving sister.'"

The captain finished writing then passed the note to Julianna for her signature. She examined his neat penmanship. "Very legible. Posting it won't be a lot of trouble for you, will it?" She tipped her head, amazed at the captain's generosity. But, then again, that quality was part of why she loved him so.

"No trouble at all." His charming smile sent her heart racing. "If we discover posting it in Chicago is impossible, we can wait until we arrive in Manitowoc or..." He chuckled.

"What's so funny?"

"I should just take it with me back to London and hire a messenger to deliver it to Flora. Probably speedier that way."

He was leaving. How quickly she'd forgotten—or wanted to forget. "How long will you stay in Wisconsin, Captain?"

"A couple of weeks. And I believe we can do away with formalities in our private conversations. Call me Daniel."

"Daniel." She smiled. "A noble name. It suits you."

"I'm sure I don't do the name justice."

"Ah, but you do." An indescribable sadness stole over her. "I just wish you weren't leaving me so soon."

"Now, Julianna..." He stretched his arm across the table and touched her wrist. "You're going to be just fine. It's not as if I'm dumping you off on the streets of Manitowoc. My family has always embraced guests, both expected and unexpected. You'll stay at the farm on which I grew up."

"The very one you ran away from at age fifteen." She gave into the threatening pout.

"I was a boy, longing for adventure."

"And you found it."

"Indeed." He smiled.

"But it cost you your real family, didn't it?"

"Julianna, please…" He spoke her name so softly it tugged at her heartstrings.

"I've gotten quite selfish, haven't I? But you see, I can't recall anyone caring about me welfare—*my* welfare—until that day Jeremy dragged me into your office."

He expelled an audible sigh and stared out the window. The sun seemed to follow their ramble westward. "Listen, I may as well tell you this because you'll most likely find out anyway." Daniel swung his gaze back to hers. "My mother is a stubborn, Norwegian woman who planned out my entire life without any regard to what I thought about it. She did the same to my father. He could have been a successful politician, if she hadn't convinced him to farm."

"Your father said that?" *How disrespectful!*

"No, *Bestefar*—my grandfather—told me the story. He was my father's father. *Bestefar* is also the one who encouraged me to pursue my dreams in spite of my mother's plans."

"What did your father say?"

Daniel lifted one broad shoulder and pursed his bottom lip indifferently. "He defended *Mor*, of course."

"As well he should."

A sad smile played upon his lips. "Even when I visited seven years ago, *Mor* hadn't changed her mind about what my future held. She was determined to keep me on that farm." A muscle worked in his jaw. "She even said God told her that my destiny was a life in Wisconsin—in Manitowoc."

"Maybe she really heard from Him."

"I might have wondered if the Ramseys weren't within earshot of *Mor's* remark. George recognized it as being a manipulative ploy. He advised me never to return to Wisconsin, that if I did, *Mor* would ruin my future. I agreed. But then I received word that Poppa was ailing." Daniel glanced out the window. "And, in spite of my disagreements with my mother, I feel it's my duty to make sure she and my sisters are well taken care of if he dies."

"See? You are a noble man."

Daniel looked at her again and gave a wag of his auburn head. "Either that, or I'm a very foolish one."

CHAPTER 13

*T*HE CLOCK IN the small station bordering the Lake Michigan shoreline read eight thirty. Julianna remained on the platform until Daniel hailed a porter to assist with their baggage. After overseeing it onto the steamship *Shioc*, named for a Wisconsin river, Daniel had said, he helped Julianna board.

"I love the smell of Chicago." He inhaled deeply as he leaned on the ship's rail and gazed out over the water. "It's a city rich with history and yet so new because of all the rebuilding that went on a few years ago."

"Rebuilding?" Julianna clutched the rail with both hands.

"Yes, after what's now called the Great Chicago Fire. It happened in 1871. I've visited Chicago many times with the Ramseys. We'd stay in luxury hotels and visit the theaters and dine at the best restaurants. But they're all gone. The fire left the sturdiest of brick buildings in piles of rubble and twisted metal. Hundreds of people lost their lives, and tens of thousands of people were left homeless."

"How dreadful." She looked out over Lake Michigan. "And with all this water right here? Couldn't they figure out how to put out the fire?"

"The lake saved many people from burning alive, but the wind was blowing eastward and the flames were so intense that they reached out over the water. Sadly many people drowned. Firemen did what they could."

"I'm afraid I don't care to hear that story, Captain." She lowered her voice. "I mean, Daniel." But threading her hand around his elbow gave her a measure of security. "It's worse than Jeremy's tale about the woman and child, frozen in time under the sea."

"Why is it worse?"

"I suppose because it's true."

"Oh, Julianna, don't fret. Nothing will happen to us tonight." Daniel gave her hand an assuring and gentle squeeze. "But before we part for our cabins, let's sit down and enjoy the mild evening weather. The fresh air feels good after being in those stuffy railroad cars."

"I couldn't agree more."

They found two unoccupied chairs and sat. Julianna watched the couples promenading on the deck with moonlight growing brighter in the sky. She got one last glimpse of the lake before a shroud of darkness fell.

"You know if one gazes over the lake, one could imagine it's the sea."

"I suppose... if one didn't know better."

She sent him a sharp glance and he chuckled.

A crew man walked along, lighting the many lanterns adorning the boat. Suddenly it felt rather romantic to be sitting on deck with the man she adored.

Daniel turned to her. "This steamship doesn't cruise too far from shore and avoids the rougher waters, so many people from Chicago enjoy the mild excursion to Milwaukee, Manitowoc, or Green Bay, where they dine or visit friends before sailing home again."

"I suppose it's a memorable affair if one enjoys being out in the middle of a lake in the dark."

Daniel laughed under his breath.

An hour or so later, he walked her to her small but functional cabin. Julianna managed to undress and slip into her berth. By morning they would be docked in Manitowoc, and she'd begin her new life…on a farm.

After a light breakfast the next morning the steamship docked at the depot on the Manitowoc River. Daniel helped Julianna disembark. Directly across the water construction was underway for a sailing vessel. Numerous warehouses lined the wharf, and a tall grain elevator stood proudly at the foot of the bridge. Steamers and schooners were unloaded or loaded as the case may be. Workers shouted to each other while passengers hurried toward their destinations.

Taking Julianna's elbow, Daniel led her toward the baggage clerk to collect their things. Then they made their way toward a multi-passenger horsecar. Daniel felt glad he didn't have to engage in conversation at the moment, although he knew he hadn't been good company at breakfast. Since he'd awakened, thoughts of Poppa had plagued him. Was he still alive?

Daniel helped Julianna board the conveyance. Minutes later they set off, crossing the bridge on the south side of town. He'd find the livery down this way. As they turned onto Eighth Street, sudden amazement caused Daniel to blink. Since his last visit his hometown had sprouted more businesses, many quite impressive. Spying the hotel, he called for the driver to halt. Bending close to Julianna's ear, he said, "You can wait in the hotel lobby while I procure a carriage to take us out to the farm."

She replied with a nod.

When the horsecar stopped, Daniel held Julianna's gloved hand and helped her alight.

"Couldn't I just come with you?"

Uncertainty settled in her eyes before she gazed down the unpaved street aligned with uneven planked walkways. Daniel realized Manitowoc must seem uncivilized to her compared to London. Still, and in spite of his obligations to her, Daniel had no time to dally. He wanted to get to his parents' farm post haste.

Inside the hotel's lobby the air felt pleasantly cool. The young man at the desk greeted them with a smile and agreed to store their baggage nearby. Daniel found an empty table near the windows.

"Will this do?" He held a chair for Julianna. She adjusted her skirts and sat.

"I suppose." She didn't look at all pleased.

He ordered tea for her. "I won't be gone long, and I'm sure you're perfectly safe here. All right?"

Apparently her rolling of one shoulder would be all the acquiescence he'd get.

"I'll be back." Daniel gave her hand a gentle squeeze, telling himself he was doing the right thing by asking her to wait here.

With purposeful strides he headed for the door. Outside the hotel he squinted into the bright sunshine then walked the distance to the livery stable. Reaching it, he entered the large barn, spotted the office, and strode over to it. Daniel removed his hat and searched for the proprietor.

"Well, as I live and breathe! Daniel Sundberg...is that really you?"

He narrowed his gaze. The brawny fellow sauntering toward him didn't look familiar.

"Josh Schulte." The man stuck out his meaty right hand. "You and me went to school together, although I'm a couple years older."

"A pleasure to see you again." Daniel honestly couldn't recall the blond man—or even the boy of the same name. "I'm in need of a carriage or wagonette and a couple of your finest geldings."

"Sure thing. Got just the vehicle right here." He pointed to a covered black buggy with room enough behind the front seat for luggage. "As for horses, you lookin' to buy?" Schulte tipped his head and grinned.

"Perhaps." Daniel wondered over the transaction. Were his folks in need of more horses? "Do you know my family?"

"Sure do."

"Can you tell me how my father is faring?"

Sympathy spread across Schulte's square face. "Not so good, I'm afraid. He had some kind of apoplexy that left him... well, senseless. It was touch and go for a while there. I know your mother did everything she could to make a go of the farm."

Daniel figured that meant nothing got planted this spring.

Schulte set his hand on Daniel's shoulder. "I'm real sorry to be the one to tell you."

He pushed out a polite smile despite the sorrow that pierced him through. "I appreciate it." He cleared the emotion from his throat. "And if it's all right with you, I'll rent the wagon and team for now until I find out the situation with my mother and sisters."

"Fine by me." Schulte stood with his hands on his hips. "But just one of your sisters is left at home. Agnes." He gazed at the stable's beamed ceiling. "She must be 'bout ten now." Looking back at Daniel, he grinned. "Your older sister, Adeline, got married last summer. She and Will Dunbar just had a baby boy. You know, Will's the foreman at Dunbar Manufacturing."

"Where is that located?" Daniel couldn't recall.

"West of here, at the least navigable end of the river."

"And what do they manufacture?"

"Anything you can think of that's made out of timber. Doors, window sashes, beams for ship-makers. It's quite the enterprise."

"Is that right?"

"Adeline married well. Will's a hard worker."

Daniel could scarcely believe his sister was old enough to marry.

144

Last time he was home, Adeline had been in her teens. "It's hard to imagine my sister grown up, married, and a mother already."

"You been gone too long." Schulte cocked a brow. "Don't tell me you're one of them Norwegian bachelors."

Daniel grinned. "For the time being."

"You don't say. Any prospects?"

Obviously the man wanted more information. But Daniel wasn't about to share his life's story with some person he may or may not have known in school. "Let's just leave it at that."

"No, huh?" Schulte chuckled. "Well, there are plenty of single ladies here in town. I'm married, and we got a son."

"How nice for you."

The man shuffled his feet. "How long will you be staying?"

"Just a couple of weeks, depending."

Schulte seemed to understand. "I wish your father the best. Enjoy your stay."

"Thank you."

"And I hope your pa is feeling better."

"Again, thanks."

While Schulte went to hitch up the team, Daniel meandered out onto the walk. His gaze wandered east where tall masts bobbed above the rooflines. Plenty of activity on the piers this morning. Numerous steamships, like the *Shioc*, on which he and Julianna had arrived, made Manitowoc a regular port of call. They took on grain, feed, and flour from the various local mills, as well as coal and lumber.

Schulte called to him, and minutes later Daniel held the horses' reins in his palms. He urged the team forward and down the crowded street, past the blacksmith shop, Knapp's Carpentry, and Edwin Cruthers, Attorney at Law. If he turned east at the next block, he'd still find numerous shipping offices, which took up the entirety of one street. Also there, leading to the waterfront, were taverns and the not-so-well-respected rooms for rent.

But steady ahead on South Eighth Street, the post office, bank, and sheriff's office, all built with Cream City brick, shipped from Milwaukee. Although blackened from years of weather, the buildings still looked as structurally sound as Daniel last remembered.

Next came Grainger's General Store, and Daniel thought the place had to be run by the next generation of Graingers, the very ones with whom he'd attended school.

At the corner dressmaker's shop Daniel slowed. An onslaught of memories collided with him. For as long as Daniel could recall, *Mor* knitted, crocheted, and sewed accessories for the shop, which had changed ownership several times. *Mor* once debated over purchasing the business. It had been her childhood dream to one day own a store.

Then suddenly he saw her—his mother. The color of her hair had gone from blonde to white with age, and her figure was thicker than he recalled from his last visit seven years ago. Other than that, she looked the same save for the purplish-blue slashes below her eyes. Hadn't she gotten enough sleep last night? Obviously not with Poppa ill.

Daniel pulled the vehicle to a halt in front of the hotel across the street. Just as he prepared to jump down, a girl handed *Mor* a broom, and she began sweeping the wood-plank walk in front of the store. And that's when he noticed the sign above it: *Sundbergs' Creations*. So, *Mor* had finally gotten her store. Poppa had forfeited his dreams in politics for her, and now *Mor* had gotten her way again—and that's always how it went, as Daniel recollected.

He leaned a forearm on his knee and stared. The girl must be his baby sister, Aggie. Why weren't she and *Mor* on the farm, working?

Daniel decided to find out.

He climbed down from the wagonette and tethered the team to the hitching post.

"Captain, what took you so long?"

He turned, hearing Julianna's breathless question. Her eyes were round, frightened, and pleading. Before he could ask, a blond man with round spectacles exited the hotel right on her heels.

Julianna stepped nearer to Daniel. "Captain, this is Mr. Mark Dunbar."

"Ah..." Daniel figured out what had happened. Already Julianna had garnered unwanted attention.

But then the man's last name gave him pause. "Dunbar?"

"I'm Will's younger brother." Mark held out his right hand. "I'm the manager here at the hotel."

"Nice to meet you, Mr. Dunbar."

"It's Mark. No need for formalities. We're practically brothers." He stared at Daniel with a mix of awe before his gaze fell on Julianna and stayed there.

She pretended not to notice and stared down the block, although the rapid rise and fall of her chest indicated her discomfort. Then he caught Julianna's eye. "I'll hire a porter to load our things, and then we'll head off to the farm."

"Beg your pardon, sir. Did you just say the farm—as in the Sundberg farm?"

"Yes, although..." He cast a glance across the street and saw his mother reenter the shop. "I just saw *Mor* and Aggie—"

"That's because they live and work here in town now. Earlier this year, after your father had his stroke, your mother was forced to sell the farm. She purchased the building across the street and opened her own shop, figuring she'd earn a wage, and the new location is closer to Dr. Harris's office."

"She sold my family's farm?" The news hit Daniel like a thunderbolt. Why couldn't she have hired able-bodied men to help with the plowing and planting? Why did she have to sell it? No wonder his father never recovered. He'd been taken from the home that he himself had built—the home he loved. Daniel didn't think he'd ever forgive his mother for this, yet one more selfish act.

"Couldn't be helped," Mark said.

Drawing in a slow, deliberate breath, Daniel stuffed his emotions. Offering his arm to Julianna, he said, "Let's go say hello to my mother, shall we?"

Julianna had to run to keep up with Daniel's long strides as they crossed the busy thoroughfare. However, she didn't complain. The faster she escaped from Mark Dunbar, the better.

After he'd refilled her cup of tea, she'd seen that certain, interested light in his eyes—same as she'd seen in Jeremy's eyes. It meant only one thing, and Julianna didn't share their interest. On the other hand, when the captain looked at her that way, it meant she'd likely get herself thoroughly kissed. That she didn't mind at all. Unfortunately she'd made a promise. Another kiss between them must never happen again. Daniel was going to marry his countess.

But it seemed he wouldn't be leaving for the farm.

"*Mor?*"

The older woman sweeping the walk swung around. Her gaze widened when she saw Daniel, and then she dropped her broom.

"Daniel!" She folded her hands over her heart.

"Hello, *Mor.*" He closed the distance between them and placed a very perfunctory kiss on her cheek.

The woman threw her arms around his midsection. "You're home. You're home." She seemed delighted, and Julianna wondered if she were really as manipulative as Daniel claimed.

"I am so happy now that you are home."

Julianna heard the accent in the woman's voice and recalled that Daniel said his family was Norwegian.

"This is hardly home to me, *Mor*, in more ways than one."

"I will explain everything later."

"Fine."

Daniel eyed the store. Julianna followed his line of vision and noted the lovely knotted light-blue shawl hanging inside the window.

"But I'll say now that I'm disappointed to hear you sold the farm."

"Come inside. You can see your poppa, and we will talk."

"Just a moment." Daniel turned to Julianna. "*Mor*, I'd like you to meet Miss Julianna Wayland. I brought her here—"

"Your *forloveden*?" A slow and pleased-looking smile spread across Mrs. Sundberg's tanned face, although Julianna had no idea what she'd said in Norwegian.

"No, *Mor*, she is not my fiancée."

A wave of embarrassment worked its way from Julianna's cheeks to her hairline.

"I hired Julianna to assist you on the farm while Poppa is ill. Now that there is no farm, I'll have to make other arrangements for her."

Other arrangements? Her blush suddenly turned to chagrin as she realized what a burden she'd been on the captain. All the while she ignorantly assumed he enjoyed her company as much as she enjoyed his. But now she truly understood that he'd been merely acting like a gentleman, like the honorable man he was.

"Oh, not to worry, Captain. I'll be more than happy to work here in a shop full of pretty ladies' things."

"But I do not need any help here." A little frown puckered Mrs. Sundberg's brow, and Julianna felt a stab of panic. "School is out for the summer, so Agnes is working at the store and assisting me with Poppa's care. Besides..." Her weary blue eyes met Julianna's gaze. "I cannot afford to pay you, Miss Wayland."

Julianna felt the blood in her face begin to drain, and the word *unwanted* permeated her being. Daniel had planned to leave her off on his parents at their farm. But now there was no farm, and Daniel's mother didn't need Julianna's help.

Pivoting, she scanned the unfamiliar scenery. How very far away from London and New York she felt. At least in New York there were similarities to London, paved streets, art galleries and museums, churches made of red brick with steeples so high they brushed the sky. Here, nothing save for the hotel was even two stories tall.

"If it's a job you're looking for, Miss Wayland..."

She turned again to find Mark Dunbar's eager expression. He must have followed them across the street.

"I'd be happy to inquire for you at the hotel. I have a good rapport with the owner." He tried to conceal his shy grin. "He's my dad."

"Oh?" Julianna forced a little smile just as Mrs. Sundberg moved in to give Mark a hug.

"God morgen, Mark."

"Good morning, Mrs. Sundberg." He glanced at the captain. "I see our collective prayers have been answered. Your son has come home."

"This is not my home," the captain muttered. "And I thought you said your family is a wood manufacturer."

"Yes, sir. We own Dunbar Manufacturing as well as the largest lumberyard around." Mark's grin widened. "And the hotel too."

Mrs. Sundberg's eyebrow dipped as she looked from Mark to her son. "Have you two met?"

"Just minutes ago." The captain shifted his stance on the wooden walk. "And, as for Miss Wayland's position in your store, *Mor,* I'll guarantee her wages."

Julianna stared at Daniel, knowing she couldn't accept such an offer. She had quickly become a burden to him when all he wanted to do was see his poppa and return to New York. He'd be out of her life forever, soon. If she was, indeed, meant to forge her own way here in America, she had to begin now.

"Thank you, Captain. But I think I'll take Mr. Dunbar's offer of, at least, an inquiry."

"You will?" An ear-to-ear smile stretched across Mark's face. "That's…that's fine. I'll go speak to Dad right now."

"Thank you." Julianna pushed out a smile and fixed her gaze on the younger man. Her initial fear of him melted away. He was, after all, related by marriage to Daniel's family, and she'd witnessed Mrs. Sundberg's maternal embrace just now. If he should happen to express interest in courting her, Julianna would just have to inform him that it was no use, that she'd already given her heart away. There was only one man in this world she'd ever love.

She looked back at Daniel. She loved him—and she'd never, ever change her mind!

CHAPTER 14

*D*ANIEL WASTED NO more time in getting to his father's bed-side. As he followed *Mor* through her shop and to the back apartment, his world tipped precariously on its axis.

No farm? The very home in which he'd grown up was owned by others outside their family? He couldn't say why the thought aggravated him, although he blamed *Mor*. Why couldn't she have purchased a shop earlier in her life and allowed Poppa to pursue politics, like *Bestefar* had suggested? *Mor* enjoyed controlling everyone's destiny—and look where it had gotten Poppa!

Mor paused with her hand on the bedroom doorknob. "As I said, he's sleeping now, Daniel. He ate some porridge this morning, and I washed him up."

"Fine. I'll be quiet. But I still want to see him."

She replied with a reluctant nod then pushed open the door. It creaked on its hinges.

The room was dark, the draperies pulled shut against the brilliant summer sunshine. Once Daniel's eyes adjusted, he made his way to the bedside in the unfamiliar room. Gazing over the specter-like face of his father, Daniel questioned whether this poor creature really was his strong, capable Poppa.

"When it first happened," *Mor* whispered as she stepped in next to him, "we didn't know if he would survive the night. But here he is, and we rejoice each day that we have with him."

Daniel thought his father looked as bad as human existence allowed. Quite literally Poppa was withering away—and right under his mother's eyes.

"Why didn't you write to me immediately?" He'd spent the winter season in England courting Reagan. However, George would have forwarded on her letters.

"I did. I sent several missives to the Ramseys' home in New York City. You did not reply."

"I only received the one—just last month. It was dated earlier in the year." Daniel doubted his mother would lie. "The others must have been lost in transit." It was a common occurrence, and yet Daniel had received several letters and telegrams from George. He'd never once relayed news from Wisconsin or indicated that *Mor* tried to reach him. George would never keep information such as that from him. Why would he?

Of course he wouldn't.

But then someone wasn't being honest…

He gave himself a mental shake. He couldn't think about that now.

Returning his focus to his father, Daniel bent a knee by the bed. Carefully he smoothed Poppa's thick blond hair back from his forehead. It felt like oiled straw. The man looked dead already, but the slow rise and fall of Poppa's chest attested to the fact he still breathed.

"Poppa?" Daniel felt compelled to arouse him in spite of his promise to his mother to keep silent. "Poppa, it's me, Daniel. I'm here now."

When no answer came, Daniel peered over his shoulder at *Mor*. "Do you mean to tell me that he just lies here? Day after day?"

"Mostly. Agnes and I prop him up with pillows sometimes."

Like an infant? How pathetic!

"I think he's been waiting…waiting for you." *Mor*'s voice broke. "To see you again."

She whirled away and ran from the room. A shaft of light from the hallway window fell over Poppa. His mouth hung slightly open on a head that looked like a skull dipped in transparent flesh.

"Oh, Poppa…" It pained Daniel to see him this way. Better for him if he'd have died months ago. To linger this way must be a taste of hell—except Daniel knew his father had a strong faith in God.

So why hadn't the Lord received him in paradise then?

Poppa's eyes fluttered open.

"Poppa, look at me!"

Slowly his eyes slid until they found Daniel's gaze. Disbelief pooled in the blue depths of the older man's eyes.

"It's really me, Poppa. I'm here now. Everything is going to be all right." If he wanted Daniel's permission to die, he had it.

Poppa's jaw moved up and down, his lips twitching as though he wanted to speak.

Daniel waited, but it seemed Poppa had given up. A surge of anger—or was it guilt, perhaps both, surged through Daniel. Something more had to be done.

He got to his feet and raked his hand through his hair. Maybe if he had stayed around on the farm Poppa wouldn't have overexerted himself and fallen victim to apoplexy. The idea only fueled Daniel's belief that Poppa should have gone into politics.

"Y–you have come home."

His father's raspy voice pulled Daniel from his turbulent thoughts. "Hello, Poppa."

"*Du er for sent*," he mumbled in Norwegian. "You are too late."

Julianna had never seen Daniel so distressed and determined. But where was he going? She ran out of the store after him.

"Captain Sundberg!" She waved, hoping to catch his attention.

At last he glanced her way. "I'll be back," he called as he steered the wagon down the dirt road.

"Where's he going?"

Julianna turned to Daniel's youngest sister, Agnes. They'd been forced to make their own introductions after Daniel and his mother strode briskly to the back of shop and disappeared there, leaving the establishment in Agnes's care. Funny, but Julianna hadn't been much older when she worked in the Potters' store.

"I have no idea where your brother is off to." Julianna glimpsed the hurt in Agnes's blue eyes—eyes that resembled Daniel's.

"He didn't even say hello to me. He walked right by me."

"Oh, now, he didn't mean anything by it." She hooked arms with Agnes and sent one last glance down the street at the retreating wagon. "You said yourself that you were just a baby the last time he saw you." Julianna swung a smile at the pretty, round-faced girl. The indigo print in her ivory gown matched her eyes. "But seeing how you're a young lady, he probably thought you were just another customer in the store."

Agnes's hurt expression vanished. "Perhaps you're right, because he didn't even recognize me."

"Exactly."

They reentered the shop just as Mrs. Sundberg walked in from the back. She looked around for any patrons. Seeing none, her shoulders sagged slightly. Julianna could tell the older woman had been crying, although Mrs. Sundberg quickly blinked away her sad expression and pushed out a smile.

"Did your husband's condition worsen?" Julianna thought that would explain Daniel's hasty departure—except where had he gone off to? The doctor's office... the undertaker's?

"No." She wrung her hands. "It's just that Daniel..." Mrs. Sundberg pressed her lips together as if to forestall further comment.

"He's a fine man, Mrs. Sundberg." Julianna couldn't help gloating over him. "And he's a good captain. Why, I saw with my very eyes how he keeps the bawdiest of sailors in line."

"Really?" Agnes looked impressed.

"Except I am not a bawdy sailor." Mrs. Sundberg raised her chin, looking quite insulted.

"Oh, I didn't mean to imply that you are!" Julianna instantly regretted the remark. "I only meant to brag on your son. I thought it would make you proud."

"We're proud of him, aren't we, Momma?" Agnes bobbed her blond head. "We've prayed for him every night since Poppa got sick—prayed that God would keep Daniel safe on the sea and that he would come home." Her smile widened. "The Lord has answered our prayers."

"It seems so." Julianna marveled that these two ordinary females petitioned God specifically and He gave into their requests.

"*Ja*, and I am grateful."

Mrs. Sundberg's countenance softened. Her face was round and sweet, like Agnes's, but her lard-blonde hair bespoke her age. Worry lines etched around her tired-looking eyes, and her pale complexion cued Julianna in on the many sleepless nights the older woman must have endured in the months past.

"Daniel looks just like my poppa did." Wistfulness spread across her features. "So brave and strong... and *stubborn*."

"Oh, he is that, all right."

Agnes giggled again, and Julianna felt herself blush for admitting such a thing to Daniel's family. He might not appreciate it.

"But he's also kind and extremely generous." She removed the tan traveling hat she'd been wearing and carefully repinned her hair. "He's been good to me, seeing after me welfare...I mean, *my* welfare. Why, among sailors he's known as the prince of sea captains."

"Is that so." Mrs. Sundberg narrowed her gaze. "And you are not Daniel's *forloveden*—beloved?"

"Me?" Julianna shook her head and glanced at the tips of her black leather boots. "No." She wished she were with all her heart. "He's going to marry a countess."

Agnes gasped, and when Julianna looked up, she saw the raw surprise flash in Mrs. Sundberg's eyes.

"A countess?"

Julianna nodded. "And I heard she's very rich and beautiful."

"I wonder..." Delight spread across Agnes's features. "Will we be invited to the wedding?" She sucked in a breath. "Oh, Momma, wouldn't that be grand?"

Doubt crept across Mrs. Sundberg's face. "I do not think we will be invited, Agnes." Straightening the folds in her dark brown skirt, she cast a glance at Julianna. "Daniel has a new family. They despise our simple way of life—and, I think, they despise us too."

"You mean Mr. and Mrs. Ramsey?"

"You have met them?" Looking interested, Mrs. Sundberg stepped toward her.

"Oh, I've met them, all right. Mrs. Ramsey seems like a good woman, but Mr. Ramsey is a pompous a—" Julianna choked on her poor choice of words. "He's arrogant. That's what I meant to say...arrogant. And he's got a conniving way about him, asking me all sorts of personal information that I would have rather not shared."

When silence met her tirade, Julianna supposed she spoke out of turn.

"But I shouldn't have said all that."

"Why?" A hint of a grin pulled at Mrs. Sundberg's mouth. "I have met the Ramseys also, so I know you speak the truth. God help me, but I agree with you."

Relief poured over Julianna, although she knew Daniel wouldn't have approved. He obviously cared deeply about his other set of parents. "Please don't tell Daniel that I spouted off the way I did. He's been good to me, and I don't want to offend him."

"It will be our secret." Mrs. Sundberg glanced at her daughter. "Right, Agnes?"

"Yes, Momma." She smiled, first at her mother and then at Julianna.

Several moments lagged, and Julianna took the time to glance around the shop again. Once more she eyed the pretty shawl near the large front window.

"Did you make this, Mrs. Sundberg?" Walking to where it hung on display, she stroked the light-blue yarn. It was silky to her touch.

"*Ja*, I did."

"It was my idea to use blue." Agnes stepped in beside Julianna. "Do you like it?"

"It's beautiful."

"Then you must try it on." Mrs. Sundberg crossed the store's scuffed, walnut-brown wooden floor. Extracting the shawl from its hanger, she set it around Julianna's shoulders. "Now look in the mirror."

Julianna did as Mrs. Sundberg asked and felt awed by her appearance. The shawl made even her wrinkled traveling dress look comely.

"Now pinch your cheeks like this." Agnes gave a quick demonstration. "It puts a little color into your face."

Julianna copied the girl just as the door of the shop opened. Mark Dunbar stepped inside. He smiled at Julianna, but then seemed to forget what he was about to say.

The Sundbergs simultaneously looked from him to Julianna and back to him again.

"Mark?" Mrs. Sundberg moved toward him. "Do you wish to purchase another necktie?"

"No...no, thank you." He snapped from his daze. "I just came to tell Miss Wayland that..."

Julianna rehung the lovely shawl on its padded wire.

"...my father would enjoy meeting her. And we'd like to invite you to dinner tonight."

"Tonight?" She faced him again.

"At our home. I'm sure my mother would like to meet you as well."

"Oh, but I just arrived here in Manitowoc, and I'm afraid I'll need to get settled." Even as the words tumbled from her mouth, Julianna wondered where she would stay.

"Tomorrow night, then? Will you accept?"

"Well, I..." She glanced at the smiling faces of the Sundbergs. If she refused, would she offend them? "Of course." She looked back at Mark. "It's such a kind offer. Thank you."

"Tomorrow night it is." He smiled again, revealing white, even teeth. "We don't live far away, so I'll come to call for you after I'm finished at the hotel—about five o'clock. If the mild weather holds, we can walk to my parents' home."

Julianna tried to seem more enthusiastic than she felt. "Thank you, Mr. Dunbar."

"Please. Call me Mark."

"Very well." Embarrassed by his obvious interest, Julianna stared at her folded hands. All she wanted was a position at his family's hotel, not a husband.

"I am sure you are very busy this morning, Mark."

Hearing Mrs. Sundberg's voice, Julianna looked up to see the older woman ushering him out the door.

"Thank you for calling, and we will see you again soon."

She closed the door on him, and Julianna watched as Mark Dunbar made his way back across the street.

"He's sweet on you, Miss Wayland." Agnes hugged herself and laughed. "As sweet as sugar candy."

Mrs. Sundberg smiled. "He is a good man. Hard-working too."

"I'm sure he is all that and more." Julianna decided that now was as good a time as any to set things straight. "But I'll never get married, and so I mustn't waste that fine man's time."

Agnes came forward, wearing a pout. "But why won't you get married?"

"Because I love another man. I gave him me heart."

"Ask for it back."

Mrs. Sundberg grinned at her daughter's childish comment and set an arm around Agnes's shoulders.

"And you and this other man?" Mrs. Sundberg slowly began. "There is no future for the two of you?"

Julianna shook her head. "I'm afraid not. But I love him just the same, and I'll never love anyone else."

"Hmm…" Mrs. Sundberg eyed Julianna in a way that made Julianna wonder if she could read her very thoughts. "Can I guess who this man might be?"

CHAPTER 15

*J*T JUST COULDN'T be too late. It couldn't be!

Daniel marched toward Grainger's General Store. After sending a message to George, asking for names of specialists in either Milwaukee or Chicago, Daniel decided to purchase supplies.

He reached the store and entered. His eyes adjusted to the darkened establishment, and as he gazed around, he felt surprised by the familiarity. The same barrels were lined up near the counter, containing various grains, sugar, nuts, and coffee beans. On the adjacent wall were all the canned goods and syrup. The floor was still cluttered with wooden boxes and crates containing sundry other goods.

"May I help you, sir?"

Daniel politely removed his hat and glanced across the way to see an elderly woman with a spry step approaching him. "Mrs. Grainger?"

"Why, yes. And who are you?" She stopped and tipped her head upon which her gray hair had been neatly arranged.

"Captain Daniel Sundberg, ma'am. I'm visiting my family."

Surprise flashed across her face. "Well...welcome home."

"Thank you." This wasn't home!

A look of sorrow spread across the older woman's countenance. "What a shame about your father. Such a young man too."

"You're very kind. Actually, my father is the reason I'm here."

"Oh?"

"I'd like to order a wheelchair for him, and I want the best there is to offer."

"Well, there's no need for a special order." She straightened her shoulders and pulled her head up. "We've got a few in stock."

She waved him into the back of the store. Daniel followed on a wave of amazement. However, when he stepped into the back room, he realized how much the general store had expanded. Now, instead of just a few guns, there were rifles and pistols displayed along one wall. Various ammunitions were advertised from inside a glass counter top. And there was farm equipment galore. Daniel couldn't help thinking how much Poppa would have loved to see it here, all shining and new. But perhaps he had...

In the far corner, opposite the collection of firearms, was a vast array of medical equipment—including three wheelchairs.

Daniel inspected each of them and chose the one best suited for his father's comfort. A caned back and padded seat.

"You're a good son," Mrs. Grainger said as she wrote up the sale. "I know your mother will appreciate this."

Daniel wasn't sure about anything that had to do with his mother, so he said nothing as he paid the bill. All he could think of was that his father couldn't lie in darkness and linger. Getting him out of bed and outdoors into the fresh air and sunshine would help. Dr. Morrison had always said so.

"I think your mother's cupboards have been a little sparse these days." Mrs. Grainger pretended to arrange some candy on the counter. "I brought over some rhubarb sauce that she can add to your father's daily consumption of porridge. As you're aware, I'm sure, rhubarb has some medicinal qualities."

"And with enough sugar, it's actually edible." Daniel chuckled inwardly and scanned the wall of various canned goods before gazing back to the more-than-helpful proprietress. "I could use some assistance, Mrs. Grainger, selecting items that might be useful for my family."

Her eyes sparked with enthusiasm. "It will be my pleasure." She stepped out from behind the counter and wiped her hands on her tan apron. "And while I'm filling a crate or two, it may interest you to know that my son-in-law is the butcher next door." She sent him an encouraging smile.

"Well, then, I'll load my father's wheelchair into the wagon before returning for foodstuff."

"You're not only generous, but you're a smart man too, aren't you?"

"I certainly try." This time Daniel actually laughed. The old woman was quite the sales person. "Thank you, Mrs. Grainger. I'll be back shortly."

❦

"And this is my workroom." Mrs. Sundberg lifted an arm, indicating that Julianna should precede her into the room.

"Goodness," she breathed, feeling a bit awestruck. Bolts of all different colors and fabrics were neatly stacked on shelves against one wall. A black sewing machine, built right into its own cabinet, occupied some nearby floor space, and in the corner of the room was a spinning wheel surrounded by baskets of puffy wool.

Julianna neared the spinning wheel for closer inspection.

"That belonged to Danny's *bestemor*—his grandmother." Mrs. Sundberg came to stand beside her. "When I first met the Sundbergs, they allowed me to use it to spin. After I married Sam, my father-in-law gave it to me as a very special gift. I spin almost every day. It relieves my mind of our troubles for a time."

"That's a good way to let out the tension." Julianna wandered to the sewing machine and ran a finger along its sleek black top. "Me sister told me that my mother was a seamstress. I can sew too, but I've only done mending."

"Then I will have to show you how to use the machine." Mrs. Sundberg smiled. "It has made my life so much easier. I purchased it a few years ago. Crops were plentiful then, and I was able to use the funds I earned from my knitting to buy it."

Agnes burst into the room.

"What is it? A customer in the store?"

"No, Momma. Daniel has returned, and he's got a wagonload of goods for us and a wheelchair for Poppa. Quick. Come see!"

Julianna glimpsed the frown puckering Mrs. Sundberg's brow as she followed Agnes out of the workroom. "I'm afraid you'll have to get used to Daniel's generosity. He purchased a new wardrobe for me so I could have a chance at a nice start in America."

"He should not have done all this." Mrs. Sundberg stopped at the front window and peered out while Agnes ran to greet Daniel.

Julianna laughed softly when he lifted the girl off the ground and twirled her around in his arms. She noted Agnes's expression of admiration as he set her back down on the walk.

"Your son sees to the needs of others, Mrs. Sundberg, whether it's his crew or a lowly housemaid who'd accidentally boarded his ship—or his family."

When Mrs. Sundberg's frown didn't abate, she added, "Daniel's a good man, and that's thanks to you."

She gave a little snort, dismay or disbelief?

"You gave birth to him and raised him until he was fifteen. I don't know about Daniel, but when I was fifteen, I was grown and taking care of me sister who enjoyed tippin' the bottle with her friends, if you know what I mean. I'd make sure she stayed safe while she was inebriated."

"That's a lot of responsibility for a fifteen-year-old." Slowly Mrs.

Sundberg turned to Julianna. The woman tipped her head. "You said a housemaid accidently boarded Danny's ship?"

Dread ran down the length of Julianna's body, from head to toes. She shouldn't have said such a thing. She patted the knot of hair at her nape. "It's a long story. Maybe for another time."

Mrs. Sundberg blinked.

Then Daniel came through the door, carrying a wooden wheelchair with black leather padding on the seat. He set it down, and Agnes came around him.

"Momma, look what Danny brought Poppa. Now we can take him on a walk outside."

"Your poppa cannot go outside." She glared at Daniel. "The doctor ordered—"

"I care very little what that senile old man sputtered. I just talked to him myself, and he wasn't even sure what day it is." Daniel wagged his head. "I'm going to have a specialist examine Poppa."

Mrs. Sundberg drew back. "But Dr. Harris is the only doctor in town."

"That ought to change too."

Julianna sucked in her lower lip as she watched the exchange. She thought Daniel was awfully hard on his mother. It was obvious that she'd been doing the best she could.

"Now if you'll excuse me, I have a wagon to unload."

"Can I help, Danny?" Agnes looked up at him with an eager shine in her eyes.

Daniel smiled. "I believe you can." He reached for her hand, and she clasped his palm.

Julianna tamped down feelings of jealousy. How she wished it could be her holding Daniel's hand in such an affectionate way. Still, she couldn't help but smile as brother and sister made their way outside.

She turned to Mrs. Sundberg, noting the tears filling the older woman's eyes. "Don't be offended. Daniel only wants to help."

Mrs. Sundberg didn't reply but whirled around and ran to the back of the shop, through the curtained doorway, disappearing into the cozy apartment she shared with her husband and Agnes.

❦

"It only makes sense that we each take a room at the hotel. *Mor* doesn't have room for us here."

Julianna saw Daniel's gaze darken in a way that let her know he was none too pleased with the situation. "I don't mind sharing a room with Agnes."

Daniel shook his head and gazed across the street. Earlier he'd shed his jacket while unloading the groceries, and now he looked less formal as he leaned against the white, wooden outer wall of his mother's shop.

Julianna sat down on the bench beneath the front window. She'd trailed Daniel outside since his mother and sister refused to let her help, insisting that she was a guest. "I'm already indebted to you. I can't let you pay for me stay at a hotel—my stay," she quickly amended.

"Nonsense, Julianna." He folded his arms. "You owe me nothing. I've told you that before."

"And I thank you for that." She sent him a smile. "But you can't take care of me forever. Eventually I will have to make my own way." Gazing down the street and having a clear view, now that the morning crowd had thinned, she eyed the hotel. "Which reminds me…" She gazed up at Daniel again. "Mr. Dunbar invited me to dinner tomorrow night so his father can meet me and decide if I'm worthy enough to hire."

Daniel's auburn brows arched with interest. "To which you said…?"

"I agreed." She grimaced. "But won't you come along with me?"

"What happened to making your own way?" He barely contained his grin.

"I know it sounds contradictory." Julianna felt a jab of chagrin. "However, after thinking over his offer, I realized that I don't want to serve strong drinks because of what's become of me sister in that line of work. How do I say such a thing eloquently? I don't want to make a complete fool of meself." She blinked. "*Myself.*"

He narrowed his gaze, and Julianna recognized the look: the good captain was considering her request. She held her breath, hoping he'd consent.

"All right," he said after several long moments.

Julianna exhaled.

"I'll accompany you tomorrow night. I'm sure I can extract another invitation. But I can guarantee Mr. Mark Dunbar won't like it."

"What do you mean?"

Daniel moved to sit beside her, and Julianna scooted over to make more room for him.

"I'm sure you realize that you've caught the man's interest." The bench dipped slightly beneath his weight, and his shoulder brushed against hers. "Perhaps he'll want to court you."

"Yes, I've noted his interest, but I don't return it—and I've very politely told your mother and Agnes why."

"Excuse me?" He bent his head forward and fixed his gaze on her.

"I didn't mention any names." Julianna looked away, although she knew Mrs. Sundberg had guessed the truth. If Agnes had also, she had not made it known.

"Julianna, you would do well to marry Mark Dunbar. While I was in town, I discovered his family is quite wealthy. I'm sure my sister will never have to worry where her next meal is coming from."

"If I ever marry, it'll be because you asked me."

"Stop that talk right now." There was an unmistakable edge to his voice.

Julianna pressed her lips together.

"This isn't funny, Julianna."

She rolled her eyes. "I don't find it funny at all. I'm just being honest."

"I'm not the only man in the world with principles." He kept his voice low, but she heard sternness enough for a shout.

"So you've said." Except Julianna hadn't met anyone even close to Daniel's caliber. Jeremy had been nice enough, but he wasn't noble and brave, and those blue eyes—

"Julianna, I mean it." His gaze bore into hers.

"I know," she whispered, trying desperately to quell the deep sadness within her. "I never imagine a future together. I know better than that."

His features softened, and for a fleeting second she thought he'd span the inches between them and kiss her.

Instead he stood to his feet and strode to the end of the boardwalk. With his back to her he leaned against the corner of the store. Men on horseback rode by, stirring up dust on the street. A buggy passed, followed by two rattling wagons. Manitowoc's main thoroughfare certainly differed from London's.

Several minutes passed before Daniel turned and came toward her. He sat back down. "We're not isolated on a ship that I command any longer, Julianna. This is the town in which you might choose to reside for the rest of your life. Don't risk your reputation—and I'm not referring to anything concerning your past," he added quickly. "I mean your present. No one knows you here, and if they judge you by your clothing, they'll think you're from a good family. They needn't know anything else unless you tell them or show your feelings for me. If that happens, your name might be irreparably marred."

Julianna knew what he meant. "Like the woman in that story called *The Scarlet Letter*?"

Daniel pulled his head back and his brow furrowed.

"But I thought she rather deserved it. After all, she'd taken up with a married man."

"But you see? That was the author's point. Jesus Himself said, 'He that is without sin among you, let him cast a stone.'" Daniel sagged against the wall. He stretched one leg out in front of him. "It's not our job to condemn others. It's God's authoritative right."

Julianna's jaw slacked. "You know more about God than I imagined."

"No, not really. I just remember that bit of teaching from my boyhood." He arched a brow. "And you know more about literature than I imagined." With a smile he added, "How do you know about Nathaniel Hawthorne's book?"

"The Pigeon Lady read it to me, although I took a turn here and there for practice."

Daniel shook his head. "Now, there, you see, that's what I mean, Julianna. Don't mention that pigeon person, drunken sailors, your ever-inebriated sister, Olson Tolbert, or any other shady people from your past. Pretend they never existed."

She mulled it over. "But to pretend they never existed is to pretend I never existed." She laced her fingers and stared into her lap. A hot, thick breeze licked her hairline. "Which, perhaps, wouldn't be a bad thing." She'd often wondered why God allowed her to live when Mum had died. At the moment she felt quite useless.

"I suggest you refrain from any self-abasement, Julianna. You're an intelligent, determined, and beautiful young woman." He inhaled audibly and tucked his hands behind his head. "Granted, you're far too sassy and outspoken for your own good. Nevertheless, I have every confidence that you were put here on this earth to make a difference."

"Do you really think so?" No one had ever told her such a thing.

"I wouldn't have said it just to be kind."

"Yes, you would have." She turned her head to catch the warning glint in his eyes. "But I suppose I sassed you just now."

"I suppose." He arched a meaningful brow.

She swallowed a laugh. Moments later she decided that now seemed like the perfect time to broach a subject that had been weighing on her mind for some time.

"Speaking of kindness, Daniel…and about God being the one who condemns, not us…"

"Yes?"

"Well…" She wetted her lips. "Do you think you've been a bit terse with your mother?"

"Terse?" He straightened his spine. "How can you ask me such a thing after I filled her cupboards with groceries?" His jaw muscle worked. "I purchased a wheelchair for my father, and it will make her life easier. I'm also calling a specialist to examine him. How is that terse?"

Julianna blinked. "Captain Sundberg, if you were a shark right now, I imagine you'd have bitten me head clear off! That's what I mean about terse."

He blew out a breath as if tamping down his irritation. Seconds later his gaze darkened with contrition. "I'm sorry, Julianna." His shoulders relaxed, as did his features. He lazed back again, and she enjoyed his nearness once more. "I've told you what's gone on in the past."

"Yes." She realized once again that they shared a lot of each other's secrets. "But your mum has no say over your future now. You're a grown man—and one who's quite successful."

A rueful-looking smile curved his lips.

"And, besides, the farm is gone, so you never have to worry about her pestering you about it again."

He seemed to give the matter a moment's thought. "I know what you're saying is true, and yet there's a part of me that's very angry with *Mor* for letting things get this way."

"You think it's her fault?"

"Of course it's her fault. Had Poppa become the politician God wanted him to be, then he wouldn't be lying in that bed, weak and helpless...maybe dying."

"You mean politicians never suffer with apoplexy?"

"I'm sure they do, but..." Daniel brought himself forward and rested his forearms on his thighs. He clasped his hands. "There's a lot you don't understand."

"I understand that you're breaking your mum's heart. All she sees is your kindness to me and your charm toward Agnes. But toward her, you're stiff and cold. You rarely make eye contact, and you speak harshly when addressing her."

"You collected all that information in the span of four or five hours?"

She nodded. "I had to judge people by their actions in London if I wanted to survive."

He sent her a curious glance.

"If I didn't know you better, I'd swear you hated your mother."

Daniel threw a glance heavenward. "That is not true. What sort of man hates his own mother?"

"I don't know." Julianna saw the pensive light in his eyes and figured she'd said enough on the subject. Looking down, she ran her hand along the soft fabric of her colorful skirt. She felt cooler, now that she'd taken something of a break. "Well, I suppose I'll go tell your little sister that she'll be sharing her bedroom with me."

He looked up at her. "I still say you'll be more comfortable in your own room at the hotel."

Julianna gave her head a shake. "I've been alone all me life. It's nice to be around your mum and sister." She headed for the door.

"Besides, your mum said she'd show me how to sew on that black machine of hers. And Agnes said she'll show me how she spins wool on a wheel that once belonged to your grandmother."

"I know the very spinning wheel you're referring to. As a boy I used to watch that wheel go round and round, and I'd daydream of being a sea captain at the helm of a whaling ship, like in the book *Moby Dick*."

"And you got your wish."

"Hmm..." Daniel's smile looked somewhat wistful, but it didn't last long. "You're sure you don't want me to book a room for you at the hotel?"

"Positive."

"All right." He got to his feet. "I'll carry your trunk inside."

CHAPTER 16

*T*HE NEXT DAY Julianna stepped onto the walk and squinted into the late afternoon sunshine. "What in the world are they doing over there?" Several men were on top of the hotel's roof, and three ladies in bonnets were standing in the street directing them. All at once a large red, white, and blue flag was dropped over the front of the building. A collective sound of appreciation emanated from the ladies before they clapped their gloved hands.

"They're getting ready to celebrate the Fourth of July." Daniel took hold of Julianna's elbow and guided her across the boardwalk. They waited until two men on saddled horses rode by before making their way to the other side of the street.

Then they began their stroll to the Dunbar's home. Daniel had somehow gotten himself invited to dinner, a fact that still held some amazement to Julianna. She'd said a prayer this morning, just to see if God would listen, and just after breakfast Daniel strolled into the shop, pulled her aside, and announced he'd been invited to dinner this evening too. Daniel hadn't even asked.

So God really hears prayers...

"Are you aware of America's war with England—"

Julianna trained her thoughts to the present and to what Daniel said.

"—how we fought for our independence—and won in 1776?"

She glanced up at him. "Sort of. I always heard the Americans were rebels and disrespected British law."

"True, but separation from the Church of England is really what Americans initially sought. Then it became a question of our individual freedoms. Since we won, the country celebrates July Fourth as our Independence Day. Come next Wednesday, this entire street will be lined with tables of food."

Julianna liked the sound of celebrating with all sorts of food, especially since she felt so hungry at the moment.

"The day will begin with a parade. Since my mother's store is located on the corner of Main Street, we'll have front-row seats."

"I love parades." She smiled, recalling how she'd squeeze through the crowds, along with all the other ragamuffins, and seat herself on the curb so she could glimpse the clowns or wild animals in cages as they passed by.

"Then there will be picnics by the lake, a pie-judging contest, followed by a pie-eating contest." He grinned. "Later in the afternoon there's a horse race, games for the children, and a baseball game for the ambitious young men."

"Baseball?"

"Similar to the English game called rounders."

Julianna knew the game well, although she herself hadn't ever played it. "The Fourth of July sounds like a fun-packed day."

"Oh, it is—at least that's how I remember the holiday here in Manitowoc. I'm sure many things have changed since I last participated."

They turned the corner, and a large home appeared on a hill a short distance away. The sun glared down on them, and Julianna adjusted the white, frilly bonnet trimmed in sky-blue ribbons. The color matched her gown, the same one she'd worn the first day at the Ramseys' home.

She cast another look at Daniel. Beneath the brim of his fashionable hat he squinted as they made their westward trek, but obviously the summer sun didn't bother him in the least. And Julianna felt especially proud of him today, proud that he'd been nicer to his poor, dear mum. She was dreadfully worried about her sick husband, that's for sure, and it seemed Daniel had come to realize the fact. He'd been patient with her this morning when she threw a conniption as he rolled Mr. Sundberg outside into the backyard for some sunshine and fresh air. Later, when the man from the bank came to call, Daniel took care of the matter. Mrs. Sundberg dissolved into tears as she thanked him. Daniel replied by taking his mother into his arms and promising everything would be all right. The scene touched Julianna deeply. And it made him a hero in Agnes's eyes.

But then Captain Daniel Sundberg *was* a hero.

"What are you staring at, *Miss Wayland*?"

Hearing his curt tone, Julianna blinked and faced straight ahead. "Oh, nothing. The sun's just in my eyes."

"Ah, well, my mistake." He leaned closer. "I had read the discomfort on your face as adoration."

"Don't flatter yourself," Julianna quipped. But he hadn't misread a thing.

"Remember what we discussed yesterday—and our agreement."

"Yes, sir, *Captain*."

"And none of that sassiness. I expect you to be on your best behavior tonight."

"I know what you expect, and you needn't speak to me like I'm a child. I know how to behave meself." She swallowed. "*Myself*."

A hint of a grin played at the corners of his mouth, letting Julianna know he wasn't all that upset with her.

They reached a tall, wrought-iron black fence that encompassed the Dunbars' home. Daniel opened the gate and allowed Julianna to pass through first. He closed it behind him, and they strolled to the front door.

Mark opened it before Daniel could knock.

"Welcome." He smiled at Julianna before swinging his gaze to Daniel. The two men shook hands. "Please come in."

Entering the foyer, Julianna carefully removed her bonnet and smoothed her mussed hair. Her eyes soon adjusted to the dimmer light, and she took in the lovely, floral oil paintings on the walls.

"Our intimate dinner party has grown considerably." Mark took Julianna's bonnet and shawl and waited patiently while she removed her gloves. He placed both accessories on the mirrored hallstand's oak bench. Next he took Daniel's hat and asked for his jacket. "Much too warm for formalities."

Daniel agreed.

It was then that Julianna realized Mark wore only a white shirt and black waistcoat over dark trousers.

Daniel handed over his jacket, and Mark hung it on a peg. "Will and Adeline will join us." He looked at Daniel as he spoke. "And they're, of course, bringing baby Jacob."

"It'll be good to see my sister again, and I'm looking forward to meeting both Will and my first nephew."

Julianna wondered, and not for the first time since her arrival, why Daniel ever traded his own nice family for the Ramseys.

Mark led them into the parlor, and Julianna admired all the nice furnishings. Then he indicated a set of double doors. "Would you care to sit on the terrace? It's cooler out there."

"Sounds delightful." Julianna could feel drops of perspiration forming along her hairline. She glanced at Daniel and saw his affable nod.

"I always prefer the outdoors to sitting inside," he added.

"Good. Come this way." Mark waved them onto a bricked area surrounded by tall evergreens. Comfortable-looking wooden furniture had been neatly arranged in a half-circle.

Julianna arranged her skirts and sat down as gracefully as she could, given her fashionable bustle. It took some extra arranging, but she managed. She glimpsed Daniel's dimpled grin and wondered what he found so amusing. Let him wear all these petticoats and try and be ladylike. He'd last five minutes.

Mark took the chair beside hers. "Have you been able to see much of Manitowoc yet, Miss Wayland?"

"Some of it. Agnes and I took a stroll up and down Main Street this afternoon so I could see all the shops and business. It's quite rustic, if you ask me."

"Compared to London and New York, it is," Daniel added.

Mark pulled his chin back slightly.

"Oh, but I don't mean that as an insult. Merely an observation."

"The town is growing." He gave Julianna a hopeful grin. "Immigrants arrive daily. We're becoming quite diverse. Why, a new German family recently joined our church."

"How very interesting." Julianna smiled politely.

"Your family's businesses must ship a lot of cargo." Daniel sat back in his chair. "Lumber, I presume?"

"A goodly amount, yes. And our manufacturing plant exports numerous products."

"What about imports?"

"On the rise daily."

"How about the railroad as a mode of transportation?"

Mark rolled a shoulder. "Shipping is our first choice. Our mills are west of here, on the river."

"Makes sense."

As the men continued discussing a topic that Julianna cared little about, she bided time by watching Daniel. She admired his commanding manner and how he knew so much about everything. She added *brilliant* to her list of his many attributes.

His gaze slid to hers, and he widened his eyes. She blinked and caught his warning.

"And how about you, Miss Wayland?"

She felt her face flush with embarrassment as Mark stood to his feet.

"Would you like a glass of berry punch?"

"Punch?" Julianna grew instantly wary. "Is it a strong drink? I don't imbibe."

"Oh, no." Mark shook his head. "It's made with ripe berries and fresh, cold water." He shifted his stance. "My family and I don't serve spirits."

"That's a relief." She smiled. "And, yes, I'd enjoy a glass. It sounds very refreshing."

He crossed the terrace and entered the house.

"What am I going to do with you?" Daniel shook his head and sat forward. "I can't very well marry you off," he whispered, "when you're giving me moon eyes."

She clucked her tongue, hoping she hid the fact that his remark stung, except she knew he spoke the truth—partially, anyway. "I told you, I'm not interested in marriage. I only want a job at the hotel, for pity's sake." She took to studying the landscape instead of the man she loved more and more each day.

"Julianna…"

Despite the gentleness she heard in his tone, she refused to face him.

"You'd be wise to cultivate all possibilities that fall in your path."

She didn't answer, and silence settled between them. In the next moments Julianna heard the sound of happy voices greeting one another, followed by the rustling of skirts. She turned to see a young woman resembling Agnes and Mrs. Sundberg making her way onto the terrace. Julianna guessed it was Daniel's other sister.

He followed her line of vision.

"Adeline! How good to see you again."

He embraced the buxom blonde, but Julianna noticed she didn't share his enthusiasm.

"My, but you're all grown up now. Married and a mother." Holding her at arm's length, he shook his head as if in disbelief. "Has it been that long since I've seen you?"

"Yes, it has." She turned her slender nose up at him. "It's been a lifetime, Daniel."

"My humble apologies." Releasing her, he dipped his head.

Julianna felt taken in once again by Daniel's fluent charm.

His sister, on the other hand, wasn't taken quite so easily. "Your apologies are not accepted—although I've forgiven you for your neglect long ago." There were no traces of amusement in her voice, and her blue eyes were hard set. "I'm surprised you came back again."

Daniel glanced down at his booted feet for several seconds before meeting his sister's gaze. "I thought you would be pleased to see me."

"I thought I would be too." Her sapphire gaze turned misty. "I've missed you so much over the years. There were so many times that I needed my big brother, and you were not here for me. I was eight when you first left home, and it broke my heart. Then you returned with those *people*." Derisiveness flowed from her voice, and Julianna realized that Adeline hadn't seen her sitting just behind them. "Those Ramseys, who looked down their noses at us and talked critically of our farm." Adeline's tone softened. "I was a bit younger than Agnes is now, and I adored you, Daniel. But again you hurt me by leaving without ever looking back. Adding insult to injury, you never returned my letters—or even those written by your own mother!"

Daniel shifted, and his gaze bounced to Julianna. "I, um, don't believe you've met Julianna Wayland." He made the introductions.

Julianna could see the horror drip over Adeline's features.

"I...I didn't see you sitting there, Miss Wayland. Please forgive my outburst."

"Quite all right. Didn't bother me in the least. But I must say that your brother wouldn't intentionally hurt you. He's a noble man, kind and caring—"

"Julianna, you don't have to defend me."

"Oh, I'm not. You're able to defend yourself." She glanced from him to Adeline again. "He's quite brave, you know."

Daniel sighed audibly.

"More than likely your brother never received your letters. Perhaps Mr. Ramsey never forwarded them."

"That's quite enough, Julianna." Daniel spoke her name through a clenched jaw, and his eyes narrowed.

She knew she'd said enough.

Adeline burst into a laugh. "Now, you, Miss Wayland, I like. But you—"

She pierced Daniel with a glare and continued speaking in another language that Julianna guessed to be Norwegian. She had overheard Mrs. Sundberg and Agnes talking to each other last night with the same sing-songy inflection in their voices.

Daniel replied in Norwegian, although his tone contained the magnetism that had captivated Julianna from the beginning.

If only she weren't so drawn to him, to a seafaring man who planned to marry a rich countess.

The curse.

He caught her stare and sent a glance heavenward.

Julianna shook herself and decided not to even look at the man anymore.

"Let's begin again," Adeline suggested. "It's a pleasure to meet you, Miss Wayland."

"Likewise, Mrs. Dunbar."

"Adeline."

Julianna smiled. "Then you must call me Julianna."

"What a lovely name." A sudden frown puckered her brow. "How did you ever become associated with my brother?"

"Once you hear about it, you'll understand what a fine man Daniel—I mean, Captain Sundberg—is." She hoped she'd covered her blunder.

"Oh?" A curious expression wafted across Adeline's circular-shaped face. "I think I am beginning to understand."

Daniel jumped into the conversation. "No, no, you're not, Adeline. I merely sponsored Miss Wayland so she could come to America and begin a new life like many other immigrants have done before her."

"Like our own parents," Adeline said, looking somewhat wistful.

Mark returned with a tray containing glasses of berry punch. Three more people stepped onto the terrace, and Mark made introductions—his father, Mr. Jedidiah Dunbar; his brother, Will; and his mother, Eunice, who carried a baby wrapped in a beautifully stitched, blue blanket. Mrs. Sundberg's handiwork was written all over it.

"Welcome to our home." Mrs. Dunbar's smile lit her entire face. She looked at Julianna then Daniel. "I'm so glad you could join us for dinner."

He politely inclined his head. "The pleasure is ours, right, Miss Wayland?"

"Right." She smiled.

"And how is Sam?" Mrs. Dunbar looked at Daniel. "Any better?"

"About the same, I'm afraid."

Julianna saw Adeline's expression crumble.

"But I've requested a specialist come and examine him. I received a telegram today stating a man named Dr. Grant Ellsworth will arrive Monday."

Julianna had heard the news already and knew that George Ramsey had made all the arrangements. Mrs. Sundberg, while grateful for Daniel's help, hated to be indebted to the Ramseys for anything. She'd made it clear her husband wouldn't be happy to learn the news either. Daniel said his poppa didn't have to know.

"Do you believe a specialist can help your father?" Will put his meaty arm around Adeline's round shoulders. "We were told nothing more can be done."

"I heard the same, but I refuse to believe it, and I plan to do everything in my power to prove old Dr. Harris wrong—again."

"You never did like Dr. Harris," Adeline said.

"No, I never did. And, this time, in Poppa's case, he's made a great misdiagnosis."

Adeline stared at her husband while Julianna admired Daniel's confidence. She hoped he was right and that Mr. Sundberg's condition would improve soon.

"Have you seen my precious grandson?" Mrs. Dunbar moved her willowy frame closer to Julianna. With nimble fingers she brushed the blanket from the little one's face. "Jacob William Dunbar. He'll be eight weeks old on the sixth of July."

"He's beautiful." Julianna touched the child's tiny hand as he snoozed and noticed the folds of skin around his neck. "A healthy little one to be sure."

"I'll say." Adeline blushed. "I can barely keep up with him."

Will tightened his hold around her shoulders, and Julianna thought they made a sweet pair.

Just then baby Jacob awoke. He blinked and then stretched in his grandmother's arms. Once his eyes focused, he stared at Julianna before doing the most incredible thing—smiling, and directly at her, no less!

Julianna felt dazed and awed as she peered into the tiny face. The baby cooed and smiled again.

"He likes you," Mrs. Dunbar said.

"I like him too."

"You'll have to hold him after dinner." Adeline crossed the terrace and stepped in beside Julianna.

"I'd enjoy that."

Julianna touched the baby's hand, and he clutched her finger. "You're a charmer, all right." The boy had those sea-blue Sundberg eyes. She'd dreamed about those eyes. And in that moment she knew she'd fallen for another male—this one barely two months old.

CHAPTER 17

*D*ANIEL STOOD ON the edge of the terrace, breathing deeply of the humid summer air. Dusk had fallen. In the distance he heard the jangling of rigging as ships bobbed in the harbor, and he felt a sort of homesickness fall over him. He would sorely miss the days of mastering the *Allegiance* on the wide, open sea. Reagan, however, had made it clear she'd not abide a traveling husband.

"I'm satisfactorily filled." Jed Dunbar walked outside and stood beside Daniel. He patted his slightly rounded belly. "I ate far too much."

"Your wife is an excellent cook."

"Thank you. I'll pass on the compliment to her."

Daniel replied with a polite grin. Except for his sister's earlier outburst, things had gone well. At the dinner table he watched Julianna with surreptitious glances and noted her demure manner. He wanted to chuckle. If the Dunbars only knew how spry she really was...

"Beautiful evening."

"Especially pleasant." The wind had turned, and now an easterly breeze wafted off Lake Michigan, cooling the summer air and tugging on Daniel's shirtsleeves.

"Miss Wayland seems like a nice young lady. Good of you to sponsor her, Captain Sundberg."

"She deserves a chance at a good and decent life here in America." He meant it sincerely. "As you heard her say during dinner, her former employer was quite oppressive."

"I heard." Jed dipped his head slowly. "And how fortunate for her that you offered a means of escape." His tone softened. "But I believe it was no coincidence. God orchestrated all of it."

Daniel found it hard to believe that God had anything to do with it.

"And no family there in England…" Jed gave a wag of his head. "Well, between your family and mine, we'll see she is surrounded by people who care about her welfare."

"I'm sure she will appreciate that." Daniel sensed the man's earnestness.

"My wife and I share your desire to offer people second chances— or even first chances." Jed turned from gazing into the starry darkness to facing Daniel. "As you're aware, Mark thinks Miss Wayland may enjoy working in our hotel."

"He mentioned the possibility yesterday." In fact, Daniel had used it as a means to procure tonight's dinner invitation. He'd told Mark that as Julianna's sponsor, Daniel needed to be kept abreast of any and all employment opportunities.

"But do you think she is too…too…"

"Yes?" Plenty of adjectives filled Daniel's mind.

"Shy."

"What?" Daniel couldn't suppress a chortle. "Shy? Heavens, no! She's quite determined, actually."

"I must have misread her personality."

Daniel thought over the past couple of hours. "I believe Julianna is purposely being reserved. She wants to make a good impression on all of you."

"Of course. That makes perfect sense." A smile pervaded his tone. "I'd gotten concerned because in the hotel business, you've got to win customers without letting them run roughshod over you."

"I suppose you're right at that." Daniel shifted his stance. He could see how the misunderstanding took place. During their dinner conversation, Julianna only spoke when spoken to and gave fragmented truths about her personal history. When asked how she'd come to select Manitowoc as her destination, Julianna had balked. Daniel jumped in, stating that since she had no relatives in America, he'd persuaded her to come to Manitowoc and help his mother and sister on the farm—except, to his surprise, there wasn't a farm to come home to.

That, of course, inspired more harsh remarks from Adeline. But Daniel had weathered them, aware that none of the Dunbars even subtly reprimanded her. It was then he figured he might deserve Adeline's hostility, given how hurt she'd been because of his absence. Daniel had never guessed it mattered much, thinking that he'd never be missed. After leaving Wisconsin, he'd gone on with his life and assumed his family members had gone on with theirs too.

But apparently they hadn't, and Daniel wasn't so hard of a man that he didn't feel remorse over it. He did. But what nagged at him was the fact he'd never received even one of his sister's letters. One could assume that in seven years a few missives at the very least would have found their way to the Ramseys' residency. Not a single one did.

Which meant George must have kept them from me…

"So, Captain, tell me about your adventures afar."

Shaking himself from his muse, Daniel turned his attention to Jed, who sat perched on the white rail encompassing the balcony area.

"Anything in particular you'd like to know, Jed?"

Before he could answer, Will strode from the house. Lamplight glowed in his wake and cast a long shadow. "Mind if I join you both?"

"You're just in time," Jed said.

Daniel saw the man smile at his eldest son and noted that Mark hadn't come outside with him. "We're about to hear of the captain's exploits."

"Ah, good." Will pulled over a chair and sat.

"Where would you like me to begin?" Daniel leaned against the nearby pillar. "I'm sure you've both known ship captains. There are plenty in Manitowoc."

"None we're related to." Will grinned and relaxed back in his chair.

"That's right." Jed rubbed a hand along his clean-shaven jaw. "You know, the last time I saw you it was years ago. You were in church with your family and the Ramseys. Little did I know back then that our families would someday be united through marriage."

"You met the Ramseys?" Daniel couldn't recall.

"Yes, and we've been praying for them—and you—ever since."

"Please..." Daniel held up a forestalling hand. "No prayers needed. I'm good and fine. So are the Ramseys."

"Maybe that just means our prayers have been answered," Will said.

Daniel chafed, although he held his tongue. The discussion of prayers and answers to them was just another form of manipulation as far as he was concerned.

He decided to call it a night. "Perhaps I should check in with Miss Wayland. She may want to go home now."

"I can save you the trip inside." Will's smile looked broad and confident. "She wants to stay. I'm afraid she's succumbed to the Dunbar charm and good looks."

Daniel narrowed his gaze. "You're referring to your brother, Mark?"

Will hooted. "No, my son!"

Laughter broke out from the two men, and Daniel grinned in spite of the chagrin working its way into his face.

"But I suppose it's no secret that Mark is taken with Miss Wayland." An amused lilt still sounded in Will's tone. "I'm sure he'd like to get better acquainted with her…if only she'd stop fussing over Jacob." He chuckled all over again. "She's been holding that baby since we finished dessert."

Daniel even laughed inwardly, picturing the whole thing in his mind. "Well," he drawled, "a bit of competition is good for a man."

Just as he'd finished the last word, Mark exited the house and walked out onto the terrace.

"We were just talking about you, brother—wondering how you were doing in there with the women."

"Just fine, actually." Mark clasped his hands behind his back and eyed Daniel. "I came out to ask the captain's permission to walk Julianna home."

Julianna, is it? Daniel narrowed his gaze in thought. This is what he wanted—he wanted her interest to shift from him to someone else. Why the prickling of jealousy, then? "Miss Wayland is free to make her own choices. My permission is not required."

"But I would hate to…to tread on another man's territory, so to speak."

"No, no…you're not treading." He launched each word from his tongue. He rubbed the back of his neck to ease the sudden tension he felt.

"Very good. We'll leave shortly." After a nod and a smile, he made for the house, but paused after a few steps. "Oh, and Will? I'm supposed to tell you that Adeline is putting Jacob to bed."

"That's good news for you, I expect." Will snorted another laugh.

"Exceedingly good news." He sent his brother an annoyed glance. "Bad enough I had to compete with you for the ladies' attention before you married Adeline, but now I have to compete with your infant son."

Will looked peacock-proud, and Daniel grinned. But the fact that Mark joked about such a thing proved he wasn't an insecure young man.

Mark returned to the house, and Jed picked up the conversation where they'd left off before Will had joined them.

"Captain Sundberg—"

"It's Daniel, please."

"Daniel…" Jed gave a nod. "Please tell us of your exciting feats." Leaning forward, he dipped one eye. "And perhaps we'll talk of some business while we're at it."

"My favorite subject." A grin tugged at his mouth. "Let's see, where shall I begin…?"

***

"You have a beautiful baby." Julianna set the little one into his mother's waiting arms.

"Thank you." Adeline gave her a warm smile. "I can tell he likes you."

"You think so?"

"He wouldn't have fallen so soundly asleep otherwise." Mrs. Dunbar looked up briefly from her needlepoint and smiled.

Julianna adored baby Jacob. "May I hold him again sometime?"

"Of course." Adeline's smile broadened. "Will and I are staying overnight, and we'll be in church tomorrow morning. Perhaps you can hold him then. But if we don't meet up by then, there's tomorrow afternoon. Will and I eat Sunday dinner with my family, and we usually stay the afternoon."

Julianna saw the sadness creep into Adeline's gaze and suspected that she thought of her poor, bedridden father. "I'll look forward to tomorrow then."

"It helps me quite a lot when others take a turn and hold Jacob for a while." Adeline tucked the blanket around the baby's feet. "As much as I love my son, I'm grateful for the respite."

"If I had a baby like yours, I don't think I'd ever set him down."

"I remember having that same idea too." Smiling, Mrs. Dunbar glanced above her spectacles. "But I changed my mind after Will came along and my housework needed to get done."

Julianna tipped her head. "You didn't have a maid or other hired help?" Hours ago she'd noticed the absence of hovering servants.

"No, I've always done my own cooking and cleaning." She looked at her needlework again. "At least for now."

Mark reentered the sitting room. "Julianna, we've been given the go-ahead. I'll get your things and walk you home."

"All right." He certainly seemed eager for her to leave. She stood from the blue velvet settee and smiled at Mrs. Dunbar. "Thank you for dinner. I had a lovely evening."

"You're welcome in our home anytime, my dear."

Stunned, Julianna gaped at the older woman. No one had ever said that to her before. She was welcome here? Anytime?

She forced her gaze to Adeline. "So nice to meet you—and all of the Dunbars."

"Likewise." She glanced at her sleeping baby, then looked at Julianna again. "Any woman who abides my older brother is a saint in my opinion."

Julianna attempted to contain a laugh but failed. "He's not so terrible, really." *Not at all, in fact.* "And I meant what I said before— I know your brother wouldn't have intentionally hurt you or your parents. Not ever. His dreams of adventure just got in the way."

"Not to mention George Ramsey's money and influence." There was no mistaking the cynicism in Adeline's tone.

"You might be correct about that, I'm afraid."

"You seem to understand my brother so well." Curiosity glimmered in Adeline's blue eyes.

"I suppose I do." Julianna looked down at the carpet so she wouldn't guess how much she loved him.

"Here we are." Mark strode to Julianna and set her shawl about her shoulders.

His touched weighed heavy with unbearable discomfort, and she stepped out of his reach. Still, she gave him a polite grin as she accepted her hat and gloves.

"Tell Momma hello for me and that Will and I will see her tomorrow as usual."

"All right."

"And tell her to kiss Poppa for me."

Julianna inclined her head. "I'll do that."

Mrs. Dunbar stood and walked her to the front door. Mark followed at a close distance. They said their farewells as Mark shrugged into his jacket.

Outside the air had cooled. Julianna lifted her skirts ever so slightly and made her way down the steps to the stone walkway.

Mark took her gloved hand and curved it around his elbow. "A lovely evening for a stroll."

"A bit on the warm side."

"We'll walk slowly so we don't become overheated."

Julianna wanted to groan. So much for marching home quickly. She slowed her pace to match his.

"Did you enjoy our little dinner party tonight?"

"I did indeed, although..."

"Yes?"

"Well, I hope your father thinks I'll make a good employee at the hotel." The topic hadn't ever come up, and Julianna wondered all night whether she'd met Mr. Dunbar's standards.

"I'm sure he does."

Mark set his hand over Julianna's. Instincts hold her to pull free, but she overcame them since he'd been very courteous and respectful thus far. A bit overeager, perhaps, but pleasant just the same.

"I'm the one who makes the decisions at the hotel. I hope to own it one day."

"And why not? You're personable. I should think you'll make a fine innkeeper."

He turned, and she caught his amused expression. "I enjoy listening to your British accent."

"That's good. I'm still adjusting to hearing Yankees everywhere I go."

Mark replied with a good-natured laugh.

At the bottom of the hill they rounded the corner. Mrs. Sundberg's shop was just a block away. They crossed the nearly empty street. But as they neared their destination, raucous laughter reached Julianna's ears. It grew louder as she and Mark stepped closer to the shop.

Then, all at once, a group of laughing, cursing, brawling sailors filled the walk. Julianna stopped short.

"It's all right. Those men are probably headed for the hotel." Mark sighed. "But my assistant, Mr. Gibbons, is very capable."

"I think we should turn back." She stepped behind Mark so the rowdy sailors wouldn't see her. Filling her memory was the Grisly Devil's groping and pounding. If these men were like him, Mark wouldn't be able to defend himself, let alone protect her.

"It's all right, Miss Wayland, really."

But the men didn't seem in a hurry to move off the corner in front of Mrs. Sundberg's store. Julianna's senses soared to a heightened alert. "We should go back."

Mark tugged on her arm.

"No." She pulled free.

"There's nothing to be afraid of. Sailors come into port at all hours of the day. They're usually honest, hard-working men."

Julianna hadn't known many of those kind of sailors. "Why have they stopped?"

Mark sighed. "They're probably looking for the nearest tavern."

"Hey, mister!" one of men called to Mark.

Julianna felt her blood turn icy cold.

"What can I do for you?"

Julianna backed away, realizing the muscle-bound man was headed toward her and Mark. She saw his fists, clenched at his side. Did he mean to start a brawl?

"Don't speak to him, Mark."

"There is nothing to be afraid of. I'm sure he's merely in need of directions. It happens all the time. You'll see."

She wasn't about to wait and find out if he was right. Spinning on her heel, Julianna took off and ran for her life!

CHAPTER 18

*B*ENEATH THE LIGHT in Jed Dunbar's library Daniel glanced at the clock above the mantel. Mark should have returned by now. However, neither his father nor Will seemed concerned, so Daniel told himself not to worry.

But worried he was. Julianna could be spirited at times. Mild-mannered Mark Dunbar wouldn't stand a chance if a situation arose.

What situation? Mark was a polite fellow. Besides, Daniel told himself, he had no cause to fret over Julianna. He was nothing more to her than her sponsor. Not her husband or fiancé—or *for-loveden*, as his family would say in Norwegian. Julianna had a new life to live. He'd made it clear that he had his own plans for the future. She understood, despite her delusions of love.

Even so, he didn't think he would ever forget her kisses that night in his quarters or the way she'd stared up at him with both eagerness and innocence shining from her eyes. A lesser man would have taken full advantage of the situation, although Daniel couldn't say he was above seriously considering it.

Would Mark be so bold? Daniel doubted it. Still, he couldn't help wondering if she'd look at another man in the same way she'd looked at him, given the right circumstances.

"Captain, did you hear me?"

Daniel jerked from his troubling thoughts and looked across the way at Jed. "My apologies. My mind was elsewhere." He rubbed his stubbly jaw, another sign the night wore on. He glanced at the two men. How could he say that the foreboding inside of him matched his disquiet before a tempest?

And yet he had no right to feel this way.

"I asked what you thought of the situation involving some of the local shipping companies." Jed sat near the bookshelves, which occupied an entire wall. "They've proved most undependable."

Will added to his father's statement from the leather chair in which he sat. "With Chicago still in the throes of rebuilding much of the city and Milwaukee expanding, I have to get my lumber shipped on schedule. And then there's our manufacturing plant. We have customers all over the Great Lakes region."

"Hmm...well, I'd say—"

Mark burst into the room. He leaned against the doorframe and panted.

Daniel immediately pushed to his feet.

"Good heavens!" Jed stood as well.

Mark peeled off his hat. Perspiration had matted his hair.

"Where's Julianna?" Fingers of apprehension climbed Daniel's spine.

"I don't know." Mark's chest rose and fell in quick succession. "I've searched everywhere."

"What happened?" Daniel moved forward.

"We had almost reached your mother's shop when a group of sailors came walking up from the direction of the harbor. I suspected they'd been drinking, but I didn't sense any danger."

Daniel closed his eyes briefly, guessing the rest of the story.

"Somehow Julianna got spooked and ran. I was detained only moments by one of the men asking if I knew of vacancies at the hotel. After I replied, I immediately took off after her." Mark shook his head. "But she vanished."

At his quizzical stare Daniel felt compelled to explain at least in part. "I'm afraid Julianna has had several poor experiences with mariners."

"That would explain why she bolted."

"Well, she couldn't have gone far." Will's voice sounded thick with concern.

"I checked up and down streets and alleys." At last Mark seemed to catch his breath. "I even stopped in front of your mother's store." His gaze met Daniel's again. "But the lamps had been extinguished, and I didn't see any movement when I peered through the front windows, so I didn't dare to knock."

Knock. The word caused Daniel to remember. He patted the front of his waistcoat for the key to his family's apartment. *Mor* had handed it to him before he left. "In other words, you never went down the walk to the side door?"

"Didn't see any reason to, no."

"I think I know where Julianna is." He removed the key from his pocket and held it for the men to see. "I have a hunch she's waiting near the door, hoping I'll remember that I have the key."

Will chuckled and Jed grinned.

A look of relief fell over Mark's features.

"Like you, she probably won't knock for fear of disturbing anyone. So, if you'll excuse me, gentlemen..."

"Of course." Jed shook his hand and clapped him on the shoulder. "We'll talk again soon."

"I'd enjoy it." Daniel quickly made his way through the foyer, where he collected his jacket and hat.

"Send word when you find her," Jed called.

Daniel replied with a single nod as he left the house. When the heel of his boots struck the stone walkway, he hurried his pace. *Please, God, let her be safe.* He couldn't recall the last time he'd prayed, but more than ever it seemed appropriate now.

He gave into a jog as his mind and heart battled between common sense and all-out panic.

Reaching *Mor's* shop, Daniel slowed so as not to scare Julianna a second time. He turned onto the walk and whispered her name. Once. Twice.

At last she stepped from the shadows. Other than a troubled expression, she looked no worse for wear.

Daniel closed the distance between them and gathered her into his arms. He held her slight frame close and his tension abated. "I was worried about you, little one."

"I was a bit worried meself."

He grinned. "Well, you're safe now." He rested his cheek against the top of her head and couldn't help enjoying the way she clung to him.

"Is Mark all right?"

"He's fine. No fight ensued tonight."

"Thank God!"

Daniel held her closer.

"I ruined everything, didn't I?"

"What do you mean?"

She pulled back slightly. "The job at the hotel. I doubt I'll get it now. I behaved like a frightened rabbit." She laid her head against his chest again. "I couldn't help it."

"Shh…" Daniel pressed a kiss on her forehead. "If you recall, I was never in favor of your taking a job at the hotel in the first place."

"But…" Julianna glanced up at him. Beneath the sharp constellations twinkling above, he glimpsed the questions pooling in her gaze.

However, they dissipated and another emotion took their place—one that told Daniel she'd welcome his advances.

He cupped her head in his hands and touched his lips to her petal-soft cheek. She turned toward him, and desire overruled his common sense. He closed his eyes and deepened the kiss and suddenly wanted so much more.

Julianna wiggled and pressed her hands against his chest, her lips breaking the connection with his. "Daniel, I..." She sounded breathless.

He kissed the lobe of her ear and searched for that sweet spot on her neck.

"Stop," she whispered. "We must stop. We made an agreement..."

She's right. Daniel straightened his spine. Guilt gnawed at him—a feeling he wasn't accustomed to. "I'm sorry, Julianna. I shouldn't have taken such liberties."

For a long moment she said nothing as she gazed up at him. Daniel knew he must, but he didn't want to let her go.

"I prayed that you'd remember you had the key to the door," she murmured at last.

Daniel noted she'd completely changed the subject.

"That's my second answered prayer of the day." Her note of incredulousness hung between them. "God must really be willing to hear me."

Her mention of religion dispelled any remaining passion. He quickly released her. "How nice for you." He couldn't keep the dryness from his tone. "But I think you've been listening to *Mor*'s preaching."

"I'd rather call it teaching, although I will admit to listening to her read from the Bible this morning."

"Hmm..." Daniel fetched the key from his pocket.

"But what do you care if I listen to preaching or not?"

Her words rooted him in place. Hadn't she felt that certain

spark between them just now? "I care, Julianna." He almost hated to admit it. "I care about you more than I want to and, definitely, more than I should."

"You do?"

He heard the hopefulness in her tone, and it touched the deepest part of him. "Yes, I do." If George even got wind of the fact he'd fallen in love with Julianna, his daughter—

Daniel halted his thoughts. *Love?*

"But you're still going to marry your countess, aren't you?"

His heart twisted painfully. "Yes, I am."

"I understand. It's business."

"I don't think you really do, Julianna, and don't attempt to lecture me on matters of the heart versus arranged marriages. It's far better to be rich than to be happy."

"How could I lecture you? I don't know about either wealth or happiness." Julianna stepped back. She lowered her gaze, and he hated himself for hurting her.

"I suspect you've had a taste of both. I'm sure you'll figure out the truth in time."

"I'll try." Her tone sounded more upbeat. "And I'll try to get another job."

"There's no need, Julianna. I've told you that before." Daniel couldn't seem to keep the edge out of his tone.

She said nothing but continued to stare at the walk.

Daniel softened. "Listen to me." He cupped her face once more and forced her to look at him. "I've got it planned that you'll work for *Mor* here at the shop for a year. I'm paying your wages—and don't argue."

He watched her clamp her mouth shut.

"You said yourself that *Mor* needs help. So I want to help my mother—by hiring you to assist in her store so she can take care of my father. Then, after a year, you'll be familiar with Manitowoc and its residents, and you'll be more than able to decide for yourself where you want to work."

Neither remark nor retort was forthcoming.

"Are you agreeable to that arrangement?"

Between his palms she managed to nod.

"All right, then. We have ourselves an agreement."

"Not that we've been able to stick to all our other ones."

Daniel chuckled softly and dropped his hands. "You don't make it easy on a man. You know that, right?"

"I can't help the way I feel...*Captain*."

He wagged his head as he headed to the door. *Sassy little thing.*

Turning the lock, he pushed open the door and allowed her to enter the apartment ahead of him. In the small sitting room he struck a match and lit a nearby table lamp.

"How did you manage to outrun Mark Dunbar tonight?"

Julianna removed her shawl. "Practice, although...I lost my pretty hat somewhere."

Daniel lifted his shoulders. "A hat is replaceable. Your life is not."

"I'm sorry I ran off like that. It's just..." She stepped closer to him. "I didn't think Mark stood a chance if those sailors felt like a brawl. You're the only man I've ever trusted to protect me. But you weren't there." She swallowed hard. "I suppose I'll have to get used to you not being there in the future. Won't I?"

Any reply lodged in his throat. He couldn't speak, except he knew he should affirm her question. His future had been mapped out, his choice for a wife selected with the utmost of care. And yet Daniel couldn't bear the thought of not being close at hand, should Julianna need him. He'd come to treasure the trust she had in him. He enjoyed their bantering. He loved—yes, loved— the way she felt in his arms. He yearned to kiss her over and over again.

A sadness filled her gaze, and his heart crimped painfully.

"Good night, Captain Sundberg." With that, Julianna strode purposefully out of the room.

⊛⊛⊛

The next morning sunshine spilled onto the boardwalk and bounced off store windows as Julianna strolled to church alongside Mrs. Sundberg and Agnes. At first she had a mind to stay back and care for Mr. Sundberg. But then Agnes begged her to come. She'd described the service, and it sounded much less formal than the service Mr. Tolbert required her to attend. Curiosity got the better of her.

Two blocks down South Eight Street, and they rounded the corner. Agnes pointed straight ahead.

"That's our church. It's called Our Redeemer."

Julianna glimpsed the tall red-brick building, looming in the near distance. "It's very quaint."

"One of the largest churches in Manitowoc," the girl added.

"It's a lovely structure." Turning from it to Agnes, she couldn't help a bit of teasing. "St. Paul's in London has a spire that reaches so high the angels have to take care, lest they injure themselves."

"That's not true." Agnes dipped her brow. "Is it?"

Mrs. Sundberg's soft laugh made Julianna grin.

"Oh, you!" Agnes rapped Julianna lightly on the arm.

The bell clanged and Mrs. Sundberg quickened her pace. "We had best hurry so we are not late."

Julianna walked faster, and Agnes kept up. Daniel had offered to stay back with his father. Mrs. Sundberg's protests were in vain, but then her gaze had misted over when she admitted that it had been months since she'd attended church services. God forbid that she keep one of her children or any of her friends from hearing God's

Word, so she'd refused help. But today Daniel had insisted she go, adding that he didn't mind keeping his father company. Julianna thought it was terribly kind of him to consider his mother's spiritual well-being over his own.

Daniel. Thoughts of him caused her emotional bruise to ache even worse. But any pain she felt was her own doing. He'd warned her. She hadn't listened.

They traipsed up some stairs and entered the church's vestibule. Mrs. Sundberg and Agnes nodded polite greetings.

"There will be time for introductions and conversations after service," Mrs. Sundberg promised.

Julianna nodded, quelling another round of nerves. Since her arrival in Manitowoc two days ago, she'd met people rather sporadically, whether on the street or in Mrs. Sundberg's store. This morning, however, she'd meet many of the Sundbergs' friends and neighbors all at once—and Daniel wasn't here to help her.

But it was like she said last night: she needed to get used to his absence. He'd said all along that he wouldn't stay. He'd offered her a new and better way of life. He would do the right thing financially by his biological family. Then, he'd be leaving, never giving her—or them—another thought.

While her heart ached like never before, Julianna felt more sorry for the Sundbergs than she did for herself. They weren't fully aware of Daniel's plan to walk out of their lives for a third and final time.

Mrs. Sundberg led the way to the fourth pew from the front. Stepping aside, she allowed Agnes and Julianna to slide in before she tucked her dark blue skirt around her legs and stepped in after them.

Glancing around, Julianna felt just as prim and proper in her new raspberry-colored dress with its white lacy trim as anyone else here. She straightened the matching hat on her head. What would

Flora say if she could see Julianna now? Why, she wouldn't even recognize her younger sister.

Mark Dunbar scooted into the pew just ahead of them, startling Julianna from her muse. He nodded a greeting to Mrs. Sundberg and Agnes before bestowing a remorseful grin on Julianna.

"Please accept my apologies for last night's, um, misunderstanding," he whispered.

Julianna flicked glances at the Sundbergs, and her cheeks grew warm. "We can talk later."

Mark wagged his head. "Not necessary, Miss Wayland. I needn't take up any more of your time." He looked around. No one else was within earshot. "You see, I left my folks' house shortly after the captain did. I wanted to make certain you were safe. I knew I wouldn't rest until I did. I arrived at Mrs. Sundberg's store shortly after the captain did, and I saw you…"

Julianna gasped, and thankfully, Mark's hushed voice trailed off. So he'd seen Daniel take her into his arms. He'd seen how she'd lingered there. Julianna stared into her lap and folded her gloved hands. She couldn't say she felt a single shred of remorse.

"Well," Mark continued to whisper, "all that matters is you're unharmed."

Agnes leaned over. "What happened, Julianna?"

"I'll tell you about it later." She looked at Mark. "Unless Mr. Dunbar would prefer to relay the incident. Perhaps he'll announce it for all the congregation to hear."

"I'd never do that." His voice grew louder, although it resembled a low growl.

"You practically just did!"

Mrs. Sundberg placed her hand on Julianna's arm. The heightened inflection in her tone had caused several pairs of eyes to look their way. Instantly Julianna regretted defending herself in public.

She should have kept her mouth shut. Daniel would be so disappointed in her—except this was all his fault.

However, in that moment, Julianna realized that as fine as her dress and hat were, they didn't make her a fine lady. She'd never fit in here, among people who were socially superior to her. Why did she ever think such a thing was possible?

CHAPTER 19

*W*ITH LITTLE EFFORT Daniel got his father dressed, into the wheelchair, and outside for some fresh morning air. Once he was satisfied with his father's comfort, he situated himself on the stoop outside the door, hoping the specialist would be able to cast a bit of insight into Poppa's pitiful state.

His gaze fell over the man who had taught him many things in life. He recalled as a boy holding Poppa's hand while they walked to the barn to do the evening milking. But now his hands were limp. His head, despite being propped with pillows, sagged to one side. Daniel looked away. It was the worst thing that could happen to a man, dwelling in that useless abyss between life and death. Worse still was that it appeared Poppa didn't want Daniel's help. Instead Poppa behaved as if he would prefer to...die.

Daniel trained his focus on the street. Businesses were closed, and not a soul was in sight. He wondered how Julianna fared. She'd looked positively lovely this morning before she left for church with *Mor* and Agnes. Maybe they'd meet up with the Dunbars, and Mark could try again with Julianna—

Except every corded muscle in Daniel's body wanted the man to be unsuccessful. Yet Daniel had no right to think of Julianna as anything more than a recipient of his sponsorship to a new life here in America.

When had he become such a hypocrite?

"A'venshur?"

Daniel glanced back at Poppa. Most of his golden blond hair had turned white with age, and his hairline had receded over the years. But his eyes were still blue. "What did you say, Poppa?" He poised, listening. In the last two days Daniel noticed his father's words were sometimes a mix of Norwegian and American. The Norwegian, it seemed, was easier for him to pronounce, given his condition.

"Dream? A'venshur?"

Daniel understood and smiled. "No, I wasn't dreaming of adventure."

"'oman? Countess?"

Daniel sent a gaze skyward. "I see gossip has preceded my announcement." He tipped his head. "Who told you?"

"A'nes."

And Julianna must have told Agnes. Irritation bubbled out of Daniel in the form of a sigh. "It's not official yet."

"Miss 'ay'and? You?"

"Miss Wayland?" Daniel was growing impatient with all the explanations of their relationship. "She happened to board my ship quite by accident. But instead of prosecuting her as a stowaway—"

"No, no..."

Daniel regarded his father askance once more.

"You. She 'oves you." He struggled to say each word, and his voice was a hoarse whisper.

But Daniel understood. "She loves me?" He lifted a stone off the ground and turned it in his palm, feeling its coarse texture. "Where did you hear that nonsense?"

"'rom Miss 'ay'and."

He laughed to cover his discomfort. "Julianna told you that?"

"*Hun liker å snakke.*"

"Yes, I know she likes to talk." Daniel looked from the stone in his hand to his father. Was that a spark of amusement in his gaze? "I'm afraid she's quite delusional."

The remark came out harsher than intended. "Poppa, the fact is, I'm the first man who has ever shown Julianna any kindness and respect. She fancies herself in love with me."

"Are you in love with her?" The question came out loud and clear.

"Of course not." *What a lie!* He ignored the prick of conscience and rushed on. "I don't know why we're having this conversation. I didn't leave England ahead of schedule because of me. I came because of you."

"You shudda not come." The blue of Poppa's eyes dulled.

"You said that same thing days ago too. Why? *Mor* sent me a telegram, asking me to come." Aggravation overrode his deep sense of hurt. Couldn't Poppa appreciate the wheelchair and everything he'd done for their family in the last couple of days? He planned to do more. The specialist was due in town tomorrow.

"She sen' many 'elegrams." Again each syllable seemed an exertion.

"I know. *Mor* told me. But I never received her messages."

Once more he wondered why the correspondences never arrived. Could it be George—or Eliza, even—concealed or destroyed them? *But why would they?*

Shaking off the thought, Daniel began again. "I've been sailing to and from England the past few years. I'm part of a fleet that competes with other shipping companies. My vessel, the *Allegiance*, has almost beaten the record for fastest time across the Atlantic." A swell of pride rose up inside of Daniel, except Poppa didn't look impressed in the least.

Not much had changed over the years.

"Farm…"

"It's gone. *Mor* sold it." Perhaps Poppa needed reminding. "I've come to agree that she made the right decision. She and Agnes couldn't keep up with all the work."

"*Jeg er en fiasco.*"

"What? A failure? You?" Surprised to hear such words from his usually optimistic father, Daniel shook his head. "No, you are not a failure, Poppa. You're sick. But I've got another doctor coming to look at you tomorrow. We'll get you back on your feet and well again. You'll see."

"*Jeg ba. Jeg ba.*"

"I'm sure you did pray, Poppa." *Like it did any good.*

"Bad crop. Two years…no food…" Poppa closed his eyes as if the admission caused him a great amount of pain.

"Rest now, Poppa. It's not your fault that the last couple of harvests weren't good. You never wanted to farm in the first place. Remember? You wanted to be a politician. *Bestefar* said you would have been a good one too." *If Mor hadn't insisted on having her way,* he added silently.

"No." The tiniest of smiles tugged on one corner of Poppa's mouth. "'olitics *Bestefar's* dream. No' mine."

Daniel brought his chin back. "Of course it was your dream. Before you married *Mor.*"

"No. *Jeg er en bonde*—I am a farmer."

Daniel felt a little stunned. All his life he believed his father's goal in life had been politics and that his mother had kept him from it. "Poppa, I used to sit at *Bestefar* Sundberg's knee, and he would tell me about your trip to Madison shortly after Wisconsin became a state."

"*Ja…*"

"*Bestefar* said that when you came back you asked *Mor* to marry you, but she refused the first time."

"*Ja, ja…*" A fondness entered in his eyes and played across his lips.

"She wanted you to have a farm—a farm away from Brown County and your family."

"No!" Poppa's chest filled and deflated rapidly. "Chief Oshkosh gave me…the land…our farm…a gift…for representing…his people."

"I'm aware of that." Daniel had known that much. "But it was *Mor*'s idea for you to farm there just as her father, my namesake, did in Norway. And just as *Bestefar* Sundberg did too." A short chuckle erupted. "Except *Bestefar* liked to trap and then trade his furs with the Indians." Recollections of his *bestemor*, an Oneida and his grandfather's second wife, and his uncle Jack and aunt Mary scampered across his mind. Would he see Aunt Mary before he left?

"*Jeg er en fiasco.*"

Daniel snapped from his reverie and peered at his father. "Stop it. You're not a failure."

"As your poppa." He wheezed as he drew in a breath. "Just one son. You. Just one chance…to raise you…admonition of the Lord. "

"And you did just that. I was admonished plenty of times over the years." Daniel grinned at his attempt at some levity. "And look at me. Look at my life. I'm a successful self-made man. That's at least in part to your credit, yes? You raised me the first fifteen years of my life."

"Self-made man."

"So?"

Poppa seemed to struggle to inhale. "Not…not God-made."

Here we go again. Daniel tamped down his mounting impatience and focused on his growing concern for his father. "Let's talk of something else. In fact, I'll do the talking. I'll tell you of one of my adventures on the high seas. This same rendition entertained Jed and Will Dunbar last night." Daniel had to grin at the memory. He'd enjoyed the Dunbars' company.

"God author…finisher…faith."

"Don't talk anymore, Poppa. It's too taxing on you."

"God...finisher..."

"Look, I know religion is very important to you and *Mor*, but—"

"Prayers...kept you safe...on the sea."

"So they did." Daniel liked to think it was his own wisdom and skill that kept him alive, but he wouldn't argue. He gave the stone in his palm a hard throw toward the street.

"*Jeg er en fiasco.*" His gaze dropped on Daniel.

"You are not a failure! Stop saying that. If you were a failure, I'd be a failure—and I'm not." *Unless you think I am because I didn't take over the farm, didn't follow in your footsteps, embrace your faith...*

Poppa clutched his chest then pulled at his shirt.

"Are you in pain?" Daniel shot up from the stoop. "Poppa?"

"Your momma...Agnes." His voice was but a breathless rasp.

"They're fine. I'm taking care of them." He cupped his father's face, disliking how pale he appeared. Had this outing been too much for him?

An instant later Poppa's eyes drifted into the back in his head.

Fear fell over Daniel like a shroud. "Poppa!"

"And let's depart, remembering what our Savior, Jesus Christ, taught us." The minister's gaze drifted over his congregation. He smiled. "With God all things are possible."

Julianna sat up a little straighter. *All things are possible.* Those words gave her that slender thread of hope she'd desperately longed for. Perhaps she'd become a fine, respected lady in time. *With God all things are possible.*

Lifting his hands, the minister added a final prayer. "May the Lord bless thee and keep thee. The Lord make His face to shine upon thee and be gracious unto thee. The Lord lift up His countenance upon thee and give thee peace." With that he closed his Bible and walked down the center aisle.

After he went by, the congregation stood to leave also. From out of the corner of her eye Julianna saw Mark get to his feet, but she refused to meet his gaze. He was the last man she imagined who would be so vindictive. Then again, what had she expected? Mark was a man like all the rest.

Except for Daniel.

The din of voices filled the sanctuary as everyone greeted each other all at once while filing out of church. They paused at the doorway to shake the minister's hand.

Outside in the sunshine men shook hands and chuckled. Women used their fans to stir the hot and humid air while sharing tidbits of news.

Mrs. Sundberg introduced Julianna to, first, the Rogers family. The slender couple each held a child while their eldest daughter, Marna, who was Agnes's age, chased after additional younger siblings. Agnes joined in, and together they managed to get the youngsters corralled and hoisted into the Rogers's wagon.

Next Julianna met Mr. Belts from the newspaper. A bit on the gruff side, the bearded man seemed generally polite enough.

Adeline and Will approached them with baby Jacob asleep in his father's arms. It was Adeline who introduced Julianna to Miss Irma Dacy, a teacher at the grade school. As an amicable chat ensued, Julianna noticed Irma had eyes for Mark Dunbar. He'd walked over to talk with Will. All the while Julianna sensed Mark tried to get her attention, but she'd give none of it after how he'd shamed her in front of Mrs. Sundberg and Agnes. Besides, Julianna wasn't a bit sorry for her behavior last night. All she wanted was to be close to Daniel, and now she had a few more memories to tuck inside the corner of her mind before she forged a future for herself—without him.

The sun was high in the sky when at last she and the Sundbergs made their way back to the cozy apartment behind the shop. The heat of the day had become stifling, and while she had no idea of the temperature, Julianna didn't think it ever got this hot in London.

"I will go and check on your poppa," Mrs. Sundberg said to Agnes as they stepped into the sitting room. The air felt cooler inside. "Then we will eat our noon dinner, for which we have Daniel to thank." She sent a smile at Julianna.

Daniel made an uncanny appearance at the doorway, leading to the hall. One glimpse of his dire expression and Julianna knew something was amiss.

He blocked his mother's entry.

"Daniel?" She gave him an uncertain smile.

He didn't return the gesture, and the hard set of his jaw, the dark blue of his eyes, told Julianna all she needed to know before he ever spoke the words.

"Poppa's gone."

"What?" A nervous laugh burst from Mrs. Sundberg's mouth. "Gone where?"

Julianna put her fingertips over her lips. Sorrow squeezed her heart.

Agnes ran across the room and hugged her mother around the waist.

"Poppa is dead." Daniel swallowed, as if grappling with a host of emotions. "I'm sorry, *Mor.*"

While Agnes buried her head in her mother's shoulder and began to cry, Mrs. Sundberg remained nonplussed.

"How? When?"

Daniel's features softened. "He had another spell of…of apoplexy or something. He went very quickly. I was with him."

Mrs. Sundberg inhaled a sob. "He waited for you, Daniel."

"I might believe that except he told me I shouldn't have come home."

Julianna saw the hurt in his eyes.

"I think maybe he did not want you to see him this way. He wanted you to remember him as your strong poppa who could do anything. Still, he wanted to see your face one last time. We both prayed for your return. But I mostly sent the message to you because I–I needed you. I am the selfish one, just as you always said, Daniel." She dissolved into tears and clutched Agnes's shoulders. "And now my Sam is gone."

Daniel came forward and embraced them both. He looked over their bowed heads and met Julianna's stare. She glimpsed the helplessness in his gaze and longed to wrap him in an embrace of her own.

Pulling his gaze from hers, he peered at the top of his mother's head. "I was wrong, *Mor*. You're not selfish. I was disrespectful, and I'm sorry about it. Please accept my deepest apologies."

His tender admission caused Mrs. Sundberg to cry harder. She pushed past Daniel and ran to her bedroom.

"Sam! Oh, Sam…"

Julianna choked, hearing the note of desperation in Mrs. Sundberg's voice. Over the last two days she'd seen the love that the older couple felt for each other. A number of times she wished Daniel could have been there to witness it too. It was a pity he'd opted to sleep at the hotel.

Agnes threw her arms about Daniel's waist and sobbed into his chest while Julianna stood by not knowing what she could do. She felt like the dutiful housemaid at Mr. Tolbert's, awaiting her next orders.

Adeline and Will walked in just then. All Daniel had to do was give a little shake of his auburn head, and his sister somehow knew her father had passed.

"Oh, no…Poppa!" She ran for the bedroom.

Daniel sidestepped to get out of her way.

Will held baby Jacob in one arm and slowly strode across the sitting room. "Sorry to hear the news." He placed his hand on Daniel's shoulder. "But your father had a strong faith, so you can take comfort in knowing that he's in heaven, where there's no more pain and no more tears."

Heaven's like that? Julianna thought it sounded like a wonderful place.

"I appreciate the sentiments. Thank you." Daniel forced a polite smile, but Agnes sounded inconsolable. She clung to Daniel, hiccupped, and cried some more. He held her tightly against him.

Julianna knew just how it felt to be in Daniel's embrace, although not in a sisterly way, of course. Nonetheless, she imagined Agnes would eventually find some solace in her big brother's arms.

At that moment Mark Dunbar entered the apartment. He removed his hat and glanced around the room. His gaze finally settled on Julianna.

She rolled her eyes. The man had a poor sense of timing, that's for sure.

"It's Mr. Sundberg," Will said. "He's gone."

"I'm so sorry…" He looked at Daniel. "He was a good man."

Daniel merely nodded, and Julianna thought that Mark did indeed look sorry.

He shifted his weight from one foot to the other. "Would you, um, like me to fetch the undertaker?"

"I'd be most appreciative," Daniel said. "Thank you."

"Miss Wayland? Would you care to walk down the street with me? Mr. Paulsen's funeral home isn't far."

"I should say not!" She turned her back to him and folded her arms. At Daniel's curious stare, she averted her gaze, but she caught

Will and Mark exchanging glances. "Mrs. Sundberg might need me." She hoped she sounded less abrupt.

"Then I'll be back."

Mark took his leave, and the weeping in the other room grew louder.

Will threw a glance in that direction. "I had best see to Adeline. She sounds awful upset."

Daniel inclined his head. "Good idea."

Will walked across the sitting room and offered baby Jacob to Julianna. "Would you mind holding him?"

"Not at all." At least she'd have something to do now.

She cradled the babe and smiled into his sleeping face. Then realization struck. Now that Daniel's father was dead, there was no more reason for him to stay in Wisconsin. Dread, fear, and sorrow knotted in her chest. Another life awaited him, one of luxury and influence. Daniel would be leaving soon.

And Julianna couldn't fathom how she'd ever get along without him.

CHAPTER 20

*J*ULIANNA CLUTCHED THE sidebar when the covered buck-board carriage hit a particularly deep rut. "This is quite the bumpy road, isn't it?" She'd been trying off and on to ignite a conversation and lighten the mood.

No reply…again. Thank goodness the jangling of reins and the horses' rhythmical steps over the dirt road muffled the silence. Still, the solemnness in the air matched the day's high humidity, but what more could she do?

She glanced over her shoulder into the backseat. Agnes slept, and Mrs. Sundberg stared out at the passing scenery. Next to Julianna Daniel sat rugged and stiff, reins in his hands. She felt the weight of his sorrow. For the last day and a half he'd been so quiet, barely saying a word to anyone. Julianna wanted to help in some way, but it wasn't as if she could take his pain away. He had lost his beloved father, not that she knew anything about losing a father. But she'd had friends die over the years, people who had meant a great deal to her, like the Pigeon Lady. She'd had a story for everything.

Mrs. Sundberg coughed as dust rose up from the road, and Julianna turned to be sure she was all right. She appeared to be. And, out of her family, she was the one handling things the best.

Julianna had only seen the older woman weep that one time when she learned of her husband's death. Ever since Mrs. Sundberg had been a pillar of strength. She had greeted the neighbors and close friends as they brought dishes of food to the door along with their condolences. Then, after the short memorial service yesterday, Mrs. Sundberg had stood in the receiving line with her shoulders square and her eyes dry. Adeline and Agnes, however, had wept on and off, and today Agnes was exhausted.

Julianna's shoulder bumped against Daniel's, and she murmured an apology. But he didn't answer. He just looked straight ahead as though he were lost somewhere deep inside himself.

Shifting her gaze, she saw a barn, surrounded by a lush, green field. Then she spotted several black and white cows chewing lazily by a wooden fence. "I've never visited a farm before, much less spent a few days in the country." Despite the sadness that filled the jostling carriage, Julianna couldn't help but feel a tad excited about this new adventure.

Mr. Sundberg had requested that his remains be buried in his family's cemetery, located on the farm in Green Bay to which they now traveled. Daniel's grandparents and uncle had been buried there also.

The road curved around a thicket of trees. Their leafy branches formed a lovely green canopy overhead.

"Can you see the other buggies?"

Julianna swiveled and saw Mrs. Sundberg crane her neck, while beside her Agnes stirred.

Sitting taller, she caught sight of the backend of one of the carriages before the road looped around the other way. "Yes, they're up ahead, not too far in front of us." The older Dunbar couple and Mark rode in the first black buggy that led their caravan of three. Next came the vehicle carrying Will, Adeline, and baby Jacob, followed by the one in which Julianna and the Sundbergs sat. The hearse had left for Green Bay late yesterday afternoon. The interment would take place this afternoon. Everything needed to be done with some haste, due to the July heat. Julianna found it amazing that in spite of mourning, Daniel had seen to everything.

Daniel slowed the carriage then turned onto a shady lane that took them up to a lovely white house. It seemed dwarfed by the vast countryside. He pulled off to the side and halted the team of horses near the barn. A barking dog welcomed them, along with several pecking chickens.

He jumped down from the buggy, and Agnes awoke. Then he helped her, his mother, and Julianna alight.

A willowy woman jogged from the house to meet them. When she spotted Mrs. Sundberg, she opened her arms.

"Mary! Oh, Mary…"

Julianna saw Mrs. Sundberg's chin quiver before the two women embraced. Adeline and Agnes stepped into the queue for hugs.

"I'm so glad I visited last month." Mary's round eyes grew misty. "I got to spend time with my big brother."

The Dunbars sauntered over to say hello, and then Mrs. Sundberg introduced Julianna.

"She's become a valuable assistant to me." Mrs. Sundberg looped her arm around Julianna's.

At the compliment Julianna's confidence grew.

"Welcome to my home, Miss Wayland."

"Thank you."

Mary's dark eyes matched her deep brown dress, and her gaze flowed to Daniel, although she didn't move to greet him.

He inclined his head. "Hello, Aunt Mary." His tone sounded stiff and formal.

The thick summer air suddenly crackled with unmasked tension. Julianna looked from Daniel to his aunt. Her mouth was set in a firm line, the only indication her feelings weren't amicable toward him.

An instant later Mary spun on her heel and waved everyone inside. "Please come. You've journeyed a long ways, and I prepared some refreshments. Reverend Wollums is waiting for us."

Daniel hung back. "I'll bring in the luggage."

Julianna turned to him and found his expression unreadable. "Can I help you?"

"No, go on ahead," he urged. "Stay with the ladies. *Mor* needs you."

"What about you?"

He began unbuckling the many valises, secured behind the buggy. "I just want to get this over with and get back to New York—and back to my *real* life."

Another reminder that he'd leave soon. Julianna's heart grew heavy.

"My father was right." Daniel met her gaze, and she detected a sharp glint in the depths of his blue eyes. "I should never have come in the first place."

❦❦❦

Julianna sat in the shade of a beautiful willow with baby Jacob in her arms. A short distance away the Sundbergs, Dunbars, and a host of friends gathered within the confines of the cemetery's white-picketed fence. Daniel stood off to one side, his stance resembling that of a sea captain overlooking his crew. Julianna sighed. If only he'd see that his family wanted his love and attention, not his money, although he had completely lifted his mother's financial burden. But it wasn't enough for them, and Julianna understood why. They envied the loyalty that Daniel felt toward the Ramseys.

In truth, Julianna did too.

She turned her attention to the darkly clad minister. "For those of us who abide with Christ, this isn't a good-bye to Sam Sundberg. It's a mere farewell. Death cannot hold believers in its icy grip." Reverend Wollums looked to the sky. "Some day we'll see Sam, not in the rays of the sunshine under which he lived and worked in this life, but in the glow of Christ's glory." His gaze returned to the mourners. "So let not your heart be troubled, and don't be afraid. The Lord Jesus knows of your sorrow." He stared at Mrs. Sundberg for a long moment before his gaze roamed over the others. "Let us pray…"

Heads bowed, and Julianna saw that Daniel had respectfully lowered his.

"May the Comforter, whom the Lord Jesus sent, give us all peace in this, our hour of sorrow. Amen."

Everyone took fists of dirt and, one by one, tossed it into Mr. Sundberg's grave. Then they filed out of the cemetery, many heading for the house.

Adeline came over and sat by Julianna. She peered at her son, saw that he slept soundly, and smiled.

"Well," she said with a sigh, looking toward the freshly dug grave, "Poppa isn't suffering anymore."

Julianna wondered. Questions burned deep within her. "How do you know?" The question sailed out before she could think better of it. "How does Reverend Wollums know? For that matter, how can anyone really know what happens in the hereafter?"

Adeline didn't seem put off in the least. "The Bible tells us exactly what happens."

"The Bible." Julianna nodded. "I started reading it on the ship. Unfortunately I didn't get very far."

"Keep reading." Adeline's lips curved upward. "You'll find the part where God's Word says that it's appointed unto man once to die and after that the judgment." She looked toward her father's grave. A few mourners lingered, Daniel being one of them. "Some will meet Christ as their Savior, and others, who refused to believe, will meet Him as their judge—and the judgment will be eternal separation from God in a place called hell."

Julianna thought she may have lived in hell for a while.

"The Bible says there will be weeping, wailing, and gnashing of teeth."

Now she was certain of it. Julianna grimaced. She hoped never to return to that dark, horrible place again! "So what do I do if I don't want to go to hell?"

"Only believe."

"In what?"

Adeline smoothed her dark brown skirt over her legs, and then smiled into Julianna's eyes. "Believe that God so loved the world—and that includes *you*—that He gave His only begotten Son, so that whosoever believes in Him—again, Julianna, you're part of *whosoever*—should not perish but have everlasting life."

"I'm not sure I'd be included. I haven't lived a very nice life."

"Well, Mary Magdalene certainly didn't live a nice life." Adeline leaned closer. "She was a woman of ill repute back in Jesus' time. Nevertheless, He favored her and considered her His friend. And the woman at the well—she had been living with many men who were never her husbands. However, Jesus Christ, the King of kings and Lord of lords, deigned to stop and speak with her in public."

"Really?" Julianna thought it quite remarkable. Mr. Tolbert certainly wouldn't have dealings with such women—at least not in public.

Adeline dipped one brow. "Anyone can be saved and become a Christian."

Julianna looked at the baby she held and touched his wispy reddish-blond hair. She supposed Daniel looked something like this as an infant. "Is your brother saved?" At Adeline's momentary hesitation she glanced up.

"I don't know," Adeline said at last. Her gaze seemed honed in on Daniel now. He'd taken a seat on a stone bench and watched as two men heaved shovelfuls of dirt onto his father's grave. "Momma and Poppa raised us to be saved, but it's an individual decision."

"Hmm…" Julianna decided right then that she wanted to be saved. "Well, I believe."

Adeline's troubled expression transformed into one of gladness. "I'm happy to hear that."

"And Daniel might believe too." Julianna stared at him, and her heart ached because she sensed his deep pain and sorrow. "He's like Jesus in many ways. He's kind-hearted and generous."

"He's hardly like the Savior. Daniel chose a life of wealth over his own family."

"He worked hard for that wealth. George Ramsey merely gave him the opportunities. And aren't you glad that your brother has the means to help your mum right now? I'd go so far as to say he's been a *godsend*."

Adeline's eyes darkened, and Julianna wondered if she'd crossed the boundaries this time. Seconds later, however, Adeline's taut features calmed. "You're right. I should be more grateful than resentful."

"Why don't you go talk to him, Adeline? He's as sad as you are about your father's passing. I'll stay here and hold the baby."

She laughed. "Oh, you'd come up with any excuse just to hold my son."

Julianna smiled at the jest. Then, again, there was a lot of truth to it.

Standing, Adeline brushed the dried grass from her dark skirt and strode toward her brother. Julianna sent up a prayer. *God, if You can hear me, please let these two make their peace.*

⊛⊚⊛

Daniel felt a presence beside him and assumed it was Julianna—until he heard his sister's voice.

"Thank you for helping Momma out these last few days. I noticed Agnes is wearing a new dress. She hasn't had one in over a year."

He glanced at her. "Of course I'd help out. What kind of a man would I be if I didn't?"

"Well, I must confess that I've wondered."

Daniel clenched his jaw. "You wondered? Why, because I chose a way that wasn't in *Mor*'s best-laid plans? Poppa's too, so I recently learned."

"Yes, I suppose so."

Hearing the doubt in Adeline's voice, Daniel turned. "I never wanted to farm. I made my desires known, and they went ignored. After Uncle Jack was killed, *Bestafar* encouraged me to forge my own path in life, and I did." His gaze fell on his grandfather's grassy grave. "I'm sorry I missed his funeral—*Bestamor*'s too."

"You've missed a lot, Daniel." Adeline's voice sounded tight now. "You missed my wedding and the birth of my son."

"I'm sorry, Adeline."

She inhaled a sob. Daniel set his arm around her shoulders.

"Momma and Poppa had such a tough time these last two years. There were months before my marriage that we had no food in our cupboards."

He set himself firmly against another wave of guilt.

"Will and I were always friends in school, and for a long time I wondered if he'd married me out of pity. I know differently now," she quickly added.

Daniel glanced at her in time to see a pretty blush radiate from her face.

"But even after I'd married into a prominent family, our parents were proud and stiff-necked about accepting any charity from me."

Daniel ground out a laugh. "Some things never change, I guess."

"And many other things do."

Daniel held her gaze. "Such as?"

"Such as I still need my older brother."

"Bah!" He didn't believe that for an instant.

"What about Momma and Agnes?"

"I've already opened an account for *Mor* at the bank, and she can draw from it whenever a need arises."

"Daniel, they need your emotional support too." She shifted. "And why don't you call her Momma like we do? It hurts her that you've chosen to refer to her in a formal and more distant manner."

"I'm a man. I don't need a 'momma.'" He heaved a sigh. "What's more, I don't need a lecture from you, Adeline."

"What about Julianna? Are you going to leave her here, just like that?" She attempted to snap her gloved fingers.

"No, not *just like that*." Daniel hated being put on the defensive this way. He'd made financial arrangements for Julianna too.

"Do you love her?"

Every muscle in Daniel's body tensed. "That's none of your business."

Adeline grew quiet beside him, but not for long. "Agnes said you're marrying a princess."

"A countess—and it's not official yet."

"Yet? So it's true? You'll be leaving soon?"

"Yes, it's true."

He could feel his sister begin to seethe. "How can abandon your family a second time?"

Daniel weighed his reply. "I don't consider it abandonment. Hardly that, Adeline."

"You walked away the last time, with the Ramseys, and didn't give us another thought."

"I gave you plenty of…thoughts over the years."

"We prayed for you every day." Adeline choked on the words. "For your safety—and that you'd come home again. But if you'd given us any thought at all, you would have answered my letters. Momma's too."

The fight went out of Daniel, and he pulled his sister close. Placing a kiss on top of her head, he held her while she wept. "I'm sorry I neglected you, Addy." The fact she cried so hard signaled Daniel to her mourning their poppa rather than her disappointment in him.

"Don't leave, Daniel."

"Now, now…you have your husband to care for you. You have your adorable son to raise and…to boss." He chuckled. "That's all a woman wants in life, right?"

"Argh!" Adeline broke free from his hold. "You are so dense, Daniel Sundberg."

He shrugged. "Perhaps." He searched her tearstained face. "But did it ever occur to you that I want exactly what your husband wants—to be successful and influential within his community, and—and to raise a family." From the corner of his eye he could see Julianna, sitting beneath a tree, rocking his nephew. The glimpse was almost surreal, and Daniel's mouth went dry as he imagined her as his wife, cradling their child.

But, no!

He refocused. Marrying Julianna wasn't written in the stars, as George liked to say.

"Will wants to be a successful man." Adeline's admission helped to tame Daniel's wayward thoughts. "But he would never sacrifice his family to do so."

"Adeline…" Daniel repositioned himself on the cool stone bench. "There is an almighty God in heaven who won't violate my will.

225

Why do you—why does my family—believe that they can decide what's best for me?"

When she didn't answer, he continued on.

"You don't know me at all. None of you do." If honest, he'd have to confess that Julianna knew him the best. "And let's be honest. You and *Mor* and Agnes—and Poppa, when he lived—don't want to know or accept me for the man I am. Yes, you'd like to dictate to me, manipulate me, but I refuse to succumb. That's my only fault. I'm not responsible for the poor crops, just like you're not responsible for the raging tempest which took the lives of four of my crew last year."

Adeline's eyes grew round.

"I wouldn't dream of laying that burden at your doorstep." He leaned his elbows on his knees. He still felt badly for the souls lost during that harrowing voyage. "And yet my family tries time and again to encumber me." Daniel recalled his poppa's last words. He died believing he failed, as a farmer and a father. He never gave Daniel a chance to list his successes.

Then again, he'd probably consider those triumphs wood, hay, and stubble.

But Poppa was wrong.

"Adeline, either God is in control of everything or nothing."

"He controls everything—even the bad is for our ultimate good."

Daniel turned and gave her a pointed stare. "Thank you."

She blinked. "So you're saying it's God's will that you leave us again?"

"Yes." Part of him chafed at the idea, and yet he believed he spoke the truth. He pushed to his feet then reached for his sister's hand. "Come. Everyone's expecting us up at the house." As long as he was here, he might as well continue his charade of the dutiful and faithful son.

CHAPTER 21

*M*ISS WAYLAND, MAY I have a word with you?"

A tray of coffee in her hands, Julianna resisted the urge to glance heavenward at Mark Dunbar's request.

"Here, allow me to help you with that."

"I've got it." Little did he know that she'd carried hundreds of trays in her life. Walking into the small dining room table, Julianna carefully set down her burden. "What can I do for you, Mr. Dunbar?"

"Could we step outside? I must talk to you."

She gazed around at the milling people and decided speaking outdoors might be best if he had more chastisement on his mind. Thank God Mrs. Sundberg and Agnes had forgotten all about Sunday's incident at church because of Mr. Sundberg's death.

Giving him a slight nod, she peeled off the apron Daniel's aunt lent her and followed him back through the kitchen and outside. People had congregated on the lawn too, so Mark headed toward a thicket of trees.

"Adeline often speaks of her grandparents' farm, now her aunt's home." Mark slowed his steps. "But I'd never been here until now." He pointed up ahead. "I believe that's the apple orchard."

Julianna stopped dead still in a patch of shade. "I think we're out of earshot now. What can I do for you, Mr. Dunbar?" She had little use for this young man.

"Miss Wayland, I want to beg your forgiveness for my pomp and self-righteousness on Sunday morning."

She blinked. She hadn't expected an apology.

"When I saw you and the captain"—his gaze dropped to his black boots—"I immediately assumed the worst instead of considering how frightened you must have been and that the captain had merely been comforting you."

He'd assumed correctly the first time, but Julianna knew better than to admit it.

She considered him and judged him to be sincere. She softened. "The part of London where I come from…" She carefully chose her words. "…can be rather dangerous, particularly after nightfall, and it's largely due to the number of bawdy sailors coming in and out of port."

"So that's why you fled." Understanding flashed in his sky-blue eyes. "Well, let me assure you that I'd be able to defend you against any mariners with mischief on their minds."

His remark did nothing to assure Julianna at all. If anything, it bespoke of his ignorance in such matters.

"Well, thank you, but…you don't have to apologize to someone like me."

"But of course I do. I was wrong and I can admit it. I behaved like some—"

"Puritan?"

Seeing the confusion mar his brow, she realized that only Daniel would understand her quip. Her gaze flitted to the terrace where he stood, talking with Mark's father and brother. Then, as if feeling her glance land on him, Daniel looked her way. His eyes pinned her, and a warmth spread over her body like soft butter on fresh bread.

"I'm truly sorry, Miss Wayland."

She blinked and forced her attention back to Mark. "Thank you, Mr. Dunbar."

"It's Mark, remember?"

"Mark." She gave him a polite grin.

"I hoped that you'd find it in your heart to forgive me, and, perhaps, we could…well…" His face looked suddenly sunburned. "Maybe we could get to know each other better and become more than friends."

Julianna fought against a grimace. "Mark, you'd best know now that I've decided never to marry." At his puzzled, even disappointed expression she rushed on. "It has nothing to do with what happened a few nights ago. I made my decision before I arrived in America."

"I don't understand."

She didn't know how to explain it either without looking like the wanton hussy that he'd assumed she was after last Saturday night.

"Is there someone else?"

"Well…" Julianna focused on the lush green grass so her eyes wouldn't stray to Daniel and give away her secret.

"You should have said so."

"Yes, I suppose I should have."

"The man's in London, I presume."

Let him presume all he wanted. Julianna just shrugged.

Mark took her elbow and guided her toward the house. "The captain doesn't know, does he?"

"Know?" She stared at Mark.

"That you've left your heart in London?"

"Oh…he knows."

"He didn't give any indication when I asked to walk you home."

"The captain is confident that I'll forget about my true love now that I'm here in America."

"Ah…" Mark bobbed his head.

"But I won't."

"You're sure?"

"Positive. So don't waste your time with me when there are young ladies like Miss Irma Dacy available."

"Irma?" Mark's blond brows drew inward.

"Yes, I met her on Sunday morning. She's a teacher, isn't she?"

"That's right."

"You know her, then?"

"Of course. I've known Irma all my life. We went to school together."

"I was very impressed with her."

"Oh?"

Julianna nodded. "She's so intelligent, up on current events. Why, I'll bet she even reads the newspaper."

Mark chuckled. "I'm sure she does."

"Not many women do, you know, unless the articles pertain to fashion or good table manners."

"Really?" He seemed to gauge her remark.

She elaborated. "Well, let's just say that the women I associated with in London would never spend a free minute with a newspaper." *That was the truth!*

Daniel crossed the yard and met them just before they reached the house. His probing gaze briefly met hers. Was he making sure she was all right? She smiled to say she was, and Daniel looked at Mark.

"Thank you for making the trip." He extended his right hand.

Mark gave it a firm shake. "You're entirely welcome. Your father was a good man, a friend to all."

Julianna thought Daniel had to force the polite smile on his lips. Once more she sensed his hurt over losing the father he hadn't known and his guilt because it had been his own fault.

"In the end you did what you could for him."

Daniel hesitated. "Yes, well…" He inhaled deeply and glanced around at the leafy treetops. "Death comes swiftly, doesn't it?"

"It can, but in your father's case he suffered for many months."

Why did Mark have to say such a thing? Julianna felt like kicking the man in the shin.

"At least you were able to see him before he passed."

Daniel nodded. "Well, now, if you both will excuse me, there are some other guests here whom I haven't seen in half a lifetime."

"Of course, Captain."

"And, Mark, if you'll excuse me also, I need to finish helping Daniel's aunt."

"Certainly, Miss Wayland." He bowed courteously.

Turning, she sent Daniel a roll of her eyes and then caught his amused little smirk before she reentered the house.

☙❦❧

Hours later, after all the guests had left and the kitchen was cleaned, the Sundbergs bid Julianna good night, and she entered the smallest of the three upstairs bedrooms. The Dunbars opted for a hotel room in the city, and Julianna had thought that Daniel would prefer it too, but he chose to stay in the room in the basement. Mrs. Sundberg said she'd stayed there after she was hired to care for Sam's stepmother. Sam had rescued her from a bad situation involving her aunt and uncle and they'd fallen in love. Julianna enjoyed hearing the tale as she helped wash and dry the supper dishes. In fact, just thinking of it made her smile.

She peeled off her brown traveling dress and hung it in the wardrobe. She didn't own anything black—not anymore, since the people at the dress shop in New York tossed her maid's uniform into the hearth with their noses pinched. Standing only in her undergarments, she felt cooler, although this upper room felt much warmer than even the kitchen downstairs.

Moving to the washstand, Julianna splashed her face and bare arms before glancing around. She'd been told that this was Miss Mary Sundberg's bedroom at one time. Now Mary occupied the largest one, and tonight Agnes and her mother would share the room that had once belonged to Mr. Sundberg and his brother, Jackson. Their bunks, however, had been taken down and replaced with two sturdy frames and mattresses. Julianna had offered to share that room so Mrs. Sundberg could have some time to herself, but Agnes insisted upon her mother's company and had, for the last two nights, slept in the same bed as her mother. The little girl was taking her father's death quite hard.

Once in her nightclothes Julianna extinguished the lamp and sat by the opened window, hoping to feel a breeze. None came. But in the stillness, sounds of buzzing and then an animal's throaty moan off in the distance filled the darkened space outside. Were they signals of danger? Living all her life in a busy city that didn't sleep in spite of nightfall, Julianna never heard such noises. And the suffocating heat up here made her restless.

Padding across the floor, Julianna found her wrapper and pulled it on. She walked into the hallway and saw no lights shining from under the other bedroom doors. Quietly she took to the stairs with the moon's glow guiding her path. When she reached the bottom, she opened the door, and cooler air fell over her. How could the Sundbergs sleep in such high temperatures?

Making her way through the kitchen, Julianna headed for the yard. The day's heat and humidity had abated somewhat, but it was hardly what she'd consider comfortable. The buzzing noises, however, had lessened now that she'd come downstairs and outside.

"What are you doing still awake?"

She startled at Daniel's voice and pulled her wrapper more tightly around her. Then she spotted him, sitting several feet away on one of the benches they'd used for the guests this afternoon.

"I couldn't sleep." She strode toward him. "All that racket was annoying me, and along with the heat, I couldn't bear it a moment longer."

"What racket?"

"Can't you hear it?" She sat down on the bench beside him. "The buzzing and croaking, and—" She heard the moaning again. "What was that?"

Daniel's soft chuckles reached her ears. "That, little one, is a cow, lowing."

"A cow?" She sat back. "I never heard a cow do that before."

Beneath the moon's shine she saw him smile. "The buzzing you hear comes from cicadas. As kids we called them tree crickets. They're in the treetops and sing loudly on particularly hot days."

"Lovely music." Julianna didn't even attempt to hide her sarcasm. "No wonder it sounded louder from my bedroom window with a tree nearby."

He didn't reply but sat forward and stared at his folded hands.

"Are you thinking about your father?"

"Mm-hmm." He released a long audible sigh. "I've been wondering what went wrong and when it happened."

"His illness, you mean?"

"No. His disappointment in me." Daniel paused. "My parents always talked about the farm and how it would be mine someday. I let them know I didn't want it. I didn't want to become a farmer. After Uncle Jackson fell at Gettysburg, *Bestefar* Sundberg, my father's father, encouraged me to go after my dreams before...before it was too late, such as in the case of Poppa. *Bestefar* told me my father could have been a great politician if he hadn't married *Mor*."

Some of this Julianna had heard already, but she sat by quietly and listened, sensing his need to talk about it.

"I left home, thinking I'd take on the whole Confederate Army single-handedly. But the war soon ended, and that's when I met

233

George Ramsey. I admired him because of his wealth, and since he never had an heir, he more or less adopted me."

Julianna wondered if that had been a blessing or curse. After all, he'd had a perfectly fine family here.

"George insisted I write my parents and let them know I was alive, which I did. Then he sent me to school. Just before I turned twenty, I'd had enough of the classroom and wanted to jump into the business end of things. George decided to whet my appetite and took me on one of his business trips to Chicago. Eliza came with us that year. We were there a year before the Great Fire." A moment's pause, and then Daniel continued. "Since we were that far west, I asked if we could visit my family here in Manitowoc. I wanted to show them how refined and educated I was. I wanted my family to see I had a bright future ahead of me, and it didn't involve farming."

"It doesn't sound like that visit went very well." Julianna had heard it mentioned a time or two.

"No, it didn't. However, it served its purpose." Daniel crossed his legs, placing a booted foot on his opposite knee. "George helped me see that my family couldn't appreciate my talents. They wanted to oppress me with their religious views and use guilt to control me because I didn't want the farm. The Ramseys and I left, and I decided I didn't want anything more to do with my parents. The Ramseys were all the family I needed. But recently I discovered George isn't the upstanding man I thought."

"What do you mean?"

He looked her way and opened his mouth as if to reply, then shook his head. "Never mind. I shouldn't have said anything. They are only suspicions. I have no proof."

"Proof of what?"

"Forget it, Julianna."

She bristled at the sudden sharpness in his tone. "Fine."

"You understand now why I left?"

"Not really. What about your sisters? You might have stayed for them."

Daniel lifted a broad shoulder. "They were so young. And when I last saw them seven years ago, they appeared healthy and happy. I figured they'd grow up and get married and live happy lives. What had I to do with any of it?"

Julianna recalled Adeline's hurt and anger when she'd seen him Saturday night. "Perhaps you were too hasty in erasing them from your life."

"I wondered that very thing when I received *Mor*'s message about Poppa being so ill. I was prepared to right all the wrongs and prove that I was a dutiful son by lending financial support to *Mor* and my sisters. Of course I soon learned that Addy was married. As for my father, I wanted to give him the best medical care possible. Even so, he told me with his dying breath that I shouldn't have come back, that he was a failure—a failure as a father—because I'm a self-made man and not a God-made one." Daniel's voice waxed thick with emotion. "He was disappointed in me right up until the end."

Julianna's heart broke for him. "Oh, he didn't mean it."

"A man doesn't waste his last breath on words he doesn't mean."

She recoiled at his sharp remark.

"Oh, I'm sorry." A weighty sigh. "I didn't mean to burden you with this."

"I'm not burdened, Daniel." She leaned sideways and touched his hand. He caught her fingers and brought them to his lips. Warm tingles flowed down her limbs. How did he manage to make her feel so completely captivated by a single gesture?

She didn't pull her hand away when he held it between the two of his.

"I regret disappointing my father and, apparently, blaming *Mor* for something that was never her fault."

"Families are an oddity, aren't they? Not that I'm any expert." She moved closer to Daniel, and her arm rested up against his. She felt its sinews through his shirtsleeve. "I still worry over Flora from time to time, in spite of all the heartbreak she caused me with her drinking and...her lifestyle."

"It's insanity, isn't it?"

"Mm-hmm..." *And so is sitting out here in the darkness with you.*

Julianna somehow knew that if she wanted it badly enough, Daniel would take her in his arms and kiss her again. She wondered if this was how Mum felt, so willing to give herself over to one man.

At the notion something deep inside of Julianna pricked enough so that she slowly withdrew her hand. Suddenly what she wanted and what she felt warred within her being.

She swallowed. "I–I should go back inside."

"Yes, little one, you should." He stood and helped her to her feet. "You'll be lucky if you don't catch a chill out here."

"A chill?" She smiled. "I've slept outside on cold bricks in the rain and sleet. I think I can manage in hot summer weather."

He didn't reply, only dropped his gaze to the lush grass beneath his boots.

She moved toward the door, although her heart begged her to stay.

"Thank you for listening to me ramble on, Julianna."

"You're welcome. I enjoyed listening." Something occurred to her then. "Just remember that your father was very ill before he died." She faced Daniel once more. "I took a turn spoon-feeding him his porridge, and I thought he seemed...well, exhausted from life. Perhaps he didn't mean what he said about failing."

"Perhaps you're right." He gave a half bow as though they stood in an elegant ballroom. "Again, thank you."

"Again, you're welcome."

She stood there, her gaze locked with his, as moonlight spilled all around them. She swallowed down her desire to be held in his arms, knowing no good would come of it. Not tonight. Not ever. While he might care for her, he planned to marry someone else.

"Good night," she whispered. *I love you!* she longed to scream.

Instead, she forced herself to walk to the house. How she managed to turn the knob, enter, and close the door behind her she would never know.

CHAPTER 22

Y<small>OU SEEM TO</small> be in better spirits today."

Daniel paused from cleaning the fish he'd caught this morning and glanced at *Mor*. "Yes, I guess I am feeling better."

"Mary saw you coming with the string of brook trout." *Mor* lowered herself into a nearby chair on the porch. The day had just begun, but her eyelids drooped and the lines around her mouth looked more pronounced. "She is preparing the stove in the kitchen."

"Good. Fresh trout will make a tasty breakfast." He turned the fish in his palm. "You look worn out, *Mor*."

"*Ja*, I am, Daniel. For months I dozed in a chair beside your father. I never slept. Now that I can lie down in a bed, I still cannot sleep. My body hurts and my heart is broken. I will miss your father so much."

He believed it and realized now that Poppa and *Mor* always had a close relationship, although there were times they didn't see eye to eye. He'd been wrong about a number of things. "I had always thought that you wanted Poppa to farm but he wanted to be in politics."

"Oh, *ja*, Sam would have made a good politician. His gift was mediation."

"*Bestefar* told me that you were the one to persuade Poppa to farm."

Mor's brow furrowed. "When did he tell you that?"

"After Uncle Jack fell at Gettysburg."

"No, that is not correct." She dropped her gaze. Her white-blonde hair was in its usual braid that ran around the circumference of her head. "Your *bestefar*'s mind slipped a little after Jack was killed. Suddenly he only remembered a time that happened before you were born, Daniel. Slowly it returned—for a time. But the truth about your poppa is he loved that land outside of Manitowoc. He loved this land too, but the farm we had to sell only months ago was special because it was ours—Sam's and mine—and we built a life for ourselves there. Sam loved the feel of the soil, loved to plant and watch things grow. He saw firsthand God's creation and experienced God's provision."

"Except for the last couple of years."

Mor managed a nod. "Yes, these have been lean years—and not just for us, Daniel. But for Mary too. Out of need she has sold much of her land and clung to only a few acres, including the pond and orchards. She bartered acreage for a farmhand's labor; otherwise she could not stay here alone."

He squinted into the sun. "I had wondered about it."

"For us, everything changed when your father had a stroke. Things grew desperate." Obvious grief constrained her voice. "It nearly killed me to sell the farm, even though your poppa agreed to it. He knew I couldn't manage."

Guilt threatened, but Daniel tamped down the feeling as he cleaned the last fish. Somehow he knew *Mor* spoke the truth. He'd been wrong to blame her all these years for stymieing Poppa's political career. If he'd taken the time to think it over, he would have realized his father made his own choices. Sam Sundberg had been a man to follow his convictions—which was what probably irked *Bestefar* in the first place.

A grin tugged at Daniel's mouth. But then he glanced at his mother again. "*Mor*, I suggest you rest today."

She lifted a hand in protest. "No, I am all right. Just sad."

"I want you to rest." Unable to help a tiny smile, Daniel lifted the cast iron frying pan in which he'd placed the cleaned fish and pushed to his feet. "I don't want to see you washing dishes or cooking. Nothing. Understand? You've been through an extremely difficult time."

An annoyed glance was her reply.

He decided to pull rank. "I'm the man in the family now, right? So I'm telling you to take it easy." Daniel knew his mother wouldn't rest unless someone ordered her. Even then, there wasn't any guarantee she'd mind the command. He glanced at the fish then regarded *Mor* again. "I'm taking these inside so Aunt Mary can fry them up. May I get you a cup of coffee while I'm in the kitchen?"

A light chuckle escaped her. "Your aunt will not allow you to set one foot inside her immaculate kitchen like that." Her gaze roamed over his soaked attire. "Did you fall into the water?"

"No." Mirth tugged at his mouth. "It felt so cool, I decided on a quick swim. It did wonders for me."

"*Ja*, I imagine so. It will be another hot day today."

"Perhaps after you eat, you should swim too. Take Julianna, Agnes, and Mary with you."

"Maybe I will." A smile lingered on his mother's lips. "But first coffee would be good," she replied in Norwegian. "*Takk.*"

"You're welcome. And I mean it about resting today." Daniel knew that wound-up-tight feeling. "You know," he began, "there were times on the sea when I would tie myself to the helm and battle a tempest for days without sleeping. Survival instincts took over. Adrenaline surged through my veins. Then, after the storm passed and an officer relieved me of my post, I'd try to sleep, but I couldn't seem to cut off that continued flow of energy." He gave her a gentle smile. "Maybe that's how you feel—you're still in survival mode."

His words had an obvious affect on *Mor*, and she inhaled a sob, nodding.

A wave of compassion crashed over him. How broken and sad she seemed, and it pained him to see his strong-willed, brave, and determined mother this way. And, yes, she was all those things. Until now he hadn't appreciated her qualities—or her.

Setting the pan of fish on the grass, he crossed the lawn and lifted his mother into his arms. She sagged against him and cried into his shoulder.

"He's gone. My Sam is gone."

"Shh, Momma." Sadness, as heavy as an anchor, pressed down on him. "Don't cry."

Slowly she raised her head and stared at him. "What did you say?" An errant tear trickled down her cheek.

Daniel brushed it away. "I said, don't cry. It was a weak attempt at comforting you."

"No, not that." Her countenance brightened. "You called me Momma."

He thought back on his verbiage and grinned. "So I did." It had come out rather automatically.

"You haven't called me Momma since you left home at fifteen. I missed you so much. When you came back, you were all grown up. My boy was gone. He had turned into a man who called me *Mor*."

"It means the same thing...mother."

"Not to me. To me it signified a great wall between us."

"Because I'm a self-made man, not God-made, isn't that correct?" Hardness gripped Daniel's heart. He released his mother and stepped back.

She looked perplexed.

Daniel pushed out the truth. "Those were among Poppa's last words to me, and they will be forever etched in my memory."

"I cannot undo what he said, nor can I apologize for him." His mother wiped the wetness from her black cotton gown.

She was right, of course. And she likely felt the same way, and it angered and hurt Daniel all the more. "Even with all my accomplishments, I am still a disappointment to my parents?"

"We were never disappointed with your achievements." Wearing a sad smile, she dropped back down into the chair, as if her legs wouldn't support her a moment longer. "I moved past the fact that you did not want to inherit the farm many years ago. You chose your own way, not ours."

"But I'm not a God-made man." Daniel still didn't quite understand what his father meant by it. "I told Adeline yesterday that God is either in control or He isn't. Later I wondered, if I'm so horrible, why doesn't He take my life?"

"You are not horrible, Daniel. I am proud of your accomplishments and thankful that you are here now to help me." She smiled. "My son, the respected sea captain. If he had lived, my father, your namesake, would be so proud of you too."

He forced a smile then lifted the pan of fish and headed for the house. His mother had spoken the words he'd wanted to hear. But why hadn't they assuaged the intense yearning within his soul?

⊛⊛⊛

Songs of dozens of birds filled the morning air as Julianna traipsed behind Agnes, Mrs. Sundberg, and Miss Mary. They were all intent on a swim in the pond. The smell of dew-dampened vegetation reached Julianna's nose as they passed through the apple orchard. She'd never taken such a picturesque stroll, and it reminded her of how she and Flora used to daydream about living in the country one day.

"Momma, it's the Fourth of July; couldn't we head for home? If we leave now, we'd make tonight's festivities."

Julianna turned and spied Mrs. Sundberg's smile.

"Only one so young," the older woman said, "could travel for five long hours in the summer heat and still have energy for festivities."

Miss Mary laughed, and Julianna had to admit to feeling amused.

"But it's so sad here," Agnes pouted. "I want to feel happy again, and there will be food and dancing right outside of our store! Then, later, the fireworks will light the sky over the lake."

Mrs. Sundberg halted and faced her youngest, causing Julianna to stop as well. Miss Mary continued walking up head.

"And we should leave your aunt Mary alone so soon after she lost her dear brother?" Mrs. Sundberg's voice was firm yet whisper-soft.

Agnes's chin dropped. "But Poppa was sick for so long, and he's in a better place."

"But Mary and I—and Daniel—are not. We are mourning, so get the notion of celebrating out of her head." Mrs. Sundberg squared her shoulders. "Besides, you heard your brother at breakfast say that we will stay a week. He means what he says—and so do I."

"Yes, Momma."

Their walk continued, and soon they reached a clearing, which sported a clear, lovely pond. Julianna couldn't wait to shed her clothes and take a dip.

As she undressed, she glanced in Agnes's direction. Her heart went out to the lamb. Of course sadness abode in the Sundbergs' hearts, but she was glad that Daniel made the decision to stay here at Miss Mary's. The decision meant altering his plans to return to New York. She wondered how Mr. Ramsey would take the news of Daniel's delay. After breakfast he'd left for Green Bay to meet the Dunbar men and inform them of the change in itinerary and to send a telegram to Mr. Ramsey. Talk about fireworks…

"Too bad Julianna won't find out how Americans celebrate their country's birthday," Agnes said.

"Oh, it's all right. I'm British anyhow." She laughed at her own tart reply.

"Are you sorry you left England?" Mrs. Sundberg hung her skirt over a tall-standing bush.

"Not a bit sorry." Except she did wonder how Flora fared.

"What about the store, Kristin?" Mary's gaze lit on Mrs. Sundberg. "Will you lose business?"

"I know from the previous owners that sales are down over the holidays, so it is better that we stay here for a time where we can all be together. The store can wait."

Julianna thought she saw a shadow of worry creep across Mrs. Sundberg's features just before the woman turned and strode toward the water.

"Daniel said we're not supposed to think about money problems," Agnes said. "He's going to take care of us."

"And it's about time!" Mary Sundberg squared her shoulders. Her mouth was set in the same grim line that formed whenever Daniel was present or even mentioned. Clearly her anger toward her nephew hadn't abated over the years.

Julianna decided to change the subject as she followed Mrs. Sundberg into the pond. "It's so lovely out here. You're very fortunate, Miss Mary, to live surrounded by nature." She dipped her toes into the water. It felt cool and promised to be thoroughly refreshing. "Back in London there are few, if any, wide open spaces."

"Yes, I know I am blessed." Miss Mary came to stand alongside Julianna.

Mrs. Sundberg spoke up. "Long ago my uncle Lars owned the land on the other side of the creek that runs through the orchard." Mrs. Sundberg pointed to the place where the land came together, squeezing the pond's end so only a small portion of water flowed out before she indicated to more trees.

"After Kristin's uncle decided to leave Green Bay," Mary continued, "my father purchased the land. We planted pear trees there. Ma always wanted pear trees, and Pa loved her so much that he gave her whatever she asked for." Mary's brown eyes rounded with sorrow. "She only enjoyed the first year's harvest before God took her home to heaven. I still miss her."

"I never knew my mum." Julianna waded into the pond.

"I'm sorry to hear it." Compassion laced Mrs. Sundberg's tone. "But even tragedies in life are part of God's plan for our greater good."

"It's hard to imagine." Julianna worked her lower lip between her teeth, wondering how bad things could work out for one's greater good. But there was so much about God she still had to learn.

Once more her gaze roamed her surroundings. She breathed in, enjoying the way the air tasted so fresh and clean—another difference from London.

Agnes tossed a square of soap at Julianna and laughed when Julianna missed catching it.

"Now you have to dive for it," the girl taunted.

"I should say not. You're the one who threw it."

"Can't you swim?"

"I can swim just fine." Julianna narrowed her gaze. "But I can give you a dunking even better!"

"What for?" Agnes pointed to the soap, bobbing to the pond's surface. Her giggles ricocheted across. "The soap is right here!"

"Lower your voice, Agnes." Mrs. Sundberg wagged her head. "Young ladies should not be so boisterous."

"Yes, Momma." Agnes held her nose and dunked under water.

"I was a bit boisterous meself." Julianna felt guilty for egging the girl on. She peered at Miss Mary. "I hope we haven't disturbed your neighbors."

Agnes's head appeared above water not far off.

Mrs. Sundberg said something in Norwegian and gave Julianna a speculative glance.

"Now that's not fair." Julianna disliked it when the ladies reverted to their native tongue and she couldn't understand them. "What did you just say? I suppose you think I'm too skinny. Well, it's a problem I've had all me life. But I can say this much. I've eaten well since arriving in America."

"I would never speak ill of you in Norwegian or English. That would be most rude." Mrs. Sundberg's blue eyes searched Julianna's face.

She felt somewhat ashamed for accusing Daniel's mother of such behavior. "But how would I know that?" She'd met Mrs. Sundberg less than a week ago.

"You make a good point." Understanding pooled in her eyes. "When you get to know us better, you'll find that we are Christians who want to honor God with our speech. I spoke in Norwegian so I wouldn't frighten you. You see, Indians roam freely on this property. Mary is half Oneida, which is a particular tribe in this region."

Julianna's gaze sailed to Mary. "You're part Indian then?" She looked back at Mrs. Sundberg. "Was Mr. Sundberg part Indian too?"

She shook her head. "Mary is his half-sister, but they were very close."

"I adored my big brother, Sam." Mary's features fell.

The sorrow in Mary's voice crimped Julianna's heart. She imagined her adoration for her big brother matched Agnes's and Adeline's for Daniel.

"Prejudice against Indians is prevalent in Green Bay and else-where." A challenging spark entered Mary's cinnamon-colored eyes.

"So I ask you, Julianna, how do you feel about being a guest of an Oneida woman?"

Agnes stood still to hear Julianna's answer.

"I don't hold your heritage against you, and I hope, Miss Mary, that you're not offended by mine."

"No, I'm not." Her features softened.

Mrs. Sundberg smiled. "As for the Wisconsin natives, there is no need to be afraid, Julianna."

"Oh, I'm not afraid." Could Indians be any worse than a drunken sailor intent upon having his way?

"I am looking forward to getting to know you better." Mrs. Sundberg smiled at Julianna. "You have been a great help to me. I am glad Daniel brought you here."

"I'm glad too." She surveyed the countryside again. Glad couldn't begin to describe how Julianna felt. Surely this life in America was a dream come true!

⚭⚭⚭

"Bad news?"

"Indeed." Standing outside the telegraph office, Daniel looked up from the message he held.

Jed Dunbar clamped his hand down on Daniel's shoulder. "Anything my sons and I can do to help?"

"Thank you, but I'm afraid not." Daniel stared at the telegram again.

He'd wired George to say he'd remain in Green Bay for the next week, perhaps longer if need be. His family needed the reprieve. While waiting on a reply, he'd eaten lunch with the Dunbars. Inadequate shipping was definitely one of their concerns, and the topic occupied the table talk. Daniel did his best to advise them. But now, here it was evening, and the reply from George didn't have a happy ending.

His investigator in London had located Flora and confirmed her story about being employed by Olson Tolbert. Flora had been located, but shortly after the interview with the investigator, she succumbed to an illness caused by heaving drinking. Daniel knew Julianna would be heartbroken to learn the news of her sister's death. In the meantime George wanted him home post haste.

"I've been ordered back to New York." As he spoke the words, vexation welled in him. Couldn't George understand that he needed to settle matters here? Of course he probably worried that Daniel would fall in love with Julianna. *Too late for that!*

"A shame you're leaving," Jed replied. "We're enjoying your company." A wagon rattled noisily by, momentarily inhibiting conversation. "But if you must return to New York so soon, please stay in town tonight and be our guest for dinner."

"I think Adeline would appreciate it," Will added, tucking his thumbs into his belt loops.

"Thank you. I accept." Facing Julianna wasn't something Daniel relished at the moment, even at the expense of his youngest sister's disappointment.

"Perhaps you can give me suggestions on how to better run my hotel in Manitowoc." Mark gave him an eager smile as they crossed the busy thoroughfare. Strains from a nearby band, playing a lively march, wafted to Daniel's ears on the hot July breeze. "I want to hear about the various establishments you've encountered during your travels."

"All right." Perhaps the topic would keep Julianna from permeating his thoughts as usual.

Nevertheless, the fact remained: he would have to tell her the truth, at least about her sister's passing, some time between now and the day he left for New York.

CHAPTER 23

*T*HE FOLLOWING TUESDAY morning the luggage was loaded into the buggy, and Julianna was the last to hug Mary Sundberg good-bye.

"You're welcome here anytime." The older woman smiled into her face. "I'd enjoy getting to know you better."

"Thank you." Warmth and acceptance like she'd never known enveloped Julianna.

The Sundbergs were already waiting in the vehicle, and Daniel helped her into the backseat beside Agnes. Within minutes they were off.

The mood was lighter as the buggy rattled down the dusty road —all except for Daniel's. He'd become more of a puzzlement these last four days than ever. He acted distant and kept his gaze averted. Julianna got the feeling he no longer cared for her at all.

Well, all's the better. He would soon take his leave, and Julianna would have to forget him. An impossibility. She resided with his family, and she'd always love him. It was an awkward situation to be sure, especially if Daniel ever decided to bring his countess to Wisconsin.

They made the same two stops on the way home, once to stretch their legs and water the horses and another to eat. By the time they rolled into Manitowoc, evening had settled over the town.

Daniel halted the buggy in front of Mrs. Sundberg's shop. He helped her down and then swung Agnes from the vehicle. She giggled as her feet hit the dirt road.

"Miss Wayland?" A familiar-sounding voice came from the opposite side of the buggy, and Julianna turned. "I've been watching for you."

"Why, as I live and breathe, it's Jeremy Kidwell! What are you doing in Manitowoc?"

"I came for you." He lifted her from the buggy. "The captain said he was bringing you here, and I followed just as soon as I was able."

Despite his friendly smile, Julianna felt a measure of alarm. He glanced at Daniel, who had already made his way around the buggy.

"Kidwell." He offered his right hand.

"Hello, Captain." Jeremy shook it with exuberance.

Calm as can be, Daniel introduced his mother and sister while Julianna's heart beat fast in her chest. He came for her? What was that supposed to mean?

"I checked into the hotel, and Mr. Dunbar said I'd find you arriving shortly." Peering down at Julianna, Jeremy smiled. The late sunshine caused his carrot-red hair to glow brighter.

"How nice." Her gaze flitted to Daniel, and for the first time in days he returned her stare.

"Why don't you ladies go on inside and get freshened up. Jeremy and I will be along soon. Perhaps he'll assist me with the luggage."

"My pleasure."

Julianna followed the women into the apartment behind the shop.

"Who is that man?" Mrs. Sundberg whispered.

Agnes looked on with wide, curious blue eyes.

"He was the cook on board the *Allegiance*, the ship that brought me to America. He asked me to travel farther west with him, but

I didn't want to go. That's why Daniel offered to bring me here to work for you." Julianna glanced out the window and saw the men set off for the apartment with their arms filled with baggage. She turned back to Mrs. Sundberg. "I don't want to go with him."

"Then don't," Agnes said simply.

Julianna couldn't be sure it was that easy. Daniel hadn't been himself lately. His mother mourned her recently deceased husband and had a shop to run. Would Julianna be more hindrance than help?

"No one here will force you to do something you do not wish to do." Mrs. Sundberg took Julianna's hand. "You are welcome to continue staying here."

"Yes, stay, Julianna," Agnes begged.

She smiled. "Thank you." She glanced from her back to Mrs. Sundberg. "Thank you, both." The assurance gave Julianna a renewed sense of confidence.

Unless, of course, Daniel had a shift in heart. Perhaps he'd prefer to be rid of her. After all, he'd been supporting her financially since the ship anchored in New York.

The men entered with Mark Dunbar on their heels.

"I'm happy to see you all made it safely home from Green Bay." He and his family, along with Adeline, Will, and the baby, had left Saturday. Mark's gaze came to rest on Julianna. "That man you told me about, that love of your life who you met in London..." He clapped Jeremy on the shoulder and grinned sheepishly. "Here he is!"

Julianna felt herself pale as Jeremy set down the valises near the parlor's settee.

"Great balls of fire, Miss Wayland, I didn't realize you loved me so much until Mr. Dunbar, here, told me."

Daniel gave her a hard, quizzical stare, and Julianna felt her temples begin to throb.

"I can explain." The words were but a whisper. She looked at Mark, then Jeremy. "I'm sorry, but there's been a terrible misunderstanding."

Daniel turned. "Listen, fellas, it's been a long day. Let's leave the ladies and resume this conversation in the morning."

Julianna lowered her head and kept her eyes on one of the polished floorboards. What a mess, and all because of Jeremy's persistence and Mark's assuming nature.

Mrs. Sundberg had seen the men out the door and returned to stand near Julianna. "Let's unpack, and I will pour us some cool tea. I store it in a jar and lower it into the well where it remains very cold and tastes so refreshing."

"Momma, I'd like some too." Agnes picked up her bag and dragged it toward the bedroom.

Mrs. Sundberg's gaze remained on Julianna. "No one will force you to go with Jeremy."

"Maybe Daniel—"

"No, he will not." Kindness shone from her blue eyes, their color more pronounced because of Mrs. Sundberg's black dress. "If you want to stay with Agnes and me, then so be it."

Julianna prayed it was that simple.

An hour or so later Daniel returned. "Julianna, I must talk to you."

She steeled herself. *Here it comes.*

"Let's go for a ride. We'll take Agnes along for propriety's sake."

Amazingly the girl had overheard the suggestion from the next room. "Oh, yes...I'll come along." She trotted toward them. "I'm not too tired for another buggy ride, especially if it's a joyride."

Daniel grinned, but he still didn't look happy, and that alarmed Julianna.

"Oh, all right. Give me a moment." She collected her lightweight shawl and tied her hat's ribbon beneath her chin. As she strode for the door, Mrs. Sundberg caught her elbow.

"Make your wishes known." She spoke the hushed words close to Julianna's ear. "If you want to stay here, then tell Daniel. He will agree to it."

"Thank you." Despite the confidence her tone exuded, Julianna wasn't so sure. Daniel had been cool toward her for days now.

They left the Sundbergs' apartment and strolled to the walk and to an awaiting buggy.

"Where are we going?"

"You'll see." Daniel allowed Agnes to sit beside him in the front seat before he helped Julianna into the back. His tone sounded rather ominous, but she managed to smile at Agnes.

Daniel climbed aboard and took up the horses' reins. A nearly full moon rose above the lake in glowing splendor. When they'd gone a short distance out of town, he pulled over and halted.

"Agnes, I must talk to Julianna about a private matter. We'll stand just a few feet away, and I'll tether the horses around this sapling." He nodded toward the small but sturdy-looking tree nearby. "Will you be all right alone for just a few minutes?"

"I'll be fine, Daniel. I'm almost grown up now."

Julianna smiled at the remark and noted Daniel's amused expression…until he looked her way. Her heart ached as his expression turned back to stone. With some trepidation she accepted his hand and got down from the buggy. She followed his lead across a grassy parcel that jutted out over the lake, providing a clear view of Manitowoc's harbor.

Daniel pointed to the ship closest to them. "Can you see that steamer?"

Julianna dipped her head. "Yes."

"It leaves tomorrow at noon, and I'll be on board."

The news came as no surprise, although sorrow welled up inside her. It was then Julianna realized she'd held out a thread of hope that he'd change his mind and stay. What lunacy!

"I won't be around to fend off Kidwell. He's in the tavern tonight playing cards."

"No matter. I can take care of meself."

Daniel didn't acknowledge her remark. "If there's trouble, either later tonight when he's had one too many drinks or tomorrow after he's sobered up, you'll have to alert the sheriff."

Julianna grimaced. The last thing she wanted to deal with was a drunken seafaring man. "I'm not going with Jeremy. I want to stay here."

"I figured as much."

"Mark assumed I was pining over some man because I said I never want to get married."

"You owe me no explanations, Julianna."

The note of disinterest in his tone discouraged her from saying more. He'd once told her he cared. When had he stopped? Oh, but what difference did it make anyhow?

"I have something to tell you, and it's not pleasant, I'm afraid."

What else could there be?

"George grew particularly curious about you the moment he met you, so he hired an investigator in London."

"What?" She tipped her head. "Curious about me?"

"Allow me to finish, please."

Julianna folded her arms.

"The investigator found Flora, and she verified everything George wanted to know."

"Like what?"

"Like…" Daniel's shoulders rose with his deep inhalation. "…your mother's name and her occupation. Flora basically verified everything you'd said."

"It's the truth!"

"Yes, and it led to George uncovering your father's true identity."

Julianna felt her jaw drop. "Me father?"

Beneath the moon's bright glow, she saw his nod. "Julianna, as much as you dislike George Ramsey, he is your biological father."

It took a second to register, but then Julianna burst out in laughter. "That's ridiculous. A fable if I ever heard one!"

"I'm afraid it's the truth. George recognized you because, he said, you're the spitting image of your mother. He is—was—the sailor known as *Christopher Columbus*."

"No..." Incredulity made her head spin.

Daniel reached for her elbow.

She pulled away. "But I guess I shouldn't be surprised. Flora said me father was a scoundrel, and I knew from the instant I met George Ramsey that he was one too."

"That's not true. And if it's any consolation, George tried to find your mother and you."

"Find us? Well, he didn't try very hard now, did he?"

Daniel didn't answer.

"So the scoundrel is filthy rich while his daughter and her half-sister starve and nearly freeze to death in the winter's cold." Julianna nodded. "Sounds like something George Ramsey would allow to happen."

"Stop it, Julianna. You don't know George. He's an honorable man."

"Honorable in what way?"

"He told me that he loved your mother very much."

"A lot of good that did me—or her." Then she remembered the document she signed. "So that's why Mr. Ramsey"—the name almost choked her—"that's why he insisted I sign a contract." She'd heard about indiscretionary scandals. Mr. Tolbert had needed to sweep a few under the rug himself. "He feared I'd cause a stir and make demands."

"Yes." Daniel's admittance was nearly inaudible.

"And you knew all along?"

He paused. "Yes, I did."

"But I trusted you, and you purposely misled me." Her fists clenched. "Not that it matters. I don't want a single coin from George Ramsey. But you—"

"That's right. I betrayed you, Julianna. You have good reason to hate me. My loyalties were put to the test, and George took precedence over my family here—and even my feelings for you."

"You're a fool, Captain Sundberg. Honorable, yes, but a fool."

"So hate me for it, Julianna. That's what I want."

"Why?

"Because I can never love you, and there's no future in pining over a man with whom there is no future."

At his self-deception the fight left her. He really thought wealth would make him happy? Suddenly she pitied the man before her. "It sounds like you hate yourself more than I ever could. Besides"—she turned toward the calm lake waters—"I could never hate you."

"As you wish." His voice dripped with painful indifference. "However, there's something more you need to know."

"What is it?" Julianna remained with her back to him. Her heart already felt numb. What more could he say to hurt her?

"Flora is dead."

"What?" She spun around. "No! How can it be?"

"It's true. I'm sorry." His tone sounded compassionate, more like the Captain Daniel Sundberg she'd come to love. "Your sister died as of a result of her frequent and heavy drinking. There was nothing you or anyone could have done to save her."

Tears blurred her vision, and her chin trembled, but Julianna willed herself not to cry. "Serves her right, the lush." Anguish squeezed her heart until she felt like doubling over. Her sister. Flora. *Dead*!

Daniel stepped forward and collected her in his arms. She fell against him.

"She was probably sick a long while, little one." He murmured the words softly against her temple. "It wouldn't have mattered if you'd been there to care for her or not."

Don't cry. Don't cry. Tears never solved anything. Isn't that what Flora always told her? Flora scoffed at tears, and Julianna could still imagine the sting of her sister's slap across her face for being such a *baby*. Instead Julianna forced herself to listen to the steady, rhythmical beat of Daniel's heart.

"Don't leave me," she breathed. "Everyone in the world has left me. Please…" She pulled back and stared up into Daniel's face and blinked away more unwanted moisture. "…please, don't go."

"Listen to me." The hardened sea captain returned to his voice, and Daniel gripped her chin. "Don't beg. Not now. Not ever again." He sternly ground out each vowel. "You're a Ramsey, and Ramseys never beg."

Anger flashed and exploded through Julianna's being. She struggled out of his embrace and pushed him away. She took several steps back. "I'll never be a Ramsey, and you hear me." She pointed a finger at him. "I'm going to repay every coin George Ramsey spent on me, on me clothes, shoes, hats—*everything!*"

"I never used a cent of George's money, Julianna. I've told you that before. I'm a man of means and important in my own right."

"But what sort of man are you really once that *means and importance* is stripped away? A life on the street is only a bad business decision or addictive habit away." A cynical guffaw came from somewhere deep within her. "I've shared scraps with wealthier men than you and George Ramsey in London's gutter."

Daniel folded his arms and gave her a bored stare. "Are you quite finished?"

"Yes, but I'm very disappointed in you, Daniel Sundberg, and

I was wrong. I'll admit it now. You're not the honorable man I thought."

She ran past him and to the buggy, quickly stuffing her sorrow and disbelief so deep inside herself that she could barely breathe. But she preferred it to upsetting Agnes. Crawling up into the backseat, she actually smiled at the girl.

"Julianna? Are you all right?"

"I'll be fine." *Once the shock wears off.* "My sister died." She could say that much. She folded her hands tightly in her lap. "Now I know how you and your family must feel, losing Mr. Sundberg."

"Oh, Julianna…" Agnes scampered into the seat beside her then hugged her arm. "It hurts, doesn't it?"

"Yes," she eked out. A single tear leaked from the corner of her eye. She blinked, unwilling to shed more.

Daniel took his time returning to the buggy. He said nothing as he untied the reins and climbed in. Moments later they rode in silence back to the shop.

⚬⚬⚬

Sunshine streamed through the front windows of the hotel lobby as Daniel checked out. Mark stood behind the counter and stamped his bill PAID IN FULL. They exchanged the usual pleasantries, and then Daniel left for his sister Adeline's home. Located west of town, the saltbox-styled house looked freshly painted and well kept.

Adeline invited him in and offered him a cup of coffee. He refused. "I have a ship to board."

"Thank you for seeing me before you left."

"I knew I'd never hear the end of it if I didn't." He grinned.

She narrowed her gaze and set her hands on her rounded hips. "I would have hunted you down all the way to New York City."

"I'm sure of it." Daniel's smile grew.

Baby Jacob squawked, and Adeline lifted him from his cradle.

Daniel kissed the boy's forehead. "Good-bye, little man. Stay healthy."

Adeline slung one arm around his neck and hugged him tightly. She stepped back. "When will you return?"

"I don't know." Daniel hadn't planned on coming back, but he couldn't bring himself to say so.

"I wish you Godspeed, my brother."

He placed a kiss on her cheek.

Then it was back to town, where he returned the rented buggy and hired a man to check his valise on the steamer. He walked the rest of the way to his mother's shop, enjoying the feeling of stretching his legs before embarking on a two-day journey wrought with inactivity.

The bell above the door signaled his entry into the shop. His mother and Agnes glanced up from a garment they'd been inspecting.

"I'm leaving for New York and wanted to say good-bye."

Agnes pouted but neither cried nor said a word. She simply hugged Daniel around the waist.

He kissed the crown of her head. "Be good for your momma."

She nodded before pulling away and running out of the shop.

Daniel refused to let his heart feel anything but anticipation of his journey back home—and yes, New York was his home.

Mor crossed the distance and embraced him. "Thank you for everything."

He inclined his head. "A bank account is set up in your name. There's one in Julianna's name as well. Use it for whatever you need and want. The money's there."

Her blue eyes filled with unshed emotion. "I don't know what we would have done without you."

Daniel pulled his mother close for one last good-bye. "Where's Julianna?"

Mor worked her lips together as if to choose her next words carefully. "She is very upset, Daniel, and with good reason."

"I know." He figured she'd never want to see him again. "Tell her good-bye for me and…" He didn't want to say it, and yet he couldn't hold it back either. "Don't let her marry Kidwell, all right? She has other options."

His mother momentarily considered the request. "What do you care if she marries that man or not?"

"I care—and my feelings spread beyond Julianna." He made purposeful strides toward the door.

"We love you too, Daniel. I love you, your sisters love you—and so does Julianna."

Her words snuck up on him, engulfed him, but he wrestled to be free of emotion that would get him nowhere in life. He'd marry Reagan and pour himself into Ramsey Enterprises. That was the plan. Love had no part of it.

Leaving the shop, Daniel closed the door behind him with more force than necessary.

CHAPTER 24

A GUST OF COLD November wind blew through the nearly barren treetops. From the Ramseys' large dining room windows Daniel watched one withered remnant succumb to the battering breeze, tumble to the ground, and skip down the road. He felt as dead as that leaf inside.

The last four months had been sheer misery. More often than not Daniel's mind was in Wisconsin, not in New York. He couldn't seem to focus on bank statements; he got distracted at business dinners. And now...he ought to be listening as the Ramseys planned for the impending trip to London, but Daniel wondered, instead, what Julianna did at this time of morning. Straightening merchandise in *Mor*'s store? Except she'd moved on from the shop now.

Daniel glanced down at Adeline's folded letter. Her third so far. Since returning to New York Daniel had personally seen to it that he received his mail, and back in July, Adeline wrote that Julianna had refused Kidwell's offer. Apparently the man had left for St. Louis, where he'd hoped to join a wagon train going west. What a relief it had been to learn the news. In late September she wrote again to say that her brother-in-law Mark was courting a local schoolteacher. And now this latest missive informed him that Agnes would star in the Christmas play at school and that little Jacob was nearly six months old already. Will and his father still hadn't solved the problems concerning their companies' shipping needs, and Julianna accepted Aunt Mary's offer to move to Green Bay.

She's been so utterly depressed lately, Adeline penned. *She won't talk to anyone, not even Mor or Reverend Wollums, the pastor in Green Bay. I suspect Julianna regrets that she turned down Mr. Kidwell's marriage proposal. Perhaps living in the country will do her some good.*

Kidwell's offer? Julianna didn't regret that. Daniel felt certain of it. The man she loved was himself, just as she'd vowed. Daniel didn't doubt it for an instant. Perhaps she missed him just as much as Daniel missed her. He could only hope...

"Did you hear what I said, son?"

Daniel glanced over his shoulder and saw the lines in George's forehead deepen. "No, sorry." He turned. "My mind was elsewhere."

"It's been there quite often of late."

Daniel replied with an apologetic shrug and saw Eliza set her delicate porcelain teacup down on its matching saucer.

"We leave for England in a couple of weeks, dear," she said, "and you still haven't selected the countess's engagement ring." She looked at George wide-eyed and displeased. "The jeweler is waiting."

"Fine, fine..." George's gaze went from his wife's frowning countenance to Daniel. "Stop at the jeweler's this afternoon, will you?"

"I don't feel much like shopping." He flipped open the top of his sister's letter and stared at her neat, circular penmanship. Thoughts of Julianna so despondent that she needed a rest in the country broke his heart all over again. He regretted hurting her and his family. He regretted the rift between Aunt Mary and himself. He'd always loved her—loved all of them. He just hadn't realized how much until now.

His father's words continued to play in his head along with

Julianna's announcement that she was disappointed in him, that he wasn't so noble after all.

"Daniel, please stop moping." Impatience constrained George's voice. "It's quite unbecoming for the new executive of Ramsey Enterprises."

"And what about the countess's holiday ball?" Eliza sounded exasperated. "The countess asked me to reply weeks ago."

Irritation peaked inside Daniel. "Tell her we won't attend." *There!*

Eliza's lower jaw dropped in indignation, and George cleared his throat in objection.

Daniel softened. "Oh, I'm sorry. I don't know what's wrong with me." He tried to shake off the demons that had been riding him since he boarded the lake steamer and left Manitowoc. All he knew was that he was as depressed as Julianna reportedly felt, and it was his fault. She'd begged him not to leave her. He could still feel her in his arms. He could see her misty eyes, looking up at him, pleading…

God, forgive me! Daniel prayed that one hundred times a day. Yet he felt so empty and…*unforgiven.* He'd become the king of louts, ruthless, unredeemed…hopeless.

Do something about it! The sudden prompting within was so strong that Daniel knew he couldn't—and shouldn't—refuse.

"Eliza, will you excuse us? I need to speak with George privately in his office."

"Of course." She sent him a weak smile. One hand patted her well-coiffured brown hair, indicating her growing impatience.

George stood, and Daniel led the way into his office.

Entering behind him, George closed the doors. "What's this all about?"

Daniel faced his benefactor and friend. "I can't do this. I can't marry Reagan."

"Bah!" George waved a hand. "She's gotten over that article Mabel

Brunning sold to the *Times* along with that scandalous photograph of you dancing with that…that scamp. Eliza explained it wasn't as intimate as it appeared. You were merely being polite. The countess has forgiven you."

Daniel didn't give a hoot about that article and photograph. He'd expected a stunt like that from Mrs. Brunning. As for Reagan, she could hardly feel scandalized. Daniel suspected she'd been in far more compromising situations in his absence, although none had been published in a newspaper…yet.

"It's not that, George."

"What then?" The older man's brows knitted into a frown as he sat behind his polished desk. "You no longer think she's a suitable match?"

"That's right."

Wearing a contemplative frown, George folded his hands over a few papers. "Do you have someone else in mind?"

The question sounded more like a challenge—one Daniel would accept. "George, I'm in love with your daughter."

"What daughter? I have no daughter."

"Julianna."

"Oh, for pity's sake!" George wagged his head, evidence that he was irked.

"George, don't you care that she has your blood running through her veins? Don't you want to get to know her? Julianna is bright, witty, a tad outspoken…" Daniel nearly grinned. "And she's competent, lovely, sensitive—"

"Stop it!" The flat of George's hand came down hard on the desktop, causing the tall lamp to teeter precariously. "This is madness. Can't you see?"

"No. Pretending Julianna doesn't exist is madness, and I, for one, cannot abide it any longer." Daniel ran his finger reverently across the broken seal on Adeline's letter. "There's something else I cannot pretend to tolerate."

"Oh?"

"Your interception of my mail, from my family to me. For years they tried to reach me. You kept those letters from me, George. Why?"

Sitting back with a confident air, George said, "I burned them because you'd severed ties with those people in Wisconsin. Remember? They didn't understand you or respect your decisions. Eliza and I are your *true* parents."

Daniel bristled. "They were my letters, George, and I should have been able to do with them as I pleased. It wasn't up to you to decide to destroy them."

"I didn't want you to become double-minded—like you are now. Look at yourself. What good are you this way?"

"Indeed. What good am I?" It took great effort for Daniel to keep his temper in check. "Have you so little regard for my feelings? Am I just some sort of prize horse to you, one that you've groomed, trained, and primed for the race?"

"Don't be ridiculous." George snorted and began sorting through papers on his desk.

"I love Julianna. Do you hear me? I love her, and I can't stand the thought of my future without her."

George shot to his feet. Anger flashed in his eyes. "And you're willing to ruin my good name? Our good name?"

Daniel softened. "No one's perfect, George. Plenty of men before you have had indiscretions. It's not like you were married at the time. Besides, it happened so long ago."

"Have you any idea what you're asking me to do?"

"Yes. Own up to your mistakes. I'd like an apology for burning my personal mail, and I want you to be honest with Eliza."

"She'll leave me."

"I doubt it." So he cared enough about Eliza to want her to stay. Daniel often wondered. "Your wife is a reasonable and compassionate woman."

George tucked his hands into the pockets of his gray waistcoat and stared at an invisible spot on the plastered ceiling. "I am sorry for intercepting your mail, Daniel. I knew it was wrong when I did it." His gaze moved to Daniel's. "But I also wanted to protect you— protect you from any guilt and pain they might have caused."

"You never read them?"

George shook his head.

Daniel thought that was something. "All's forgiven for intercepting my mail, and I actually appreciate your motive for burning them."

"Good. I'm glad that's settled." He seated himself behind his desk once more.

"And the matter of Julianna? Will you tell Eliza the truth?"

"What choice do I have?" George growled the reply, and had Daniel not known the man so well, he might have been intimidated by it.

"Good. And now there's the matter of expanding Ramsey Enterprises to the Great Lakes region..."

George's eyes sailed to Daniel. "Oh?"

Daniel grinned at his sudden interest. "My sister's husband and his father are in need of a reliable shipper for their lumber and paper products. Right now the shippers coming in and out of Manitowoc's harbor are largely commissioned by investors who aren't willing to give the Dunbars the cargo space or the service they require."

"Hmm..." George ran his forefinger along his upper lip as he considered the idea.

"Let's discuss it in great length, shall we?" Daniel smiled. "On our way to Wisconsin. I'm envisioning a large Christmas celebration with snow and sleigh bells." Except he wanted to go home for

Christmas—home to the farm that his father had built. He sucked in a breath, wondering if the new owners would sell it.

"You're out of your very mind." George regarded Daniel askance. "And our trip to London?"

"Canceled. But you might promise to take Eliza in the spring so she won't feel disappointed." Daniel straightened his vest. "I hope to be happily married by then."

"To the London waif turned housemaid?"

"To *your daughter.*"

George's face reddened. "You're taking a big chance here with our company—with my reputation and yours as well."

"I disagree. I think we'll look all the better for facing facts and doing what's good and right." Daniel knew he'd be far happier for it. "I'm sure I can sway Mabel Brunning to our side."

George gave a roll of his eyes. "But don't you see, everything about your father that disappointed you, you're now embracing yourself. Selecting a bride who is far beneath your social standing."

"She's your *daughter.*" Daniel thought it bore repeating. "She's a Ramsey. And if it's any consolation, she dislikes you as much as you dislike her. Which is another thing that needs remedying."

"Bah!" George stood and sauntered to the other side of the office, where he stared at his many volumes of books. "I won't do it!"

Daniel lowered himself into a nearby leather chair. "Oh, yes, you'll do it, George, for it'll be far worse for us if I do it."

"A threat?" George swung around, his eyes wide. "You scoundrel!"

Daniel grinned. "I've learned from the best, haven't I."

With quick steps George walked to the door and left the office.

Daniel remained. He hated giving George an ultimatum, but there seemed no help for it. Daniel knew they'd all be better off once the truth was known; however, rough waters were certainly ahead.

He pondered his last bit of conversation with George. *Everything about your father that disappointed you, you're now embracing yourself.*

Disappointed in Poppa? Daniel supposed it was true. He would have made a fine politician. But he insisted in his dying breath that he was a farmer. He thought he'd failed on that account. Why? Just because the last couple of years were lean? There were many years that were plentiful... weren't there?

And that Poppa thought he'd failed as a father to Daniel—thought Daniel was a failure, despite his achievements...

A puff of incredulousness left Daniel's lungs. Maybe Poppa had been correct. Only a fool ignored the truth, ringing as loud as church bells in his heart.

<hr />

Each time Julianna heard the clanging of rigging in Manitowoc's harbor, she thought of Daniel, which proved to be nearly always. She was so glad to have moved away from there. She breathed deeply of the frozen, country air. Miss Mary Sundberg's farm appealed to her so much more. Even milking cows was an improvement over encountering seafaring men on the boardwalks. No telling which of them might be another Grisly Devil. And Daniel was nowhere around to protect her.

Then in August Mrs. Sundberg decided to spend a long weekend up here again as a break before Agnes began school. Julianna felt more relaxed, safe, and Miss Mary suggested she stay on. Julianna accepted.

However, she hadn't been able to escape her memories, and when things grew quiet around the farm, Julianna's mind wandered to Daniel. Had he found happiness in New York City with the Ramseys? Had he proposed marriage to his countess yet?

The gravel crunched beneath the soles of Julianna's boots as she traipsed to the barn to fetch eggs for supper. Both Mrs. Sundberg and Mary had taught her cooking basics, so tonight's menu would consist of fresh-baked bread and fried eggs over a beef and potato hash. They'd eat as soon as Mary returned from teaching school, which would be anytime now. In fact, she was a bit tardy today.

The sound of prancing horse's hooves in the near distance made Julianna pause. Moments later Miss Mary's buggy came into view. As she drove the team into the yard, she waved. She pulled to a halt near the barn.

"I stopped to get the mail." She held it in one gloved hand.

John Wolf, a Menomonie Indian and their neighbor who worked for Miss Mary as a part-time farmhand, strode from the barn. "G'd evening, Mary. Want I should unhitch the buggy?"

"Yes, please, John."

Julianna gave the man a gentle smile as he helped Mary alight from the buggy. His English wasn't so good yet. But Mary helped him learn to read and tutored Julianna as well. Julianna found his presence a comfort.

Mary came toward Julianna waving envelopes. "We both got letters."

"We did?" The eggs forgotten for the time being, Julianna walked to the house beside Mary. "From whom?"

"My nephew, Daniel."

Inside the warm kitchen Mary handed Julianna the ivory envelope addressed to her.

"It's probably a wedding announcement." How cruel that Daniel would send one to her. Then again, he'd shattered her heart the evening before he left. Perhaps his intention was to grind it to bits.

Mary removed her outerwear then tore open her envelope. Her cheeks were pinked by the cold, early December wind.

Julianna watched her read. Long moments later Miss Mary peered at her from over the top of the missive.

"It's an apology." Surprise laced her tone. "And an invitation to attend a special Christmas at my late brother's farm in Manitowoc. Apparently Daniel purchased the place from the man who bought it from Kristin last April." A piece of paper dropped to the floor. Mary stooped to retrieve it. "It's a ticket for the train." She looked at Julianna and smiled.

Julianna didn't know what to make of the news. "Is he bringing his countess?"

"I don't know." Mary's eyes moved to the unopened envelope in Julianna's hand. "See what your letter says."

Julianna carefully broke the seal, opened the envelope, and braced herself for the worst. She saw the familiar handwriting and easily read the note.

> *Dearest Julianna;*
>
> *I cannot tell you how very ashamed I am of my bad behavior. Last July I gave you shocking and devastating news with little to no sensitivity. I can only hope and pray you will find it in your heart to forgive me.*
>
> *I have missed you terribly. Not a single day passes that I do not see your lovely, smiling face in my mind's eye. This can mean only one thing: I am in love with you, Julianna, and cannot bear to think of my future without you.*

Julianna glanced over at Miss Mary. "I'm glad I've been practicing my reading in the evenings along with John Wolf. I believe I've improved." Even so, she couldn't be sure she'd read Daniel's letter correctly. Had he really written that he missed her—that he *loved* her?

"What is it?" Miss Mary stepped forward. "What's wrong?"

"I can't be certain." Julianna stared at the neatly penned note again and found her ticket for the train. "I got an apology and ticket too, but then..." She looked at Mary again.

"Would you like me to help you?"

Julianna inclined her head, timidly. Mary had become a dear friend as well as a fine teacher who not only helped Julianna to improve her reading skills but taught her to cook and clean and launder cloths, make cheese and soap, and a myriad of other household tasks as well. What's more, Julianna trusted Mary Sundberg. "I'm afraid I might have misread something."

Slowly she held the letter out, and Mary carefully took it. A smile curved her lips as she read the words aloud—the very same that Julianna had taken in, albeit with a good measure of disbelief.

"Well, now." Mary grinned at Julianna. "It's quite clear that Daniel isn't marrying a countess."

Julianna's eyes widened. The idea of marrying Captain Daniel Sundberg made her knees weak—although he hadn't said anything about marriage.

Mary read the remainder of Daniel's letter. He'd opened an account at the department store in town, and both Julianna and Mary were to buy themselves new gowns or the material to sew themselves dresses. The choice was theirs.

> *This Christmas will be a time when our family reunites in a special and unforgettable way—a way that will honor the memories of those loved ones who have passed on into eternity before us.*

Julianna thought of Flora, and sorrow filled her being. However, it couldn't completely override the excitement she felt about seeing Daniel again. And he loved her? She couldn't quite grasp the idea. *He loved her!*

"We have a lot to do in the next month." Mary handed back the letter. Her dark eyes shone with enthusiasm. "We'd best get started right away."

CHAPTER 25

*W*EEKS LATER JULIANNA and Miss Mary disembarked the passenger car at Manitowoc's small train depot. In a corner of the platform a small ensemble of musicians played "I Heard the Bells on Christmas Day" with the late afternoon sun setting behind them.

Julianna hadn't ever celebrated Christmas. She'd only served the Tolberts and their guests and, before that, begged in the street, as people were more apt to give a little extra during this time of year. She had never stopped to consider what the holiday was all about—not until recently when she'd watched the Christmas pageant that Mary's elementary school children put on. It was all about the Christ Child, God, clothed in humanity, coming into the world, not to condemn it, but that through Him the whole world might be saved. Julianna decided it was a glorious message, one filled with immeasurable hope—and she'd never experienced anything like it before.

Someone waving caught her eye, and Julianna spied Mrs. Sundberg and Agnes, all bundled up and standing near the steps of the platform. She tapped Mary's shoulder, and they walked the length of the wooden deck.

"Daniel wrote that he would send a carriage for all of us." Mrs. Sundberg hugged Mary and then embraced Julianna tightly. "You look much better." She put her forehead near Julianna's. "I worried about you for a while."

"I feel much better, thank you."

"The country agrees with you, then?"

"Definitely." Julianna smiled and wrapped Agnes in a hug.

"How is your business?" Mary directed the question at Mrs. Sundberg.

"It has been good." She looked pleased.

Julianna and Mary collected their bags. The train's engine chugged and belched black smoke as it prepared to move on down the metal rails. They moved a ways away so they could converse above the noise. Within a few minutes, however, a sleek conveyance arrived to transport them to the farm in big-city style. The four of them had a light laugh over the irony, although they were grateful to be out of December's biting wind.

"I always knew Daniel would own the farm one day." Mrs. Sundberg pulled her wool wrapper more tightly around herself. "The Lord told me so during my prayers one day. My mistake was relaying the news to Daniel before he was ready to hear it. I guess it pushed him away."

"But he's back now, Momma." Agnes threaded her mittened hand around her arm. "Please don't cry anymore."

Despite the bleariness in her azure eyes, Mrs. Sundberg smiled.

Mary reached across the way and clasped Mrs. Sundberg's hand. "Sam would want you to be happy, Kristin, especially now that Daniel has returned...for good, I hope."

Julianna hoped so too.

A few inches of snow blanketed the landscape, although here and there obstinate brown weeds poked their heads through the icy covering. As the carriage traveled west, Julianna glimpsed patches of plowed fields lying exposed to the elements.

"We're getting close." Excitement danced in Agnes's eyes.

"Will you be moving back to your farm?" Julianna asked.

Mrs. Sundberg shook her head. "No. It is not ours anymore. It belongs to Daniel." She sighed, sounding both relieved and wistful. "All the work is now his. I have my shop, and Agnes and I are happy in our apartment. She can walk to school, and I am not so isolated while she is gone. I am close to Adeline and Will too."

"Well, personally, I can't imagine Daniel giving up captaining and shipping." When no immediately response came, Julianna wondered if she'd been too outspoken.

Mrs. Sundberg said something in Norwegian, and Agnes and Mary laughed. Then all three sets of eyes fixed on her.

"That's not fair." Julianna feigned indignation and turned her gaze back to the passing scenery. "I can't understand a thing you said."

"Ja, we know that." Mrs. Sundberg laughed again.

Julianna bristled but only mildly. She knew the Sundbergs deeply cared for her.

And Daniel—he'd stated he loved her. Enough to marry her? What did he have planned?

The carriage came to a halt in the yard of a square-framed, two-story wooden house. It had been painted white with red trim around the windows—the same red as the barn. Chickens scurried about, and a black and gray shaggy-haired dog barked, until she recognized Agnes and wagged her tail. Three puppies followed on the pooch's heels.

"Momma, look! Pepper had babies!" The girl petted the dog and then snuggled the squirming, licking puppies. "I never thought I'd see Pepper again."

Mrs. Sundberg's smile appeared rueful. "I could not keep this animal. She would be barking at my customers all day long, and I had enough to think about with Sam being so ill." Her gaze met Julianna's. "The man who purchased the farm promised to look after our pet. Now, thanks to my son, we not only have this farm back in our family but Pepper too."

Julianna glanced around, expecting to see Daniel at any moment.

But then Adeline burst from the side entrance of the home. She appeared festive in her black skirt, white blouse, and colorfully embroidered vest. "*Velkommen*," she said in Norwegian. "Welcome!" Her smile was wide.

"What are you doing here?" Mrs. Sundberg embraced her oldest daughter. "I thought you were spending Christmas with the Dunbars."

"We'll see them tomorrow." She pulled back. "Will and I changed our plans at Daniel's request. He's indisposed at the moment and asked me to welcome you into the house and to show you, Aunt Mary, and Julianna"—her gaze flitted to them—"to the bedrooms in which you'll be staying."

"Such formality." Mrs. Sundberg clucked her tongue.

"Don't worry about your bags," Adeline told her aunt and Julianna. "The men will carry them in."

Warmth and the smell of something delicious roasting in the oven met Julianna as she entered the home. The kitchen looked clean and functional.

"While the ham is baking, Momma, you and Agnes can make yourselves at home. Meanwhile, I'll take Aunt Mary and Julianna upstairs." Adeline spoke the information over one shoulder as she walked up the open stairwell and down the hall. "You two will be sharing what used to be the girls' room." She opened the door. "Everything's been redone, from the carpeting to the new colors on the walls and the furniture."

Two neatly made canopy beds occupied the room. The walls were a pretty robin's egg blue, and heavy pleated curtains adorned the windows.

"I'm sure we'll be quite comfortable here." Julianna ran her hand along one of the polished oak bedposts.

"Take a rest before changing clothes." Adeline took hold of the doorknob. "Dinner will be in two hours."

Will was kind enough to carry up their luggage, but Julianna still hadn't seen any sign of Daniel. It seemed odd that he would be so busy that he couldn't greet his guests.

The beds looked soft and inviting, and since Julianna and Mary had been up at dawn, they decided on a quick rest. Later, after they'd washed up, they changed into their holiday clothes, Mary into a classic black outfit with a colorfully beaded bodice, and Julianna into a forest-green skirt and white blouse with green satin edging. They both set shawls around their shoulders to keep from shivering in the drafty house.

At last they made their way downstairs and into the small foyer. Someone played the piano, and Julianna heard Agnes's voice ringing out with girlish exuberance. A fire roared in the sitting room's hearth, and Julianna's heart raced with her anticipation of seeing Daniel again.

Then, an instant later, he appeared at the sitting room's entryway, and Julianna forgot how to breathe. His russet hair was neatly parted, and he appeared just as elegantly clad in his black suit and crisp, white shirt as any of the important men who visited the Tolbert residence.

Daniel hugged his aunt. "Am I forgiven?" He pulled back and peered into her face.

"Yes, all's forgiven."

"Good." After another quick hug, he gazed at Julianna, and it was then she realized she'd been holding her breath.

She quickly exhaled before refilling her lungs with air as Mary made her way into the sitting room.

"Julianna..." Daniel held his hands out to her.

Stepping toward him, she slipped her palms into his. He brought her fingers to his lips. She willed her legs to keep her upright.

"Charming as always, aren't you, Captain Sundberg?" Short of flinging herself into his arms, Julianna didn't know what to do. How did one behave when one was so dizzily in love?

He narrowed his gaze at her sass, but his smile betrayed him. "It's so good to see you again." Sincerity lit in his blue eyes.

She squeezed his hands, warm and strong beneath her fingers, and he pulled her closer to him, so close that she could smell the tangy-spicy scented soap he'd used.

His lips brushed her brow. "I've missed you." He whispered the words against her forehead.

Closing her eyes, Julianna tried to absorb this moment, one she'd only dreamed of but never believed would come true.

She felt him step back, and her lids fluttered opened. She saw questions in his gaze as he searched her face.

"I still love you, Daniel." She emptied her heart. "I always will."

"I had hoped—*prayed* that your feelings for me hadn't changed."

"They have not."

His entire countenance brightened. Then his gaze darted around the small foyer. "What do you think of the house? My father built it."

"What I've seen of it so far is cozy. The location seems perfect." She liked the fact that the house wasn't in town, near the docks, and that it was still as much of a country home as Mary Sundberg's farm. Even so, it wasn't a long distance to Mrs. Sundberg's shop. Perhaps Julianna could continue her lessons at the spinning wheel.

"I purchased this place."

"So I've heard." Julianna smiled.

"I plan to make this my home." He drew in a breath. "I think Poppa would be pleased."

"I know he would be."

Smiling, he led her toward the sitting room. "Some dear friends of mine are here. I'd like for you to say hello."

As he moved around, Julianna saw the Ramseys, standing at the far side of the glowing hearth, between it and the candlelit Christmas tree. She froze. They both gave her tentative smiles.

The room quieted, and Julianna glimpsed the stoic expressions around her, from the Sundbergs to Will and Adeline Dunbar. In that moment she felt set up and trapped. Instincts told her to run. She lowered her head, closed her eyes. *Dear God, help me face this man.*

Daniel placed his hand at the small of her back and she looked up at him. "Please listen to what George has to say."

What could he say? She hated him. Period.

But even as those thoughts scampered across her mind, she recalled the verses she'd read from the Bible recently, the very ones in which Jesus instructed believers to forgive others as they would like to be forgiven.

Ramsey stepped forward, and to his credit he appeared more nervous than arrogant. "I have already asked the Sundbergs for forgiveness. I've been rude and arrogant and highly insensitive."

"And we've forgiven him, Julianna." Mrs. Sundberg's voice carried from across the room.

Ramsey focused on Daniel for several long moments. "A good man helped me see the truth." His gaze glided back to Julianna. "Now I'm begging for your forgiveness, Miss Wayland—Julianna, if I may."

From the corner of her eye, she saw the Sundbergs and Dunbars file out of the room. They really didn't have to go. Julianna had shared the truth with them months ago.

Mrs. Ramsey spoke up. "Your last name really should be Ramsey."

Astonished, Julianna's gaze slid to Mrs. Ramsey, clad in a black velvet outfit. Was that ivory lacy collar one of Mrs. Sundberg's creations? "I know the truth," Mrs. Ramsey said simply. "George told me everything." She glanced at him in what could only be love and compassion.

Really?

"I let my pride hold me back from finding you, Julianna." Ramsey stepped closer. "You suffered for years because of me. Ambition and even fear blinded me." After a glance at the shiny tips of his shoes he met Julianna's stare. "I know I can never undo the amount of hurt and anguish that my actions inflicted on you in the past, but I can try to make it up to you in the future."

"This season is all about hope, isn't it?" Mrs. Ramsey took her place beside her husband.

He gave her a smile and a look of fondness such as Julianna had never seen coming from the man. Next he reached into his jacket's inner pocket and retrieved a document. He held it out to Julianna. Taking and unfolding it, she saw it was the contract she'd signed the day after her birthday in New York. She shook her head. "I still don't want anything from you or Ramsey Enterprises."

"Perhaps not, but will you accept anything from Ramsey, Sundberg, and Dunbar Shipping and Freight Company?" Daniel spoke the question close to her ear.

She inhaled sharply. "You're in business with the Dunbars now?"

"Yes, I am...we are." He inclined his head in Ramsey's direction. "And we have a new motto. God first, family second, and business third."

Julianna was heartened that they'd gotten their priorities straight. It meant a lot—it meant everything. Maybe the Ramseys had, indeed, changed.

"I plan to oversee the shipping and receiving of our new venture with a concentration on the Great Lakes." Daniel submerged his blue eyes into her gaze. "It might mean that I'll be gone occasionally during the summer months, but—"

"And this farm? Who will run it?" Surely he didn't think she could manage it by herself.

"I'll run it…with some help, of course." He sent her a look full of feeling. "This is no longer a working farm. I own the house, barn, outbuildings, and four acres of beautiful countryside, so there's plenty of room for flower and vegetable gardens." He smiled. "I purchased only a parcel from the new owner. My mother gave me the idea last summer. Apparently Aunt Mary did a similar thing with her land in Green Bay. The former owner gladly made the transaction, and he plans to relocate on another section of his property. He's a fine man and will make a good neighbor."

"I'm sure you'll be very happy here." Julianna held her breath.

"I will—but only if the woman I love will agree to live here with me." He adjusted his suit coat before getting down on one knee.

Julianna's heart raced when he reached for her hand.

"Please marry me. I love you, and—"

"Yes, I will." Warmth flooded her cheeks when she realized she hadn't allowed him to even finish the proposal.

Daniel didn't seem to care. He got to his feet. "You have made me a happy man, little one." He placed a kiss on her hand. "Thank you."

The pleasure was all hers. An actual giggle bubbled out of Julianna.

Then she remembered the document she still clutched in her other hand. Resentfulness, it seemed, came at a price, one that Julianna didn't want to pay. She wanted love, joy, and peace. She wanted a family, and like it or not, George Ramsey was her biological father who was asking to be a part of her life. He seemed to have truly changed. The least Julianna could do was give him a chance to prove it.

"Is this mine to keep?" She held up the document.

"Yes." Ramsey's eyes sort of zigzagged down until he gazed at the braided rug. "Again, Julianna, please forgive me for thinking a mere signature meant my daughter didn't exist. She does." He lifted his gaze. "You do—and you have. I was just an irresponsible fool."

"Say no more. I've made my decision." Julianna tore the agreement in half before moving to the hearth. She tossed the two pieces of parchment into the fire. The flames rose and consumed them. "I forgive you, Mr. Ramsey." She glanced his way and saw his features relax.

Mrs. Ramsey happily rushed forward with opened arms, and Julianna embraced her.

Daniel called his family back into the room. "Just before he died, Poppa told me that Julianna loved me. I didn't want to hear it or the other things he had to say because I had my own plans for my life. Little did I know how much better God's would be."

He sent Julianna such an intense look that her face heated all the more.

Pulling his gaze from hers, he scanned his family's faces. "Poppa was a good and noble man. I hope someday I'll measure up to him."

"I think you already have." Adeline smiled before kissing baby Jacob.

"I think so too." Mrs. Sundberg said.

Agnes crossed the room and hugged Daniel around the waist. He smoothed the crown of her blonde head. "I think Poppa would be very pleased to see us all here in the home he built for his family, celebrating the eve of our Savior's birth together."

"*Ja*, he would." Tearfully Mrs. Sundberg nodded and embraced Daniel as well.

"I'm proud of you, Daniel." His aunt Mary stepped forward and hugged him too.

Happiness filled Julianna's being. Daniel literally had his hands full—in a very endearing way.

"Family is truly the fabric of life, is it not?" He released the ladies and stepped back. "And so it is on that note"—Daniel made his way back to Julianna and reached for her hand—"that I'd like to announce my engagement to the lovely Miss Julianna Wayland...Ramsey. Together I pray that we will be able to weave together the threads of our two families into one great tapestry of love, faith, and industry."

Smiles, laughter, and applause filled the room. Daniel turned to Julianna and kissed her deeply, meaningfully. If she'd had any doubts or reservations before, they vanished. This most certainly was the happiest moment of her life.

Coming in Spring 2013, book three
of the Fabric of Time series—

Threads of Love

May 1902, Manitowoc, Wisconsin

*A*N EXPLOSION OF shattering glass sounded from directly
behind Emily Sundberg, and a thunderous weight crashed
into her. The world spun, and then she fell hard and facedown on
the dirty Franklin Street boardwalk.

Breathe! Breathe! She struggled to inhale.

"Are you all right, ma'am?" A male voice spoke close to her ear.
"I'm terribly sorry about knocking you over."

He helped her sit up, and a moment later a rush of sweet springtime air filled Emily's lungs. She let out a breath of relief.

"Are you hurt?"

"I...I don't know." Emily spit dirt from her mouth. Her left cheek
began to throb, and the world spun before her.

He steadied her, his arm around her shoulders. "Easy there."

She took several deep breaths.

"Allow me to help you to the bench. Like I said, I'm sorry 'bout knocking you over the way I did."

Emily wiggled her toes inside her ivory-colored boots. Nothing broken. She moved her jaw. Despite the pain around her cheekbone, she seemed all right. Her hand moved to the back of her head. Her fat braid had come out of its pinning, and her hat—

Her hat!

She pointed to the paved street seconds before a set of buggy wheels rolled over it, grinding the lovely chipped-shape, cream-white creation into the paved road—not once, but twice!

Emily moaned.

"Careful, now." The man helped her to stand. "There're shards of glass everywhere."

Emily thanked God she hadn't slammed her head into the nearby hitching post.

"Hooligans!" A woman's voice rang out amidst the strangely silent street. It sounded like Mrs. Hopper's. "Hooligans, ever'one of 'em!"

Definitely Mrs. Hopper's.

The man held her securely by her upper arms, and Emily's gaze fell on his walnut-colored waistcoat. "You sure you're not hurt?

"I–I don't think so."

"Well, I hope you can forgive me, ma'am."

Emily's gaze finally reached the man's tanned and golden-whiskered face. Shaggy blond hair framed his face, and blood stained the corner of his mouth. The stranger looked out of place for Manitowoc, Wisconsin, in his canvas duster and matching trousers. But odd costumes weren't totally uncommon, given the city's lively port.

And yet he seemed a bit familiar too...

"Unhand that girl, you hooligan!" Mrs. Hopper rushed forward and whacked the man on the shoulder with her cane.

He winced and released Emily. "I meant her no harm." As Emily staggered backward slightly, the man caught her elbow. His velvety-brown gaze bore into hers as if to ask yet again if she'd been injured.

Funny how she guessed at his thoughts.

"I'm just shaken." Emily glimpsed the remorse in his eyes before he bent and picked up the dark-blue capelet that *Bestamor,* her grandmother, had knit for her. He gave it a shake before handing it over.

"And what about my hat?" Sadly she pointed again to the street.

The man collected its colorful but irreparably flattened remains.

"A travesty!" Mrs. Hopper's age-lined face contorted in rage. "A travesty, I say!"

Travesty indeed! It had taken months for her to save for that fine bit of millinery with its silk ribbons, Chantilly lace, and pink roses on a velvet bandeau. Now Andy Anderson would never see it. She took the mangled remnants from the stranger's hand. "I certainly hope you plan to reimburse me for this. I paid a dollar and a half for it."

"A dollar fifty? For a hat? I could buy a shoulder holster, cartridge belt, and ammunition for that sum."

Unimpressed, Emily extended one hand of her torn netted glove. Another casualty.

Resignation softened his gaze before the man reached into his inside pocket and then placed two dollar bills into Emily's outstretched palm. "This should more than cover it. Again, I apologize."

"Thank you." Emily smiled. "Apology accepted." She folded the money and put it in her reticule, still attached to her wrist. Mrs. Sylvia Hopper sniffed indignantly, but Emily caught the approving light in her eyes. She'd known the elderly woman for a long while, as she had been *Bestamor*'s best friend back in Norway. She'd come to America just before Poppa was born, and now her granddaughter, Iris, was Emily's best friend.

A small crowd pressed in on the boardwalk to gawk, and Emily's gaze moved to the man who lay sprawled out and unmoving several feet away.

She quickly turned away. "Is he dead?"

"Probably not." The stranger bent and grabbed his dark brown, wide-brimmed hat that lay nearby and gave it a whack against his thigh. "My compliments. You took that tumble a far sight better than he did."

"Who is he?"

"A man wanted in five counties."

Emily glanced at the motionless figure again. He didn't look familiar.

"It's actually amazing that you're not out cold yourself. For a moment I feared I'd killed you."

"And you could have killed her, you low-life hooligan!"

"Please, Mrs. Hopper…" She glanced around, hating to be the subject of such a scene. "I'm fine. No need to worry."

Muttering, the elderly woman walked to where several women stood a ways down on the boardwalk, holding parasols and whispering behind gloved fingers.

Emily felt suddenly unnerved. "I guess I'm sturdy for a woman. Even so, I haven't taken a hit like that since my brothers jumped me and I fell off my horse. Those rascals pretended they were US marshals and I was one of the James's gang." Emily moistened her lips, her gaze fixed on the handsome stranger. "They flung themselves at me from a tree limb. It's a miracle we didn't all break our necks. "

A moment passed, and Emily wondered why this moment seemed sealed in time.

The man narrowed his gaze.

"Forgive my prattling." She hadn't meant to go on like that. "The fall must have shaken my tongue loose."

Despite the injury to his mouth, he grinned, and Emily could swear she'd seen it before.

"Both you fellas are paying for this damage to my front window!" Mr. Fransmuller stomped out of his restaurant and saloon. Emily knew him and his family, as young Hans had been in her class just the year before. "Look what your brawl has done!"

Emily took note the gaping hole where the two men had exited.

Mrs. Hopper limped over to the tavern owner. "There ought to be a law against such barbaric behavior in our town. Someone's going to get killed. Why, Mr. Fransmuller, you should be ashamed, serving strong drink at this hour of the afternoon. Women aren't safe to do their shopping in broad daylight anymore!"

"Just for the record, I wasn't drinking," said the familiar stranger. "Just playing cards is all."

"And gambling, most likely." Mrs. Hopper hurled another angry glare at him. "Gambling is a dirty sin."

Fransmuller frowned and wiped his beefy hands on the black apron tied around his rounded belly. "Now, Mrs. Hopper, don't start in on one of your holier-than-thou rants."

"I beg your pardon?" Mrs. Hopper brought herself up to her full height of four feet nine inches. "How dare you speak to me in such a way, Mr. Fransmuller!"

"I've got a business to run, and I pay my taxes." He threw a thumb over his shoulder. "But just look at my front window!" He gave a wag of his nearly bald head. "And you should see the saloon! One big mess!" Mr. Fransmuller marched up and stood toe to toe with the man beside Emily. "Who are you? I want your name. You're paying for half the damages to my business!"

"Yes, sir."

Emily watched as the stranger moved his duster to one side. She glimpsed the gun strapped around his narrow hips before he produced his billfold and a silver badge. "Deputy Marshal John

Alexander Kirk Edgerton at your service." After a courteous dip forward, he counted out several large-sum bills. "Will this cover my portion of the damages?"

Emily ran the man's name through her memory, and her heart beat a little faster.

Mr. Fransmuller appeared impressed. "Yes. This will do." The fight went out of him, and he nodded his thanks before walking back into his establishment.

"Jake?" She eked out his nickname, scarcely believing it was him. "Jake Edgerton?"

His gaze slid to her, and he smiled. "Well, well... Emily Sundberg." He didn't look surprised. Obviously he'd recognized her before she'd figured out his identity. "Look at you, all grown up—you even turned out pretty."

"Hmph! Well, I see you haven't changed!"

"It was a compliment."

She bristled. It didn't sound like a compliment. What's more, she recalled that Jake was part of that US marshal stunt her brothers pulled.

Jake Edgerton was trouble, trouble from the time they were thirteen and fifteen.

Mrs. Hopper moved down the boardwalk and continued her conversation with the other ladies.

"So what are you doing in Manitowoc?"

"Attending my granddad's funeral."

Emily felt a sting of rebuke. "Oh, I–I'm sorry. I didn't know he'd passed. I mean, I knew Mr. Ollie had been ill for a long while, but..."

"Happened just yesterday." Jake eyed her speculatively, and Emily guessed the questions swirling around his instigating brain.

"Just for the record," she mimicked, "I'm a schoolteacher here in town. I only get home on Sundays."

"A schoolteacher, eh?"

"That's right." She lifted her chin, feeling a sense of accomplishment. Seconds later she thought of Mr. Ollie. "Again, I'm sorry for your loss. Your grandfather was a good neighbor to our family." Emily knew that at one time Jake had been especially close to the old man. Oliver Stout, fondly called Mr. Ollie by Emily and her brothers, had been a respected attorney, one who'd boasted many times over the years that his only grandson would one day take over his law practice.

But it didn't look that way. Not if Jake was a deputy marshal.

"I appreciate the condolences, Em."

Such familiarity galled her. "So you're a gambler as well as a lawman?" Emily could only imagine Mr. Ollie weeping in heaven. A God-fearing man, the late Mr. Ollie would have never been involved in a barroom brawl!

"I partake in a game of cards on occasion."

"Family funerals being one of them?" She couldn't squelch the quip.

Jake inhaled, but then seemed to think better of a reply. Instead he guided her the rest of the way to the bench.

Emily tugged her capelet around her shoulders and sat. She eyed the crowd, praying no one would recognize her as Maple Street School's third grade teacher or Agnes Sundberg's niece or Jacob Dunbar's cousin...or Captain Daniel Sundberg's daughter. With so much family surrounding her in this town, Emily knew the odds were against her anonymity.

"Once again I am terribly sorry you got in the middle of this whole mess."

He couldn't be sorrier than she!

Mr. Fransmuller began sweeping up glass and shooing people away from the scene. Then all at once her best friend, Iris Hopper, came shrieking from the department store.

"Emily! Emily Sundberg!"

She cringed as embarrassment filled her being. So much for hiding her identity.

Iris spotted Emily and came running across the street. She held her hat in place on her head with one of her slender hands. In the other she clutched her wrapped purchases.

"What's happened? Oh, my stars!" A pale blue dress hugged Iris's wispy frame as she hurried toward Emily, while her wire-rim glasses slipped down her long nose. "I heard there was some bar-room fight and you got trampled half to death. What would I do if I'd lost my very best frie—"

Iris's gaze lit on Jake, and she slowed her steps. Giving him a timid smile, she let go of her hat and pushed up her glasses.

He touched the brim of his hat. "Ma'am."

Iris leaned toward Emily. "Is he the one who ran you over?"

"That about sums it up." Emily pushed to her feet. "But I'm fine, so let's finish our shopping, shall we?"

Iris didn't budge. "Aren't you going to introduce us?" She nudged Emily, who felt a new soreness in her ribcage.

Jake spoke up before she could. "US Deputy Marshal Jake Edgerton, ma'am."

"Deputy marshal? How impressive." Iris's smile grew. "I'm Miss Iris Hopper and Emily's best friend, going on eight years now. Right, Em?"

"Right."

"My parents were killed in a horrible mudslide in South America, where we were missionaries. I've lived with my grandmother ever since."

"Sorry to hear of your loss." Jake's gaze, the color of the brandy he denied drinking, shifted to Emily. "As for Em and me, we go way back." A slow grin spread across his mouth. "Ain't that right? And I must admit it's been a pleasure, um, running into you today."

Shut up, Jake. She looked down the block, wondering if he

had any idea how much heartache he'd caused her over the years. Because of him and his big mouth, she'd spent half her life proving her moral integrity to this entire town! Worse, Jake never forgave her.

"How're your brothers?" He gave a nostalgic wag of his head. "That summer I visited Granddad and met all of you Sundbergs was the best in all my life."

"Eden and Zeb are fine. Just fine." She couldn't get herself to say any more. "We're all fine."

"Glad to hear it."

"Emily's never mentioned you." Iris's pointed features soured with her deep frown. She leaned closer to Emily. "I thought we told each other everything."

"No? You never mentioned me, Em?" Jake's dark eyes glinted with mischief.

Tried half my life to forget you! She clenched her jaw to keep back the retort and realized that it hurt too.

His expression changed. "Maybe you ought to see a doctor, Emily."

She wished he hadn't picked up on her wince. "No, I'm fine."

"She always says that," Iris tattled. "She's always 'fine.'"

"How far's the doctor's office from here?"

"I don't need a doctor, Jake. But thanks, anyway."

"Well, goodness, Em, you certainly did take the worst of it." Iris brushed off the back of Emily's capelet. "And, oh, my stars! Just look at your hat. It's ruined."

"Yes, I know. But Jake reimbursed me."

"How thoughtful." After a smile his way, Iris examined Emily's face like she was one of her fourth graders. "If I'm not mistaken, a bruise is already forming on your left cheek." Iris clucked her tongue. "You'll be a sight at the spring dance tomorrow night. But if you need to stay home now, I will too."

"No, we're still going." Emily knew her friend looked forward to this community event as much as she did. Andy Anderson would be there, and maybe seeing her in the new dress Momma and *Bestamor* had sewn especially for the occasion, he'd finally notice her, and not just as another of her brother Eden's friends but as a young woman.

"Andy won't give you the time of day if you're all banged up. You might as well stay home."

Sadness descended like a fog rolling in from off Lake Michigan. Emily fingered her sore cheek. A bruise? On her face? Tears threatened.

"Might help if you go home and put a cold compress on it," Jake suggested. "I'll bet no one will be the wiser by tomorrow night."

"Sure, that's right," Iris quickly added. "Besides, it'll be dark." Her gaze softened. "Perhaps Andy won't see any bruising. And we can put some of Granny's concealing cream on your chin."

Emily's cheeks burned. How could Iris speak about such personal things in front of Jake?

"Excuse me, but are you speaking of Andy Anderson by any chance?" Jake hiked his hat farther back on his head.

"Yes." Again Iris seemed happy to provide all the information.

However, the last thing Emily wanted was Jake to get involved in her life. "We should be on our way, Iris. Let's catch up with your granny."

"Well, I'll be..." Jake leaned against a hitching post. "Andy Anderson...what's that rascal doing these days?"

"Andy works over at the aluminum factory." Iris pointed somewhere beyond Jake's left shoulder. "He's not married yet, right, Em?"

She swallowed a lump of chagrin.

Jake pursed his lips, seeming to mull it over, then looked at Emily. "I wondered if I'd see him while I was in town." His gaze slid to Iris. "Andy and I go way back too."

Every muscle in Emily's body tensed. If only Mr. Ollie could have waited just a week longer to pass from this world to the next. Her hopes ran high for the spring dance tomorrow night, and it galled her that Jake might have the power to destroy her well-laid plans.

"Emily is counting on Andy to ask her for a dance tomorrow night, but—"

"Iris!" Aghast, she gave her friend's arm a jerk. "I'm sure Deputy Edgerton doesn't care about such things."

"Sure I do." He straightened, still grinning. "And I'll tell you what, Em; if Andy doesn't dance with you, I'd be happy to."

"Thank you, but I can't possibly accept." She tamped down the urge to scowl.

"It's the least I can do." After another charming smirk, he glanced at Iris. "What time's the grand affair?"

"Aren't you in mourning?" He just couldn't show up.

"Of course I am." Jake rolled one broad shoulder. "But I know Granddad would want me to go."

Emily looked skyward.

Iris gave him the details, and Emily wanted to scream. She hated the thought of Jake Edgerton being anywhere near her and having any chance to intrude on her and Andy—if only there was something to intrude upon. But that's what tomorrow night was supposed to be all about. Catching Andy's eye. Telling him how she felt about him. If Andy just knew of her romantic interest in him, then perhaps he'd want to court her and...marry her.

"I know it's uncommon to hold a dance on Friday night, but it was the only time the committee could reserve the hall. I warned them to reserve it earlier so the dance could be held on the third Saturday of May, just as in years past." Iris cleared her throat. "Unfortunately, I wasn't asked to be on the committee this year."

"I'm sure I can make it," Jake said.

"Of course you must save a dance for me."

"Iris!" How could her friend be so bold?

Jake didn't seem offended. "It'd be my honor, ma'am." He smiled rather sheepishly.

For pity's sake! Emily had heard enough. More than enough! She turned and strode down the walk, passing Mrs. Hopper and the other women. Her heels clicked hard on the weathered planks. While she walked faster than a lady should, if she didn't hurry, she'd lose her composure here and now—and in front of the very man who'd nearly ruined her life!

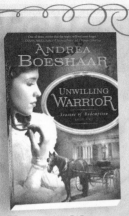

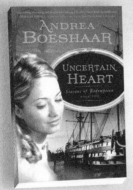
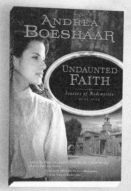